D0351204

# GIRL

## ON THE

# LINE

Also by

*Faith Gardner*

*The Second Life of Ava Rivers*

*Perdita*

# GIRL

Faith Gardner

# ON THE

# LINE

HARPER TEEN

*An Imprint of HarperCollinsPublishers*

For my mom, Susan,
and my dad, Mark,
who gave me life, love, and the words that
make it all worthwhile.

HarperTeen is an imprint of HarperCollins Publishers.

Girl on the Line
Copyright © 2021 by Faith Gardner
All rights reserved. Printed in the United States of America.
No part of this book may be used or reproduced in any manner
whatsoever without written permission except in the case of brief
quotations embodied in critical articles and reviews. For information
address HarperCollins Children's Books, a division of HarperCollins
Publishers, 195 Broadway, New York, NY 10007.
www.epicreads.com

ISBN 978-0-06-302230-0

Typography by Torborg Davern
20 21 22 23 24  PC/LSCH  10 9 8 7 6 5 4 3 2 1
❖
First Edition

# PROLOGUE

*The sun smiles* down on me, the sky deep and bright as an upside-down sea, and here I am below it all: dressed like a giant slice of pizza, thinking of death. Not because the costume is filthy and heavy, or because I only make minimum wage, or because a gum-chewing, hair-twisting trainee is staring at me with wide, frightened eyes, or because it is mortifying being in a pizza costume on a familiar street corner—though all of this is true. I think of death because just last year, I tried to kill myself. I looked ahead and saw nothing but the end credits. And here I am, not only very much alive, but wearing this ridiculous costume that stinks of pepperoni. Dancing. For the last time. Tomorrow, this gum-chewing, hair-twisting new hire with her wide, frightened eyes standing before me will inherit my uniform and I get to be promoted to the reverent position of busser.

"It's going to be okay," I yell to her over the sound of reggae music blasting out of a passing Lexus. "I promise. It's really . . . it's not that bad."

"Okay," she says, in a tone that very much embodies the opposite.

Life is punctuated with uncanny moments like these, where the past and future self collide in the daze of present tense. Where my own deeds and stories strike me suddenly as unfamiliar, as not my own. As a wise old dude once said, I contain multitudes. Right now I am a human slice of pizza shuffling on a street corner who will later peel off this costume and put my girl costume back on and go work a volunteer shift at a crisis hotline. But last year, I should have been the girl on the other end of the line.

# PART
*one*

# PAST

*I imagined suicide* would be simple: a bottle of pills swallowed on a sunny afternoon, lying alone in the lakeside grass, staring up at the shifting shapes of clouds against a sky as blue as a heartbreaker's eyes. I imagined the sound of the leaves in the oak trees whispering goodbye in a language I didn't speak, my pulse and my pain slowing to a stop. My body slackening, my eyes fluttering shut, something like the classic reprinted painting I had hung in my room, *Ophelia* by Sir John Everett Millais, dead in a brook, surrounded by greenery, covered in flowers.

I hadn't imagined the cold of the October day, the way the dry brown grasses scratched rough against my neck as I lay down, the sky gaping back cloudless and pale. I hadn't imagined there would be ants everywhere and the vague smell of dog shit wafting from the brush, or that I would forget a pen to write a note to leave behind. I hadn't imagined that I would forget to bring water, too, the way my dry throat would hurt from so many pills chafing on the way down, the excruciating minutes that ticked by where nothing happened, or how I sobbed, envisioning my family weeping at the news. I hadn't imagined dying in regret and uncertainty in thirsty grasses, no flowers in sight, only empty Bud Light cans from someone else's party. I hadn't imagined it would feel like the furthest thing from *Ophelia*. I hadn't imagined the internal thunder of nausea that rolled in, the deafening ear ringing, my stomach like someone holding a drill to it, the vomiting of bitter pills shrunken and softened by my own body. I hadn't imagined I'd have to swallow them again as they heaved up, that it would taste so disgusting, that all I would hear would be an everlasting earsplitting bell as I lost consciousness.

And I never, ever would have imagined my last thought before the darkness closed upon me like a book shutting would be, *Please don't let me die.*

It was July. I lay on a trampoline next to Jonah in his backyard; his parents were out of town. The night started when the sun and moon were trading shifts. I brought my Edna St. Vincent Millay book. We took turns reading aloud.

> *Am I kin to Sorrow?*
> *Are we kin?*
> *That so oft upon my door—*
> *Oh, come in!*

Nothing turns me on like poetry read aloud. So soon our clothes were half off, our breath shallow, sweat cooling on my face, the hot night air feeling like not enough, never enough, in the best way. His hand was on my hand. My gaze was up to where the stars swam in a black, forever sea. Dark shapes of leaves seemed to shiver our names. Life moved through me, wild, alive. I was so in love it was a scream and not a feeling. Jonah and I were eternal in that moment. We were in the eye of that hot summer night. I could feel his pulse in our grasped hands and it could have been my own.

"I want all of life to be like this," I said.

"Journey," he told me. "It can't."

I knew he was right and yet I still didn't believe him.

I wrote a note to myself that night in the back of the Edna St. Vincent Millay book.

Dear future self,
    When you get sad, don't forget the night you lay under the stars with Jonah Patterson. The way the air smelled, like honeysuckle blossoms. The warmth of him. The way the atmosphere darkened so gradually you barely noticed until it was night.

If you could look at a graph of my life, at the events and resulting moods that shaped it up until my suicide attempt, it would resemble a jagged mountaintop. Sharp peaks drop gut-wrenchingly into valleys. No plateaus. But is that a negative thing? Sometimes it's been heart-burstingly wonderful. My love can swallow the whole world. My sadness can eclipse it.

It's always been that way, since I was a kid. My parents called them "big feelings." I threw epic tantrums when I didn't get my way, screamed loud enough to wake the neighbors, bawled at sad movies. But I was also funny and made people laugh. I loved art and singing. My little sisters followed me everywhere and hung on my every word.

"When you walk into a room," my dad's always told me, "the sun rises."

Do you still feel that way, Dad, as you sit with me in this fluorescent white hospital room with a wet face, your chin in your hands? As Mom paces the linoleum floor in her running shoes, *squeaksqueaksqueak,* and asks me again why, why did I do it? I can't answer. Not just because I don't know, but because my throat is rubbed raw from where the tube went down so they could pump my stomach this morning. Out the water-flecked window, it's raining, a rarity in Southern California. Good. The world should be raining when I feel this way—like my entire body, my whole being, is one giant ache. I don't even have it in me to weep, though the want is there. I'm a shell, pumped clean and empty.

"Why, Journey? Just tell me why," Mom repeats, standing in front of the window so I'll look at her. Her bottle-red hair's a cloud around her head, her signature smoky eyeliner's not there, she's wearing exercise clothes like she raced from the gym. She doesn't even look like my mother right now.

I close my eyes, thinking, *I am such a screwup I can't even die properly.* I remember how I panicked when the black curtain pulled itself over my eyes yesterday and I thought I was dying. Then suddenly I didn't want to die. I make no goddamn sense.

"Stop asking her that," Dad says. "If you can't compose yourself, go take a walk around the block."

My dad's still wearing his badge from work that has a smiling picture of himself with much shorter hair on it and says "Seth Smith, Guidance Counselor." He's wearing the same shirt now as he is in the picture—a dorky Hawaiian number with flamingos on it.

"Compose myself?" Mom asks him, hand on hip. "Like you, you mean, sitting there in silence?"

Dad points to his tear-wet face. "What do you think these are?"

"I don't know, your cheeks?" Mom says.

"I've been crying my eyes out," Dad says.

"You want a Parent of the Year trophy?"

My dad stands up, grabs his pork pie hat.

"I'm sorry," Mom tells him. "I'm—stressed. And hangry. My blood sugar—"

"I'm going to sample the scenery" is all he says before walking out the door.

*Sample the scenery* is a classic Dad euphemism. It means he's pissed and he's going for a walk. Just like when he snores on the couch and claims he's deeply meditating.

I close my eyes, pretend to sleep, while Mom sighs. "This is what he does," she says, to no one in particular. "This is what we do."

This is the first time my parents have lingered in the same room since the family meeting ten months ago when they broke the news of their separation to me and my two sisters, Ruby and Stevie. The Christmas tree was still up; tinsel shrapnel littered the floor. My sisters' tear-sparkly eyes matched the tinsel.

"We'll always love each other. This doesn't mean we're any less of a family," Mom had said, her eye shadow suspiciously blue, her outfit showing a bit too much cleavage. Like she was already relishing the thought of singlehood.

"We'll still be the best of friends," Dad had said then, reaching over the coffee table to pat Mom's ringless hand.

Now Mom slides a stool next to me and takes my hand. She kisses it. My mom has the loveliest eyes—pale gold, an almost impossible color. Right now, though, they are cried tiny, crusted with yesterday's mascara.

"This was a cry for help," she says.

"No."

"It was."

That she would dismiss this as a gesture makes me want to scream. But I'm too raw to scream. "Well, I guess you know me better than I do."

"You're being facetious, but I actually do. Because I'm your mother. I know every part of you—even the baby, the kid you were, that you forgot. You've always had to make the biggest statement. You're upset? Throw a tantrum. Your sister is born? Start crapping in your closet and threaten to put the baby in the trash can."

"And this is supposed to make me feel better . . . how exactly?"

"This is nothing in the big picture," she whispers to me, petting my hair. "This was just—just a way to get us to hear you. And we hear you. We love you. It's going to pass. You're going to feel better."

Already I know I won't feel better.

"What if I actually wanted to die?" I ask her, not blinking.

She doesn't blink, either, but her eyes glass over with new tears.

"Then that would be the hardest thing in the world to hear as your mother." She wipes her eyes. "But luckily I don't believe you."

"Knock knock," Dad says, walking in.

What the point of the "knock knock" was, I couldn't tell you, because he's now standing behind my mother with an ice cream sandwich.

"Thought this might cheer you up," he says.

"She can't eat that after getting her stomach pumped," Mom says, standing up.

"Oh." Dad stares at the ice cream sandwich and makes a face like he feels sorry for it. "You want it?"

"No refined sugar," she says. "You bought it, you eat it."

"I'm vegan, remember?"

"You only remind me every time I see you." She grabs her purse. "I'm going to the cafeteria before I chew your head off."

That leaves Dad and me alone. He drops the ice cream sandwich in the biohazard bin. He sits on the stool next to me and folds his hands together.

"You are so brave," he says, wiping his eyes.

"Can we just be quiet for a little bit?" I ask.

*Like for the rest of my life?* I don't add.

I adore my parents. But there should be a word for the unbearable burden of their love.

The last time I almost died was the best night of my life.

My favorite band, Girl Cheese, had come to town. They're a three-piece all-female band I found online whose videos I fell in love with, who write adorable harmonizing vocals with lyrics about stuff like how delicious pizza is and thrift store shopping and bisexuality. The three girls are in their twenties and live in New York, dress like vintage princesses, and play glitter-painted instruments. I had been obsessed with them all year and they finally stopped through Goleta to play an all-ages venue. Jonah and I went. They played all my favorite songs. I bought a T-shirt and talked with Girl Cheese at the merch table for ten whole minutes. They were even cuter in person. They signed my record. It was magical.

At midnight, a bunch of us were hanging out in the

parking lot—Jonah; Marisol; her boyfriend at the time, Lloyd; a few of Lloyd's buddies, Wendy and Otis, who I know from film class. Otis said he knew of an apartment complex a few blocks away where we could sneak into the hot tub. So after a quick 7-Eleven run for Slurpees and Funyuns, we did, skinny-dipping in the dark and trying our best to keep our laughter to whispers.

Next we went out to the only restaurant open all night—a diner with tired-eyed waiters, soggy fries, and two Yelp stars. Wendy and Otis lived in my direction and offered to give me a ride home afterward. Usually I'd have to be home way before midnight, if my parents even let me go to a show in the first place. But now that my parents were separated, the rules had changed. I had no curfew. There were still rules for Ruby and Stevie, but my parents were too distracted and too guilty to enforce them for me anymore. It was after two in the morning. The streets were empty, the moon was bright.

*Dear future self,* I wrote on my diner receipt. *Remember the gorgeous night that felt like morning would never come.*

Wendy, Otis, and I rolled down the window so the barely cool dead-of-night freeway summer air blasted our faces, fresh. We cranked Girl Cheese and sang along, trees whipping by, shadows barely darker than the inky sky and twinkly star shrapnel. I remember the feeling of my heart in my chest, so strong, bursting with song; the grin on my face seemed permanent, joy coursing red through my veins. I sat shotgun, dancing.

And in one second—one second that now seems to last a year in my memory—Otis, who drove, eyed the rearview and yelled, "Oh no, you guys—"

Then there was a confusion of noise. Metal scraping, crunching, the grill of a semitruck crushed against the front of the car. Heat and the color orange exploded outside my window and a single thought accompanied by a quiet terror rang all throughout my being.

*This is it.*

Then the car was still, Otis's door crushed against the median. My side of the car was still ablaze; it smelled like chemicals melting. Wendy screamed at us to get out. She climbed out the back door and Otis and I somehow immediately scrambled over our seats and followed her. We ran up the freeway, where traffic had stopped for the accident. We ran up the wrong away, away from the semitruck turned over on its side, a river of gas lit up in flames. Away from Otis's car, where the shotgun seat was now burning. Wendy, Otis, and I held hands and watched as the whole scene exploded like an action movie and firefighters showed up and people stopped on the freeway stepped out of their parked cars to gawk and point. I shook, cold, in shock, and answered police questions. An ambulance came and took us to the hospital. Besides a small nick where my head had hit the windshield, and Otis's mild concussion that caused him to keep asking "What happened?" and forced us to explain ourselves again, again—we were okay.

We had survived, what a miracle.

We had almost died, what a horror.

The accident was only a little over two months ago now. Even though I escaped without a scratch, it did something to me. My big feelings became colossal. The world now seemed, at times, unbearable. I was sick to my stomach from fear. I cried over nothing. I thought of death constantly—haunted by it, afraid of it, obsessed with it, drawn to it. These changes were easy to dismiss, because they built up over days, and weeks, and I've always been *so much*. I was already a loaded weapon. The accident just clicked my safety off.

# PRESENT

The crisis center doesn't look like a crisis center. It's a lavender Victorian in the south part of town. Unassuming, white picket fence, painted porch with a swing on it. There's no sign on it. Just looks like someone's house. On the inside, besides an office space set up in the front with long tables, volunteers hunched over old-school phones and speaking in quiet voices, you'd think people live here. We gather in a back room set up with folding chairs, strung with a Tibetan prayer flag, lined with built-in bookcases. It smells lived-in, loved, warm, historic.

Training for the hotline is two full weekends and every evening in the first two weeks of the new year, fifty hours total. Brutal. The first day I arrive I'm greeted by the training coordinator, Davina, an Indian American woman with long braids, tortoiseshell glasses, and a brilliant smile. I know her from the in-person interview last week, where she was so happy to have me join this small bastion of new volunteers.

"Journey will be our youngest volunteer ever," Davina

tells the three of us as we sit in the folding chairs, and I can see why: two of the other volunteers are clearly retirees, older women named Willa and Francie. They're adorable. They both dyed their hair a faint blue over the white and apparently do everything together the way I hope Marisol and I will when we're granny-aged. But I feel a sea of life experience and lack thereof between us, and when Davina gets up to use the restroom right before we begin, instead of engaging them in conversation, I scroll on my phone. We're still waiting for our fourth volunteer. A part of me hopes they don't show, and I can bow out of this wild plan with no responsibility whatsoever. But then the door bangs open and a girl blazes in, guitar slung on her back and lipstick so red it seems neon, an explosion of kinky ginger hair and a nose ring and a startling smattering of freckles on her light brown skin to match. Willa and Francie go quiet, watching her.

"Sorry!" the girl says, dropping her enormous bag and guitar at her feet. She looks around the room with a grimace. "What can I say? I like to make an entrance."

This girl carries the sun in her hair. I wish I glowed like her. As if she senses my envy, she meets my gaze and smiles.

"Nice jellies," she says, pointing to my glittery, see-through shoes.

"Nice leopard-print flats."

"Gracias. I'm Etta," she says.

"Journey," I tell her.

"*Don't stop believin',*" she belts out with pop star pizzazz.

"Never heard that one before," I say.

"Seriously?!"

"No."

We giggle. Etta introduces herself to Willa and Francie. "I am in love with your hair!" she almost yells. Then they giggle. Etta has that effect on people, apparently. She's like human laughing gas.

When Davina comes back in, she hands the four of us brick-heavy binders and begins by walking us through the chapter list and outlining what we're going to learn, all the sections with their laminated pages on everything from mental illness to bullying to eating disorders. She explains how hotline shifts work. It's like a teacher going through a syllabus. Then she turns to us and asks what made us want to come here and volunteer. She asks me first, smiling, waiting for my answer. The silence seems to deepen as everyone listens. Davina asked me this same question in the interview. I wasn't expecting to have to share my answer with Etta and Willa and Francie, too. But I repeat the same story.

"I have a friend who recently tried to kill herself," I say. "I, uh . . . I just want to be able to help her if she ever needs it again. And people like her."

"Willa and I got sick of the soup kitchen," Francie says. "You wouldn't *believe* the drama that goes on there."

"Politics," Willa says, shaking her head.

"Yes, that's the word. Politics. We're just little old ladies who want to help people."

"You two are the cutest," Etta says. "I can't even handle it."

Willa and Francie giggle.

"And you, Etta?" Davina asks. "What about you?"

"I, um . . . well." She twists her hair. "I guess it's because I feel like I suck at helping people. I'm no good at it. And I—I'm afraid to. I want to be better. But honestly, I don't even know if I can. Okay, that probably makes no sense." She emits a tiny scream. "I'm so nervous right now!"

She doesn't seem nervous. She seems ebullient.

"You're doing just fine, dear!" Willa says.

"Well, whatever your reason, I'm so happy you're here," Davina says. "I promise the experiences will be intense and frightening and sometimes heartbreaking, but they are also incredibly rewarding."

"More rewarding than handing out rolls at the soup kitchen, I hope," Francie says.

"Only one roll per person, Francie!" Willa says, mock yelling.

"Oh, yes, how could I forget."

The two women giggle at some inside joke.

"You two," Davina says. "Do I have to separate you?"

More laughter. Davina lets the room get quiet before putting her hand on the binder in her lap.

"Let's open up to page two," Davina says.

We begin the work. It's not easy work. It's not work that really has right answers all the time, besides some rules that are spelled out up front. We walk through a scripted call where Davina role-plays and acts out possible scenarios, and then discusses our responses with us.

After this first day of training is over, Willa and Francie go follow Davina for a tour of the back garden. Etta and I stand up and with our bags.

"That was so intense," Etta says.

"It was."

"Do you think you're going to go through the full training?"

"Aren't you?"

"Sure. It's just . . . a lot of hours." She slings her guitar on her back. "But then again, Willa and Francie are here, and they're my favorite people I've ever met in my life."

I smile.

"Do you think they're a couple?" she asks. "That would make me love them even more. I hope when I'm their age I'm as cute as them with a cute little wife who dyes her hair blue with me."

Wow. A girl who is into girls. Took me two years of high school before I met anyone at school who was openly queer.

I think I love it here.

The next day, the second day of training, I come back and it's just Davina, Willa, and Francie.

"Etta wasn't able to commit to the time the training requires, unfortunately," Davina says. "But we'll carry on without her."

I'm kind of shocked at my disappointment. Etta was so intriguing. We could have been friends. And the next weekend, I come in and it's just Davina and another empty chair.

"Willa and Francie decided to go back to the soup kitchen," Davina says.

"Geez, people are dropping like flies," I say, taking my seat.

"I hope you're not thinking of leaving, too?" she asks.

"No way," I tell her. "Unlike my last boyfriend, I'm committed."

She laughs.

I like Davina. She has a kind, helpful air about her not unlike my therapist, Wolf—a tendency to lean in and listen and allow for thoughtful pauses after I speak. Good thing I like her, too, because this training is fifty hours. FIVE OH HOURS over two weeks. I learn about empathy and transference and validation and mirroring until my brain is bleeding. Bonus: some of this stuff will come in handy, like active listening skills—definitely plan to whip those out during excruciating conversations with my parents. I can't even imagine what this is like for Davina, who has worked here for years and led dozens of these trainings. The feedback she gives doesn't feel like criticism, but like she's simply offering another perspective. Most of what we discuss are hypothetical scenarios, page-long scripts with made-up people struggling with suicidal thoughts or abusive partners or financial stresses. If I learn anything from the binder and its endless hypothetical scenarios, it's that there are so many ways to suffer. And, as Davina points out, the binder can be useful—"a toolbox" to refer to—but most people and situations don't fit neatly in one page or one section.

After our two weeks together, I come back on a Tuesday night and it's time for me to answer my first calls. It happened so fast. It was such a whirlwind, and now I don't know if I'm truly prepared. But Davina sits next to me and smiles, sliding on her headset.

"Nobody feels ready," she says. "Don't worry. You'll be fine. I'm right here."

In the background, a couple other folks are in the middle of hotline calls.

"Busy night," she says. "But that's Lydia, JD, and Beatriz. They'll be your shift buddies."

One of them, don't know who, a hippieish woman in a long skirt, waves at us and turns back to her call.

The first call I get is not a suicidal person, an abused person, or a teen suffering from online bullying. She's not a person in financial distress or a homeless person or anything else there is a clean-cut section for in the binder. She's just . . . exhausted.

"I'm a goddamn mess," she says, crying. "I work too much. I hate how irritable I am, how tired I am, how little my own kids want to be around me."

"I'm so sorry," I say, looking at Davina, who is listening in.

*Tell me about your support network*, Davina writes on a pad of paper for me.

"Tell me about your support network," I recite.

Davina nods, like I've done so well, when all I did was read off her paper.

The woman tells me about her sister, who's been incredibly kind to her but who lives on the East Coast and has her own life. She weeps loudly and I feel for her. I feel *Fremdschämen* for her, vicarious embarrassment, because she's in such an unraveled state. Spontaneously, I ask her about other social connections she has outside of work and family. That's the first time the woman stops crying for a moment and sniffs, thinking.

"There *is* this woman Noelle in my Zumba class," she says. "We've exchanged numbers. She has kids my age, too."

"I wonder if you might try to schedule a time to have coffee with her, just to connect with another person who might understand what you're going through?" I ask.

I look up at Davina, who's giving me two thumbs up and a big grin. This is such a roller coaster. Even a few minutes into the call, I go from complete imposter syndrome panic to *I am amazing at this* confidence.

Davina writes down a question about calling her doctor. I talk to the woman about what she's happy about in her life right now and she tells me about her Chihuahua, her job as a flower shop owner, how lucky she feels to be alive sometimes.

There's a long pause where I hear nothing, no sniffing, and I wonder if I lost her.

"Hello?" I ask.

"Oh, sorry," she says. "My husband just came home. Anyway, thank you. I do feel better, just talking about it."

A little dog barks in the background and we say good-bye, hang up. Davina high-fives me.

"Look at you!" she says. "A natural."

"That was . . . something."

"Very good first call."

"I didn't feel like there were answers."

"Exactly," says Davina, smiling.

I'm still high from that call when another comes in. This woman simply whispers to me that her boyfriend is going to kill her and then hangs up. Immediately, my emotions get torn in the total opposite direction. Maybe this woman is abused. Now she's unreachable and I did nothing to help her. Davina takes me into her closet-sized office upstairs, walled with tapestries, filled with tiny cacti thriving under artificial lights. We sit on beanbag chairs and discuss.

"I hate that I couldn't help her," I say.

Davina nods. "Yes. Tell me more."

"Like, I should have said something. I should have told her to stay on the line, asked if she was safe—that's the first thing I'm supposed to ask."

"She didn't give you a *chance* to ask," Davina reminds me.

"I could have done something."

"Sometimes, everything goes wrong, and we still did everything right," Davina says. "You're here to support, not to steer. You get that? You're here to offer a kind, compassionate place for people when they are ready. She was not ready."

I thank Davina, give her a hug. She says I'm going to do great when my real shift starts next week, but I'm not so sure after tonight.

Maybe it's me who's not ready.

# PAST

The summer before last I fell stupid in love with my best friend, a boy named Jonah who lived around the corner from me since fourth grade. At first I thought falling stupid in love with my best friend was the worst idea ever. But it actually turned out to be the opposite. At first.

Dear past self, you can be so dumb, you can be so smart.

See, when you crush on someone and haven't shared history, you have this whole gap of knowledge to fill with the fluff of fantasy. We're all so many versions of ourselves, but the only version you know of your recent crush is the right-now one. You don't know who they were a year ago, what debatable fashion choices they used to rock, what the insides of their house and room look like. But with Jonah, I knew *all* his versions: the sandy-haired boy with the slight stutter and the video game collection who showed me his tree house and let me swim in his pool; the boy who was bullied by kids in elementary school, and then bloomed suddenly into this effusive, magnetic chatterbox in junior high, the one who ran for student body president, and then in high school became too cool for politics and learned guitar. Who grew his hair longer than his chin and wore band shirts and a lopsided smile. Carried a skateboard around with one hand, held mine with the other. The first time he kissed me under the same oak tree where later I'd try to die, I already knew what brand of ChapStick he wore, exactly what he'd have eaten for breakfast, and how he would pet my short hair as we made out. The only thing I didn't know was what a great kisser he'd be, but that part I guessed at and guessed right. I'd seen him smooch enough girls over the years, the way his freshman girlfriend Carla's fingers curled when he kissed her goodbye in front of English class.

I was afraid to fall in love with my best friend, afraid that I would lose him; but I was more afraid of missing the opportunity to love him back when at the end of sophomore year, he confessed he'd always loved me, always would. By the time the choice to be his friend or his girlfriend presented itself, my mind had made itself up already.

So ours was an extraordinary love, the kind with roots, the kind with hindsight, the kind you walk into with your eyes wide open. He used to love my wildness, my unpredictability. Then, after my parents broke up, my highs got higher, my lows got lower, and I became "a lot for him." He let me know that. Often.

"Babe," he'd say. "Maybe dial it down a notch?"

Or, "It's not Armageddon, you know?"

Or, my favorite of all, asked in the gentlest of tones, "Is this a period thing?"

Oh, the rage that question would evoke, even if it happened to be true.

Once the car accident happened this summer, I fell off the deep end.

It was a few weeks after the car accident that my mom took me to see Dr. Shaw. Dr. Shaw's office was tiny, brown, ill lit; it made therapy feel like it was occurring inside a hole. His desk was a city of haphazard paperwork towers, his wall a chaos of neon Post-its. He sported a beard that looked either too long or too short and he did not meet my gaze ever, just sort of glazed over it as if he were simply scanning part of the room. I saw him only once. It was my first time ever seeing a psychiatrist, someone my parents found through our insurance network. Let's just say I had been having a *lot* of big feelings—crying for no reason, wondering what the point of everything was, not caring about the future, even when I had the best boyfriend and life I could ask for. It came out of nowhere, bit me like a snake once senior year started. It was September. It was supposed to be the month of new beginnings.

"Tell me why you're here," Dr. Shaw said, clipboard balanced on khaki knee.

"I feel . . . not right," I told him. "Like everything is meaningless. I used to be so happy, I could do anything. I felt important. Then this depression hit me. This thought struck me out of nowhere: the world would be fine without me."

Dr. Shaw shifted a few papers around in his stack and reclipped them to his clipboard. *Clack.* "On a scale of one to ten, how depressed would you rate yourself right now? Ten being extremely, one being not at all."

I sat slack-jawed for a moment, the words stuck in my throat. Because I had come prepared to lie on the couch and talk about my dreams and how I felt about my mother. And now he was asking me to reduce my tornado of inexplicable emotions down to a number between one and ten.

Was that one to ten on the grand scale of happiest person in the world to saddest?

Was that one to ten relative only to my own experience? Like, how happy I'd ever been to how sad I had ever been?

If this wasn't ten, did that mean there was a way to feel worse than this? I didn't even want to know.

He said "extremely." Ten equals extremely. I was extremely depressed.

"Ten," I said.

He nodded and marked it down. I opened my mouth, ready to talk about the car accident, to say, I've always been moody, a handful, but my emotions veered to scary recently. I figured Dr. Shaw should probably know that about me.

"Recently, I was in a—"

"Let's finish the survey," Dr. Shaw said, tapping the clipboard with a pen.

"Don't you want to, like, get to know me?" I asked.

Another pen tap. "That's what the survey's for."

Oh . . . kay. I glared at the certificates on his walls, thinking, the world is a sham. This man is a crappy psychiatrist, and now we can add one more to the list of lies grown-ups tell: that psychiatry will make you feel better. That a degree and a "Dr." before your name means anything.

"Sometimes I am very spirited and/or irritable," he said.

At first I thought he was telling me this. About himself. And in my head, I was like, okay, sir. I'm the one having a session here. But after a long stare-down, I realized he was waiting for me to answer.

"On a . . . scale of one to ten?" I asked.

"Yes."

I'm feeling pretty irritable right now, Dr. Shaw. And spirited? What did that even mean? Of course I was spirited. I'd skinny-dipped in freezing ocean water on a December evening. I loved my boyfriend so much I wanted to puke on him sometimes. The right song at the right time could make me weep like a banshee, whether it was a damn commercial jingle or not. Yes, I was *spirited*.

"Ten," I said.

"At times, I feel extremely self-confident, and others, I feel full of doubt."

It was like a line from my imaginary autobiography. Sometimes I was mighty; sometimes I was a mote. I thought this was teenage-girl universal, but guess not? "Ten."

"Sometimes I am much more interested in sex than others."

I raised an eyebrow. Seemed pervy for a middle-aged male stranger to ask. There were times when Jonah complained I wanted it too much. We did it at school once during fourth period, my suggestion. But lately, Jonah had been complaining that I didn't want it enough. "Ten," I said quietly.

"Sometimes I am despairing, others I am vibrant and creative."

Lately, despair had been the word of the day. I used to dance around my room hanging Christmas lights and FaceTiming with Jonah or Marisol all night long, devouring poems, talking to myself in the mirror and putting on lipstick for nobody but me at one a.m. Now I soaked my pillow with tears for no reason.

"Ten," I said.

"Sometimes I am greatly optimistic, and others I am extremely pessimistic."

The world was such a beautiful place full of babies and flowers and parties and kisses and holidays and jewels and glittering shorelines on white sand beaches but the world was also a place of carcasses and graveyards and bullies and broken bones and darkness and in one moment a giggly car ride could turn into an inescapable inferno. So.

"Ten," I said.

He kept on with the questions, checked boxes on page after page.

Ten, ten, ten, I said.

Dr. Shaw never asked me about my mother or my dreams. There wasn't even a couch to lie upon in his office, just a creaky swiveling chair. There was no time to mention the car accident, because of the length of the questionnaire and the fact that our insurance only paid for a half-hour visit. Nor did we talk about my parents' separation, how every week now, my sisters and I traded Mom's house for Dad's, and my parents didn't even bother getting out of the car for the drop-off. How just a month after they separated, Mom had moved in with Levi, an acquaintance she knew through work. We didn't talk about any of those things.

"You have moderate to severe bipolar disorder," Dr. Shaw told me in a flat, uninterested tone, the way someone might inform you you have food stuck between your teeth. "I'm writing you a prescription for Depakote, a mood stabilizer."

I couldn't believe it. Bipolar? Because I'd said ten for everything? That's how they diagnosed things? He handed me the paper and guided me gently back to the waiting room in the middle of the dark maze of offices. I collapsed in a vinyl chair next to a stack of magazines, looking at the indecipherable prescription in my hand and suddenly seeing an answer.

Scrolling on my phone, I read the definition of bipolar

disorder aloud. "A mental disorder marked by alternating periods of elation and depression." Sounded plausible. About ten seconds later, I noticed there was a woman in the corner of the room, nearly hidden by the enormous palm plant. She was eyeing me like a curiosity.

"Sorry," I said.

She looked back down at her magazine. I wondered why she was there. Did she have bipolar disorder, too? She looked so normal. Did she sob for no reason sometimes, like while braiding her sisters' hair, or reading a Robert Frost poem to her English class? Did she sometimes hate her own boyfriend because she loved him so much it seemed to physically hurt?

*Apparently I have bipolar disorder,* I wrote in my journal.

A sense of relief seemed to lift me, a lightness returning to my body, a spirit returning to my step as I headed out of the office. It was as if Dr. Shaw had handed me a key to myself, one I had always needed without knowing. So *this* was why I was the girl with big feelings.

At the counter, I listened while the pharmacist rattled off every side effect of my new drug.

*Mild drowsiness, weakness, sleepiness; diarrhea, constipation, or upset stomach; changes in your menstrual cycle; enlarged breasts; tremors; weight gain or loss; vision changes; hair loss; an unpleasant taste in your mouth.*

A small price to pay, I thought, for feeling normal. For not weirding Jonah out anymore with my drawings of zombie girls in the margins of my composition books or by weeping and pulling my hair. For not making Marisol tell me "It's time to lay off the Sylvia Plath, buddy" and give me the name of her mom's life coach, Berry, who, of course, I never called. For not making Ruby and Stevie ask me why I was so sad all the time, and not making me answer, "Because life is sad."

Life isn't sad.

I'm bipolar.

I gave the pharmacist my money and called Jonah for a ride home. I showed him the pills, hot pink, my favorite color, like they were made for me. Jonah didn't seem sure what to say.

"You don't seem . . . mentally ill to me," he said. "You're just going through a lot."

The trees outside the window swayed with the breeze. The sky was bright and blue because in Goleta, the sky is always bright and blue. The median income is high, the schools are award-winning, the beach and mountains are paradise. I don't know why Jonah would want to suddenly make me so sad, the pinprick to my balloon.

"You were just in a car accident where you almost *died*," he said.

"Yeah, well, Dr. So-and-So seemed uninterested in that fact."

"Journey, I've known you since we were in grade school,"

Jonah said. "I know you're . . . mercurial."

"You and your SAT words—"

"Listen. Don't do that. Let me finish. Mercurial, sure. But you've always been sane. And lately, yeah, it's been bad. Worse than I've ever seen you." In a one-second glance my way before putting his eyes back to the road, Jonah looked at me with such love I shuddered. "You just went through something traumatic. If I'd been through what you'd been through, I'd be all over the place, too."

I didn't say anything. He knew me better than anyone, and sometimes that was irritating.

"And really, they just send you off with pills for that?" he asked softly. "You're seventeen."

Sometimes the way he spoke to me made me think of my dad. Huge turnoff.

"Wow, he's not only cute, he can count, too," I said.

He was quiet and chewing the inside of his cheek, a thing he did when he was in his saddest, most unreachable place.

"Is this what you want?" he asked.

"I want an answer," I insisted. "I want to not cry and scare everybody."

"You don't scare me."

"Not right *now*."

"Just . . . don't lose yourself," he said. "Like my mom."

"Your mom's clinically depressed, not bipolar," I reminded him.

35

His mother's severe depression had long been controlled by heavy meds. Yeah, it meant she was able to do basic mom stuff like hit up the grocery store and go to work and drive her kids to school. But her spirit was weak. She slept a lot and watched a lot of reality TV.

Jonah didn't say anything else. Our car rides became like that when I got stubborn and gloomy—a mean sort of quiet, him turning the music down, each of us left to our own thoughts, except of course for me telling him "Brake, brake" every once in a while as I braced myself for a stop—I'd been like that since the accident—and him whispering, "It's okay, babe."

When I got home, I thought a lot about what Jonah said and what that survey in Dr. Shaw's hands must have looked like, tens all the way down. I thought, there is no way to either tell the truth or lie on a set of questions like that. Because what is a ten? What is a five?

When I told Marisol about the diagnosis she rolled her eyes at me at first, thinking it was another phase, like that one month last year when I went to church and got really into it, or when I bought a Ouija board and thought I could see ghosts. But while my dad had some reservations, my mom was super supportive of the diagnosis. I had had some of the worst bad days of my life over the past six months—not saying it was *because* of their divorce necessarily, but it sure didn't help—and since the car accident this past summer, there had been moments when I had scared everyone with my bouts of joy that crashed into from-nowhere weepiness. Dad, of course, gently asked if I might try some more "natural" remedies before jumping to meds, but accepted it when I told him *hell no thank you*. I wanted the strong stuff. My mom ordered about every book on adolescents and mental illness you could think of and became an expert overnight. Whereas she used to be frustrated with my "drama" and my "acting out," now she seemed to have infinite patience for my mood swings. She even wanted to set up a meeting with my teachers so I could get special treatment—longer test times, forgiveness for late homework. But I didn't want people outside my most tight-knit circle knowing. I wanted to pass for normal. I didn't even like that my sisters knew, although they seemed to only understand it in the most simplistic terms: I was sad, I felt crazy, I had a condition, pills would fix said condition.

I took the pills. Two of them. Twice a day. For days, then weeks. I experienced drowsiness and a delayed menstrual period and gained five pounds like the pharmacist had warned. Sometimes I spaced out in class, but I don't know, it had happened before. I didn't cry so much, but I also didn't smile as much, either. Some days I was sure the pills were working. Some days I wondered if I'd been handed a neon-pink placebo.

◆　◆　◆

I'd started having terrible thoughts after the school year started, and I'd been too afraid to talk about them with anyone. Marisol would probably have cried if I confessed them to her. My parents would worry and call more doctors, who would prescribe more drugs.

At first it arose as a silly, overdramatic solution to problems—something benign, like the time I forgot to turn in a paper and got a reprimand from Mr. Teasley, a harried, grumpy American History teacher a year away from retirement who mentioned this fact in class frequently. He dismissed the entire class early one day just to have a "heart-to-heart" with me. Nothing resembling a heart was actually involved in this discussion.

"I've seen your kind before," he said, sitting on the edge of his desk, arms crossed. There was a weird blurry reflection of myself in his glasses. "Smart but lazy."

Nothing riles me up more than being told I'm like everybody else. "I wasn't lazy, I started the paper last week. I honestly forgot it was due today."

I had been forgetting things, writing things down wrong, procrastinating since I'd started medication. Maybe he was right, maybe I was lazy. I not only lived in a perpetual brain fog, I'd found it hard to care since school started. When the weather started turning—the air grew teeth, the leaves on certain trees yellowed—I turned with it. In the course of a lifetime, what did these papers and stupid quizzes matter anyway?

"Well, I honestly think you'll be lucky if you pull off a C this semester," he said.

He was being so patronizing I couldn't help it. Haughtily, I said the words my mom used to say to me as a child. "I can do anything I want."

"That's simply not true," he told me.

He proceeded to lecture me about my "attitude problem" and then veered into a long monologue about how happy he'd be to retire next year and move to Florida where rent is cheaper and the weather is balmy and beautiful, and never have to deal with students and their bad attitudes again. The bell rang and he kept talking. I looked out the window and watched the leaves skittering off the maples in the courtyard, students walking through patches of sunshine and laughing and putting their arms around each other and being normal humans. I had started my prescription two weeks prior. And my feelings, they were duller, but not at all in the way I wanted. *This is what life feels like lately,* I thought. *Like I'm watching it through a window. Like I'm not a part of it.*

"Earth to Journey," Mr. Teasley said, snapping his fingers in front of my face.

I looked up, his wrinkled face eyeing me with slight disgust.

"Okay," I said, forcing a smile.

"Okay?" He shook his head. "You haven't listened to a word I've said. Forget it—you're unreachable."

He waved a hand in the air and turned to his briefcase.

I slung my backpack over my shoulder and headed out the door, into the sunshine, the sound of laughter, and thought, *I want to kill myself*. I pictured it, too, in horrible flashes.

It was alarming to experience these thoughts the first time. Like some stranger had taken over my head. Like an uninvited guest had invaded me.

And then that guest unpacked its suitcase and made me its home.

The voice grew stronger.

I didn't win a poetry contest at school: "Kill yourself," it whispered.

Jonah and I had an epic fight because I thought he was flirting with Madison Jameson at lunch: "He'd be happy if you died," it murmured.

I woke up sweaty, teary, my heart a frightening drum, flashbacks of the car crash, smoke and flames: "It's a mistake you lived," it said.

Marisol forgot to call me back. I couldn't find my shoes. Look at this picture of my family from my junior high years, the way Dad's hand rested on Mom's waist.

"Nothing matters anymore," it yelled.

The voice would be quiet for hours. Then something would happen, darken my inner skies, and it would come back, tempting me with an easy answer, a black hole to jump into, a trapdoor, a sweet goodbye.

*Love is*
*a flame*
*that burns*
*your house*
*down*
*until*
*your house*
*is nothing*
*but a memory.*

That was all the mess that led me here, to this hospital room, lying brain-sick in an adjustable bed. The memories of my diagnosis and subsequent downward spiral dizzy me. Mom and Dad left the hospital. It's just me now, on my own to think about the worst thing I've ever done and wonder if I'm going to do it again.

Jonah worried about me. That's partly why I wanted medication, wanted an answer, a reason. But then it turned out even medicated, something was wrong with me. Those morbid thoughts took over. I was a cloud-headed girl with mud in her heart.

The phone was to my ear last night. I stood in front of the mirror, a bottle of Tylenol in my hand, listening to Jonah cry and tell me he didn't want to be together with me anymore.

"I'm just tired," he said. "I love you so much, but this doesn't make me happy anymore."

"We were going to be together until we were saggy and gray," I said.

"We were friends before. We'll always be friends, you know that, right? I love you, Journey."

"Jonah," I said, looking for the right words, although I knew all I had now were wrong ones. "I want to kill myself."

"Don't be dramatic."

It wasn't drama, though; at least, it didn't feel like it to me. That was the first and only time I ever said it out loud, but it had been rattling around inside me for months. I couldn't see the future anymore. I didn't know which version of myself I was.

This black hole opened up between my gut and throat, an ache strong enough to out-scream everything else, a big ball of the pain from my family being blown apart, combined with the smashing of tons of steel and red-hot flames that should have ended me, and now this—this ballooning, marooning dread. This utter loneliness and hopelessness that could, in a second, suck up all the color and breath from me.

I hung up the phone.

Yesterday, I decided I was going to kill myself tomorrow.

I compose a mental note to my past self as I lie in the hospital bed, reliving my poor life choices. It's simple. To the point.

*Dear past self,*
    *Fuck you.*

I have never met the doctor before right now, the doctor who apparently oversaw this morning's stomach pumping while I was still unconscious, but her name is Dr. Jaikumar and she is evidently very disappointed with me.

"You know how close you were to not making it?" she asks, sitting on a stool next to me and watching me with brown, blazing eyes. "If it weren't for a couple's dog who went off trail after a stray tennis ball, you'd never have been found."

I planned it that way, behind the sprawling oak at the lake. A place you can't see from the road or the main path. I don't know if I'm glad they found me. I feel like hell. I'm still ambivalent on the whole living or dying question.

"So you're saying a dog saved my life?" I joke. Joking is what I resort to when I'm all out of ideas. The joke blows right by the doctor. She doesn't even blink.

"We recommend transferring you to a facility for teenagers so you can be observed for three to five days. Since you're eighteen, you just need to give us permission and I can start the paperwork."

"What if I say no? Can I go home?"

"Or," Dr. Jaikumar says, standing up and looking down at me like the sick thing I am, "we could do an involuntary watch here at the mental ward of this hospital. But I promise you, voluntary admittance to a facility for folks your age will be much nicer."

That's no choice. When involuntary is the only alternative, voluntary isn't really voluntary anymore, is it?

I'm tempted to get salty with the doctor, but my throat still hurts, and I feel like I need to save what's probably left of my voice for something more important.

"Did my boyfriend ever come?" I ask hoarsely.

She shakes her head.

"So . . . voluntary?" she asks.

Finally, I nod. She leaves me alone in the room and I don't know what hurts more: my throbbing-with-nothing stomach, my scratched-raw throat, or my boy-shattered heart.

Just kidding. I know.

# PRESENT

Today is my first day of city college, and I wake up nervous, trying on a hundred shades of lipstick before deciding to go au naturel. I come downstairs and Dad's made my favorite apple cinnamon pancakes. I can't eat more than a few bites, though, and it's not just because Ruby is talking—loudly—about how cinnamon is legally allowed to have rodent hairs in it.

"Stop," Stevie says. "Why are you so gross?"

Dad made Stevie's pancake in the shape of a Mickey Mouse head, so this factoid is probably especially disturbing to her.

"How are you feeling, kiddo?" Dad asks me.

"Living the dream," I lie.

When he's not looking, the rest of my apple cinnamon pancake meets the compost bin.

"Delicious," I say.

I go back upstairs and change my pants three times. Then I decide on a skirt. Which means my shoes are all wrong.

Mom calls me to emphasize how proud she is of me, asks me to text her and tell her how my first day goes. *Thank you, sure, I will. I love you, Mom.*

"Journey?" Dad calls from downstairs.

"Coming."

I can't believe I'm going to college. City college, but still. As I step out into the sunshine and get in Dad's same old car, on a morning that looks like so many mornings before it, everything is different and there's no going back.

There should be an opposite of déjà vu.

My astronomy class begins with a single slide. It's a comic. A cartoon man gazes at Earth from a spaceship.

The caption reads, *Warning: the universe may threaten your sense of self-importance.*

*That's just what I need,* I think to myself, not even the least bit sarcastically. At least some part of my suicidal ideation must be rooted in a tendency to take myself much too seriously. Is it any wonder the poem "Soliloquy of the Solipsist" was written by a woman who ended her own life by sticking her head in a gas oven?

*How's your first day??* Marisol texts me later as I sit waiting for my first Philosophy 101 class to start.

*Good so far!* I text back. I want to say more. There seems so much to say—how wide and pretty the campus looks in the morning, how I drank a black coffee for the first time and I didn't hate it, all these grown-ups who seem to be accepting me as one of them even though I feel like an impostor—but I don't know how to sum it up in a text.

I can see the ellipses that mean she's typing.

*"Don't stop believin', hold on to that feeling,"* someone starts singing so loudly people shift to look at her. I look up and an immediate grin pulls at my face. Etta—the girl from the hotline—has slid into the empty seat next to me.

"Hey!" I say.

"That's right, here she is, the dropout from the crisis hotline," she says, leaning in. "I'm such an asshole, right?"

"Oh, come on."

"I feel so bad but I just couldn't swing that intensity."

"No big deal. It's not for everyone."

"Do Willa and Francie and Davina totally hate me now?"

I don't even have a chance to answer.

"I can't believe you're in this class!" she says. "This is going to be so fun."

At this moment, the man I assume is our professor is just finishing writing this quote on the board: *It is certain that we cannot escape anguish, for we are anguish.*

"Is it, though?" I ask Etta, pointing to the quote.

"Fair enough," she says. "Maybe fun is the wrong word. It'll be meaningful."

We watch as our professor writes the words *You will never live if you are looking for the meaning of life.*

"I'm going to stop talking now," Etta says.

I hope she never stops talking, though. Both times, when Etta walked into the room I was in, she shifted the dull atmosphere into some kind of magic simply by being there.

I really hope she sticks around this time.

# PAST

By the time I get discharged, the shame has rolled in. I wish I were dead from embarrassment alone. The clouds have lifted in the gray, the rain paused, and Dad gives me a ride to Ventura, where the facility that I will "voluntarily" commit myself to is. His car is older than him. It's not a classic; it's just a piece of junk. But something about the duct-taped vinyl and the many, many sun-bleached little trees hanging from his rearview feels like home. I can't tell you how many hours I've spent riding in here at my dad's side.

I wipe tears from my eyes and roll down the window, welcoming the cold air on my face. The freeway makes my heart speed up, makes me tense up and tighten my seat belt. I tried to die and here I am bracing myself for a crash, afraid of dying.

Nothing makes sense.

Dad doesn't speak, but I know I've hurt him. I've hurt everybody. God knows if or what they told my little sisters, who for some reason think I'm the coolest thing since ice cream. What kind of example would it be setting for them, to die like that? How selfish would I be to leave them? What is wrong with me?

"I'm sorry," I say in a shaky voice, but my words get lost in the highway wind.

"Sorry?" Dad asks, like he didn't hear me.

I roll up my window. "I said, I'm sorry."

"I'm sorry."

"What is this, an Abbott and Costello skit?"

He doesn't laugh. Neither do I. Even humor is broken right now.

"What are *you* sorry about?" I ask.

"I don't know," he says. "That you felt the need to do that. That I didn't help prevent it from happening."

"Isn't your fault."

"It definitely is."

The difference between my parents couldn't be better illustrated than by their reactions to today's events. My mom insisted this was all a cry for attention and everything would be fine. She left early to go talk to my teachers, straighten everything out. My dad stayed with me every second, sighing and fighting tears and taking all the blame upon himself with frequent mutterings of, "All my fault." Which gets annoying, too. Everything is about him. He can't believe that this happened for reasons that extend far beyond the radius his parenting touches.

"Not everything's about you," I tell him.

The sunset is flamingo pink, flamboyant, and I resent it. Tell me how my ugly feelings can coexist in the same world as that sunset.

"I am responsible for this," I tell him. "Me. Me and my stupid big feelings. Not your divorce or the fact you spanked me once as a kid or whatever you sit around feeling guilty about."

"I should never have let you stay out that night you got in the crash," he says.

He weeps with no sound. But right now it's Niagara Falls all over his Hawaiian shirt.

"I'm going to be okay," I tell him as he pulls into twenty-minute parking in front of the facility, whose name translates to "View of the Sea." There is no view. There is no sea.

In my journal, I keep a list of words that don't exist in English but should. Like *yuputka*, the Ulwa word for a ghostly feeling of something crawling on your skin. Or *gumusservi*, the Turkish word for moonlight gleaming on water. In Arabic, there's a term for when you love someone so much you hope to die first so you never have to see them die: *to'oborni*, which literally translates to "you bury me." I loved Jonah like that. I loved him *to'oborni*. Or, let's be honest, love, present tense, because such a thing can't switch off as soon as someone says it's over on a phone call or after a bottle of acetaminophen.

There should be a word for what I feel at the mental

ward—being afraid to die and wishing I were dead at once. But if there is one, I don't know it.

I keep thinking of my sisters. How Stevie—so little, nine, with portraits she drew of unicorns all over her neon walls—has stars in her eyes for me. And that letter she wrote that she brought home from school that said I'm her hero. She drew my picture on it with my purple hair in her composition book and showed it to her class. And Ruby—thirteen, sullen since my parents' separation, who now wears all black and listens to her headphones every waking second—told me I was "the person she hates least," which was her special way of saying she adores the crap out of me.

My sisters hole up in my room when our parents fight.

My sisters rock my hand-me-downs.

My sisters, my darlings.

Imagine if I'd died—a giant girl-shaped shadow cast over their entire lives. Just another person who fucked them up.

I'm glad Mom is pretending everything is fine at home, because I'd never want my little sisters knowing their big sister is such a basket case. I think of their sea-big, river-hazel eyes and drown in shame.

As surprised as I am to find myself in a mental ward, there's actually nothing surprising about this place. It's mundane. It's every movie I've ever seen about mental wards. It's appointments and quiet meals with strangers and TV and waiting, waiting to go home, waiting to talk to Jonah, waiting for life to feel like it's either beginning or ending again.

"Hello," Dr. Anglin says, glancing at a file folder. "Journey. What an interesting name."

Dr. Anglin's office is so blazingly white it hurts the eyes. The linoleum floors, the stark walls, blinding. I sit in a hard chair near a potted plant so healthy it looks fake shining under the fluorescent lights. I touch a leaf. Huh. Real. "My parents are rock and/or roll fans."

"How neat," Dr. Anglin says, putting the folder down on her desk. She is tan, muscular, smile-wrinkled—like someone who does fifty-mile bike rides on the weekends and gardens. "So let's talk about why you're in here."

"Yeah, the whole trying-to-off-myself thing," I say.

I expect her to laugh, but she continues her serious stare. Here it is, the chance to delve into my feelings with a capital F. You know, the big ones. The ones that used to be cute. The ones that, after the accident, confused me and ate my life up and shifted everything I knew and loved around like a terrible hurricane. The ones that drove me to medication and a diagnosis. The ones that made Jonah think I was too much, no fun, not worth it.

Every time I even utter his name, those two syllables throb like a heartbeat of hurt. I tell her I don't know when exactly suicide went from an escape fantasy to really wanting to die. That I had thought about suicide before, but I never thought I had the guts to do it until I stood staring into the mirror the night Jonah broke up with me over the phone. Before that moment, I didn't believe I had it in me. But suddenly I knew I did.

"You're on more than the amount of Depakote we'd normally prescribe for a girl your age and size," Dr. Anglin says, making a notation in my file. I imagine she's scrawled something along the lines of *patient won't shut up* after my meandering monologue.

"Yeah, the doctor who prescribed it gave me a quick quiz and then handed me my prescription. He wasn't the thoroughest."

"Mmm," she says, as if she doesn't know what to make of this.

I share with her a thought I've had since I got here, since I met the other teens here, many of whom are clearly struggling with so much more than I am. It's just a nagging little conspiracy theory circling my mind. "Hey, so, um, what if I'm not bipolar?"

She gives me a look like this is the most ridiculous thing she's heard all day. "Really."

"I mean, I've always been a little . . . much, but after I got on medication, I've only seemed to get worse," I tell her. "I mean, I never tried to kill myself before."

"We definitely need to adjust your medication," she says. "I'm switching you to lithium and pairing it with an antidepressant—hopefully that should give you some relief."

"Okay. It was just a theory."

"If I had a dollar for every time a bipolar patient told me they weren't bipolar, I'd buy a pony." She shuts my file folder and smiles at me kindly, her eyes twinkling. "That's the trick of it—you start feeling better, you think you don't need your medication, you get off it or let your dosage slide, and then you end up having an episode."

"But I was totally taking my medication."

"You will probably have many times when you feel better," Dr. Anglin says, leaning in and putting the file down. "A lot of my patients have their first breakdown in their teens, feel fine for a long time, and end up hospitalized again in their twenties. It's a long . . . well . . . journey."

Not the first joke made about my name in my life, certainly not the last.

"A lot of adjusting dosages, trying new medications and combinations," she continues, "but most people are able to live normal lives. Go to college, have meaningful relationships, children. You have a whole life ahead of you."

I nod, even though when I picture my future, I see a blank screen like the end of a movie.

Oh, Dr. Anglin. I can tell she loves her job, that she brings passion to her work, that she reads our files and then tries so hard to see us all as people. But as I leave her office, a new prescription in my file, I feel like she hasn't heard me. And that makes me even more crazy.

◆ ◆ ◆

Day two at the mental ward, the residents' phone rings. The residents' phone rings all day long. I would be lying if I said I didn't get a gross jolt of hope up my spine every time at the sound of it, peppered with self-hatred for having said hope. *Jonah,* the ring seems to scream. I've picked it up a dozen times over the past thirty-six hours I've been here and not once has it been for me. More than half the time it's been for someone named Tony. There's no one named Tony here.

I shuffle out in my slippers and pick it up.

"Nuthouse, resident nut speaking, how may I direct your call?"

"Journey?" Jonah asks.

His voice is small and sweet. I crack open at the sound of it.

"Jonah," I say, eyes filling.

"Journey," he says, sniffling.

"Jonah," I repeat.

I am so raw right now. I am so horribly new. A little pink rat, just born, disgusting, too delicate for this world. I am ashamed of myself.

"What have you done, babe?" he asks.

"I made a really stupid mistake."

"A *mistake*?"

"I mean, I meant to. But—"

He's crying. I'm crying. Two girls walking arm in arm down the hall in their pajamas are crying.

"I've been so worried," he says.

"I'm fine. No damage."

"Why did you *do* this?"

I can hear his tone turning, the anger creeping in.

"How could you really do this to everyone?" he asks. "You were just going to *leave* me?"

"You broke up with me. You left me."

"That doesn't mean I wanted you dead!"

"I know. *I* wanted me dead."

"Journey," he says weakly.

"Or I thought I did. I was just . . . It's hard to explain," I say. "I've been going over and over it in my mind. Like, when did I fall off the deep end? Was I always like this? Was it when my parents split, and everything kind of shattered into a million pieces? Or after the car accident, when death became this . . . reality? Is it the medication I'm on? Is it that I'm not on *enough* medication?"

He doesn't answer, but I hear him blowing his nose, so I know he's there.

"Is it me?" he finally asks. "Did I do this to you?"

"Of course not."

"You threatened on the phone, but I—I didn't think you'd *do* it."

"You thought I was bluffing."

"I thought you were being Journey."

"Meaning?"

"You have a tendency toward hyperbole," he says.

"You are the meanest boyfriend in the world," I tell him, jokingly. My breath catches in my throat. I close my eyes, tight. "Are you still my boyfriend?"

"Journey," he says.

"Oh no, oh no, oh no," I say, tears hot in my shut-tight eyes. "No."

"I'm afraid to have this conversation with you," he says softly. "Afraid to talk to you honestly, because I don't know what you're going to do."

"I'm on suicide watch in a mental ward," I say. "So there's no safer place. No time like the present to break the news to me."

"Now's not the time to have this conversation," he says. "Let's just . . . let's just focus on you getting better, okay? Because I love you and I want to see you better. And if we were to get back together, you'd need to be better."

"So we *are* broken up," I say slowly. "But we *could* get back together."

"Just . . . focus on you," he says.

My heart thumps. I stare at the wall, where someone wrote BICH and someone else wrote LEARN TO SPELL MORAN! and someone else wrote YOU MISSPELLED MORON, MORON. I look up and close my eyes. The air-conditioning dries the tears on my face and gives me chills.

"Okay," I say. "I'm going to get better. I made a mistake. I'll never do this again, I promise."

"I'm so glad you're alive," he says.

"I'm supposed to be home soon. Maybe you could come over—"

"Let's take it one day at a time," he says.

"Wow, how wise. Did you think of that?" I ask.

He sighs.

"I'm sorry," I say quickly. "Thanks for calling. I love you. I miss you. I'm sorry I'm me."

"I'm just so glad you're okay," he says.

"Me too. I love you."

"Take care of yourself," he says.

I hang up the phone.

So I'm discharged the next day and given back my shoe-laces and my hairpins (apparently the folks who run this place thought I might hurt myself again with these items; self-destruction by hairpin, death by shoelace) and a brown paper bag just like the ones my parents used to send me to school with as a kid.

Inside are two bottles containing slightly-less-pink pills and some little blue ones to go with them.

I try to end my life by swallowing pills, and now, to fix this mess, they give me . . . more pills. Why, hello, irony. How've you been?

> *Why is the answer*
> *colored pink, bitter*
> *as little roses?*

*Why is the answer*
*deadly*
*in large enough doses?*
*What if*
*this isn't*
*the answer*
*at all?*

Goodbye viewless, sea-less View of the Sea.

Stepping outside, automatic doors swishing behind me, the whole world seems more full-color than usual, the air clearer, the clouds freshly laundered. Must be the rain that came and went and washed everything clean.

This week is Mom's week for us, but I ask if I can stay at Dad's for two reasons: One, it's home, the home I grew up in, and I want to be in the homiest home there is right now. Two, I don't want to see my sisters or Levi and have to fake anything. So Dad picks me up for an excruciating ride back to his house. Excruciating because of the self-help audiobook he puts on called *Self-Hugging for Beginners* that is 100 percent serious and also so cheesy-bad that in another context it would probably be the funniest thing I ever heard. The narrator sounds wayyy too into it. "Repeat after me: I love myself. I am worth loving. Love is worth having. I cannot have without love." Why Dad thinks this will drive me further from suicide and not closer to it, I don't know. My dad has an endless supply of self-help books and takes a DIY approach to psychology. He's always been skeptical of me being on meds and having a bipolar diagnosis. He thinks I'd benefit from herbs. Tinctures. Essential oils and the like.

"When was the last time you looked in the mirror and said, 'I am a hero and/or heroine'?" the I-had-four-cups-of-coffee-too-many narrator asks.

"Heroin sounds nice," I say.

"Shhhh," Dad says. "Stop joking and listen."

I flip down the visor, look at myself with my frizz-puff of a hairdo and my dark eyebrows and my cracked, chapped lips and think, *If that BS is true, the word hero and/or heroine has lost all meaning.* Flip the visor back up. I stare out the window and tune the audiobook out.

Back to Goleta: land of citrus groves, purple hills, and one glittering, cold ocean. Where neighborhoods are quiet and lawns are close-clipped. Where people smile and say hello and houses have multiple stories. We pull into the driveway of the home I grew up in with its brown, drought-thirsty lawn, the mailbox shaped like a lantern, the flat stump where a violet-leaved chokecherry tree used to be and now the sun shines, relentless.

"Thanks for the ride," I say, unclipping my seat belt. As I reach and pick up my backpack from the back seat, I notice an unfamiliar purple sweatshirt—too big to be Stevie's, too colorful to be Ruby's.

"My friend Gary's," he says when he sees me looking.

"I'm going to go lie down," I tell him.

"Is this your new pharmaceuticals?" he asks. "Are they making you sleepy?"

"I don't know anymore."

Really I just want to be left alone. Ever since I failed to kill myself (which is how I think of it now. "Attempted suicide?" Come on, I failed) I haven't had a moment. The house smells weird when we walk in, a mixture of garlic in the air and lemon cleaner and windows that haven't been opened. Like someone else's house.

My room is at the end of a hall, a rectangular room with a long closet and a canopy bed I've had since I was six that has since gone from pink with violet mosquito netting to black with red lace. There is crap covering my love seat, my desk, my dresser top, and most of my floor. Clothes, papers, schoolbooks, paperbacks, some weird painted baby dolls that Marisol gave me for my birthday, makeup, purses, scarves, pens. Basically, *gaze upon my living quarters and behold my wreck of a psyche*. Jonah used to say we needed hazmat suits to hang out in my room. Though usually, strangely enough, the sight of my beloved mess makes me feel calm. It might look like a "sea of garbage" to my dad or hazardous waste to my (ex-)boyfriend, but to me it makes perfect sense. I know where everything is. It's mine.

Today, though, the room feels small. I see trash I should throw away. Food wrappers. Flattened cardboard boxes. I push a pile of shoes off my bed, climb under the rumpled comforter. Plug in my phone and turn it on for the first time since I tried to kill myself a few days ago. I'm just checking messages. Not from anyone in particular. But my throat goes dry when I see nothing from Jonah. I scroll to our last texts to each other.

Call you in a minute? I wanna talk "in person," he said.

One of Jonah's only flaws is his tendency to put quotation marks around phrases that warrant no quotation marks.

Oh dear I don't like the sound of that, I responded.

I didn't know that was the end. My eyes hurt looking at it. I scroll back, swallow the lump of pain in my throat.

Twenty-seven texts from Marisol beginning with her asking if I saw the latest episode of a reality show about people with weird obsessions that we are obsessed with. The last one, apparently, is about a guy who is in love with a finger puppet. Then there are texts asking why I am not answering. THIS IS THE GREATEST TELEVISION THAT HAS EVER TELEVISIONED, she writes. Have I lost interest in the show, how could I, it's OUR THING!

Then she asks me if I'm okay, what kind of food poisoning did I have, the puke kind or the poop kind? Was it salmonella? Botulism? Did I want soup?

I have a lot of Sometimes Friends: folks I know through shows I go to now and then or who I've known throughout years of being corralled together in public school. Their numbers are in my phone, we text and talk online, maybe eat lunch together or hang out after school. But Marisol's a Forever Friend. An adopted sister. Two hearts, one heartbeat.

Me: Who told you I have food poisoning?

Her: She lives!!!

Me: "Lives" is being generous.

I snap a picture of my tired-as-hell face and send it.

Her: Poor bb

Me: Have you talked to Jonah?

Her: No, y?

Me: I tried to off myself. Was at a psychiatric hospital. Good times. Oh yeah, also he dumped me.

Shit. I probably shouldn't have broken the news to her like that. If only there were an *unsend* button. The text sits there for about a nanosecond before my phone starts ringing. My ringtone is a cat meowing.

"Is this just your way of getting me on the phone?" she asks.

Because it takes an emergency to get Marisol on the phone. She is strictly a texter.

"Not a joke," I tell her.

"On my way right now."

Before I can respond, she hangs up. Less than ten minutes later, my doorbell rings.

I can tell she's already been crying as she leans over and hugs me, kind of lying on me, more like. I inhale an aromatic burst of cinnamon gum and fruity shampoo. Marisol has the thickest mop of shiny, curly hair she dyes red over the dark brown. She calls her fashion sense Pajama Couture, as she somehow manages to live in Ugg boots, yoga pants, and long sweater things and still seem fashionable. She's also a brilliant writer and speaks three languages fluently. Her mother is French, her father is Puerto Rican, she has dual citizenship to the EU and the US. Not that I'm bragging or anything.

It's just that I have the best friend in the world.

Sometimes I think I don't deserve her.

We sit up and I tell her the whole damn story while her hand pets my arm. I tell it all out of order. It may or may not make any sense at all. Marisol knows it's been rough since my parents split up, and then the accident happened. She gave me many long hugs when I had tears and helped me breathe when I almost had panic attacks. But since school started in late August almost two months ago, I haven't told her much beyond the diagnosis and that I'm medicated. She was deep in SAT and college prep world. I was busy losing my mind. When we hung out, we let silences expand between us—we shopped, or we saw movies, and I apparently hid my struggles well. So I have a lot to explain right now, starting with the ugly thoughts that have taken residence in Casa Journey's Brain since the school year started and ending with trying to die. As I yammer on, every once in a while she says, "Stop." Or "You did not." Or just "Journey?!"

It's the first time I've told the whole story out loud and it's served with a heaping side of shame. Even though I know it's true, I can't believe I tried to kill myself just days ago.

What's that word I'm looking for? For something you know is true but you still can't believe?

"Oh man," Marisol says, rubbing her eyes behind her ruby plastic frames. "I am the worst friend in the universe."

"What? No."

Seeing her cry physically pains me. I should have kept this a secret. This is why I never told her my stupid suicidal thoughts in the first place.

"It has nothing to do with you," I tell her.

"I should have seen this coming," Marisol says. "I've just been so busy—and since the accident, you've been so . . ."

"Insane."

"I was going to say *volatile*. I've been worried, JoJo, not going to lie. But then you went to a psychiatrist and got your diagnosis and I . . . I don't know. I thought things were going to get better. And I've been so in my own world, researching colleges and studying for SATs." She wipes her eyes behind her glasses. "I feel so selfish."

"It wasn't up to you to save me."

"I didn't need to *save* you—but I should have been a better friend."

"You've been working so hard for school—I was not about to come and distract you with my ridiculousness."

"I could *tell* something was wrong with you. I'm used to you being dramatic. But you've been so dark and so quiet. I don't know. I dismissed it. Selfishly. I didn't think you'd . . ."

She lets out a sob and grabs my wrist for a second like I'm a balloon about to float away.

"I didn't think I would, either, at first." I hug my knees, lay my head on them, breathe deeply to quiet the stabbing feeling in my chest. "It was almost like . . . like I dared myself to. I dared myself to die."

Marisol just shakes her head.

"Believe me, I know I sound crazy. I guess I am crazy. I came home with a fresh batch of crazy pills." I watch her, waiting for a response. Waiting for her to agree or disagree. Because I honestly don't know if I'm crazy or not anymore.

I never feel crazy inside myself—someone else has to come along and see it, name it. Crazy is always something someone else defines.

Marisol gets up, blows her nose loud as a trumpet. She sits next to me on the bed again, watching me like I'm something astonishing. Not the good kind of astonishing, either.

"Hon, you scare the living crap out of me."

"Why?" I ask, a crack in my heart.

"Just . . . you oscillate so wildly," she says. "Maybe that's why I've backed off since the year started and our conversations mostly revolve around reality TV. I'm sorry. I'm just . . . exhausted sometimes."

"Explain."

"Like that time last year you showed up at my house joyriding your dad's car. You told me to get in, like it was nothing. I mean, yeah, it was one of the funnest nights of my life. But you don't have a license. And, like, I was terrified."

"He showed me how to drive it. He was out of town. I'd never do that anymore, anyway, after the accident."

"Or like that time last spring you called me and said you thought maybe there was a guy with a knife outside your house. My mom and I showed up and looked around your yard. Do you remember? We were freaking out. I still don't know if you really saw a guy with a knife or not. That truly scared the crap out of us."

"There was a shadow, and I'd been watching that true crime show—"

"Or Jonah. Like he was your whole world. Your whole. World. You barely talked about anything else the past year. You kind of pushed me to the wayside and girl, you know I love you, but what the hell is this?"

Marisol points to the corner of my room, where a small pile of three infant-sized sundresses sit in a corner.

"Baby clothes."

"For who?"

"My baby someday."

"This is what I mean. You are just so . . . much," Marisol says. "It's why I love you. Why everyone does. You're such a damn flame, we all want to be around you."

I smile weakly, eyes welling up.

"Keep the flame, but please, JoJo," she says, holding my hand. "Don't burn the goddamn world to the ground."

After she leaves, I bawl into my pillow so badly it's soaked. Feels good, in a way, letting it go, like bad weather doing its thing, washing the skies clean. The old refrain circles back in my brain like a hellish nursery rhyme—*I don't know how to live. I wish I were dead*—even though I know, I know it's a lie. What I really want is to get past all this.

> Dear future self,
>   How did you survive?
>   How did you do it?
>   Are you even there?
>   Do you even exist?

If only there were a pill I could take to stop me from thinking about Jonah.

I haven't been back to school since it all happened last week. Usually Jonah would have been messaging and coming over. He called me twice, asking how I was, but seemed distant, made excuses for having to get off the phone. He didn't laugh at my dark jokes. At the end of phone call number two, he told me I was his best friend, but asked me for space. He said it would be good for me, like he was doing it for my benefit. He sold it to me so well I believed him, until I got to thinking later, and decided, wait a second, I don't want space from him. I want the opposite of space.

Hey . . . can we talk?

I don't want space.

Really? Two hours and not even a response? I can see you read my text.

Never mind, fine, you're right, we'll have space.

Sigh.

Space is stupid.

He said he still loves me when we last talked. I know he still loves me. I don't want to screw up any hope I have of us getting back together. So I don't send any more texts after that, even though I really, really want to.

Texts I didn't send:

Last I checked "best friends" text their friends back.

That was a proper use of quotation marks by the way, WHICH YOU SUCK AT USING.

Remember when you ghosted Carla after dumping her in ninth grade? Don't even think about pulling that crap with me.

Saying you want space from someone is just a nice way of saying you want nothing.

I wish I had succeeded in killing myself.

No I don't. I know I don't. I remember vividly the panic right before the world went black, and I was so scared to die. But why does my mind keep going there; why does it keep thinking these "screw it all" thoughts? Lithium dulls the feelings maybe, but it seems like it does nothing for thinking the thoughts. It tires me, it makes my brain a snail, it makes me sleep longer. And is it me or are my hands trembling?

◆　◆　◆

I've been home from the hospital two days. I tried to kill myself on a Friday. I spent a lovely weekend getaway at the lie that calls itself View of the Sea and came home yesterday. It's only *Tuesday*. I feel a decade older than a week ago.

Since I got home, Dad shuffles around me somber as a monk, accommodating as a butler, observing heavy silences in my presence, ordering me whatever food I request, suggesting hot baths. It pains me to see him like this, but his sympathy for me is so loud. I do appreciate the quiet of his house, but I miss my sisters. Mom took them for the week and it's weird to be here without them. I've been texting with my mom since I got here. She asks me how I am, tells me we should sit down and talk about the future soon, sends me pictures of the dog, fills me in on boring details around my makeup homework she emailed me, asks me how I am again. I can tell she doesn't know what to do with me. It's like she wants everything to be fine so bad she will insist fineness into existence. I tell her I'll return to school Monday, November 1, which is in thirteen days. I argue I need this much time to let the medication stabilize. Thirteen days seems an eternity away right now. Thirteen days, a mini forever. The whole world could be gone by November.

In truth, I wish I never had to go back to school. It's such a charade at this point. I'm knee-deep in senior year; I've received warnings from three of my teachers that I might not swing Cs. Before I decided to off myself I was planning to take a gap year, get a job, maybe travel, find myself, figure out what's next. Going back to high school and faking like I care sounds like such a pointless endeavor. But I won't think about it now. I can avoid the world for thirteen more beautiful days.

I check my phone again. And again. No text from Jonah. But there is a text from Marisol. It's the longest text I've ever seen. It says *I LOVE YOU* so many times I get bored of scrolling.

Now I'm worried for YOUR mental health, I text back.

"Watch some TV with your old man?" Dad asks, poking his head in the doorway of my room. He's asked me to keep my door open these first couple days back, and, humiliating as it is, I oblige.

"Sure," I say, putting my phone down with a *clack*.

I sit wrapped in an afghan on the couch in the living room, watching nature in HD, Sprinkles perched between Dad and me. Right after my parents separated, both of them went out and adopted their dream dogs. They each claimed the other had been the one standing in the way of their dream dog for years. I have no dog in the dream dog fight, nor do I care, but I do find it amusing that we now have two dogs in our lives. Sprinkles, the one on my lap currently, is an older three-legged chow, and I would amputate a leg of my own for him. Mom and Levi's dog, Chewbacca, is a Newfoundland, one of the world's largest breeds, and dumb as a brick of cheese. Dad sits brushing Sprinkles's fur, eyes glued to the nature show. The man is a live-action thesaurus of complimentary adjectives.

"Marvelous," he says when a giraffe outruns a lion.

"Brilliant," he says about a snake that finds solace from the blistering desert inches below the sand's surface.

"Isn't it so breathtaking?" he asks me when the bird of paradise performs its ridiculous mating dance. He watches me for a reaction so eagerly.

All right. Okay. I get where this is coming from. Dad's trying to get me to join the Life Is Good Club. And I see it, I see what he sees. A bizarre, full-color splendor of creatures and landscapes so unique they transcend imagination, and yet are real. But what I see much more clearly is a bleak, never-ending game of predator versus prey; weather that is downright unlivable due to man-made climate change; and a boring, pathetic song and dance everyone and/or everything does in the name of sex.

But the last thing I want to do is bum my dad out. This is the first day since I came home that he hasn't cried.

"It is . . . breathtaking," I say.

Not a lie, either. Technically life does take your breath away. Eventually, it takes it all.

That's what Wolf told me to focus on during my first day of therapy with him: my breath. It's Friday, my one-week suicide attempt anniversary . . . and yes, I have a new therapist now, named Wolf. I tried to call him Dr. Baumgartner but he said, "Call me by my first name, Wolf."

"Wolf?" I asked, leaning forward in my leather armchair.

"It's my first name," he insisted.

He looked very . . . square. Especially for a person with a moniker so lupine. Like some guy who stepped right out of a *Life* magazine from 1958. Buddy Holly glasses, a corduroy sports jacket, graying, slicked-back hair. A Dennis, maybe. A Norman. A Henry.

But Wolf? No.

"I would think if anyone could fail to be surprised by my name it would be someone named Journey," he told me.

"I know, right?" I said. "And yet, here we are."

The silence was long as he studied me, hand on his chin.

"I'm like, 'Aaaah, don't eat me!'"

This silence was longer. His brows creased, he gave me a confused look, and I felt like an idiot but kept talking because, well, that's how I roll.

"Because you're a 'wolf.' Never mind. Wow, this is awkward. So yes, hi. I'm Journey. I talk nonsensically when I'm nervous."

"You're nervous?" he asked.

I was. My palms were damp, my pulse a gallop.

"My track record with psychiatry is not good. There was the time I saw Dr. Shaw and he was like, 'You're crazy, take these pills,' and I was like, 'Oh, okay.' After that I went away and tried to kill myself. So then there was Dr. Anglin, who was like, 'Here are some new crazy pills,' and I was like, 'Maybe I'm not crazy?' And she was like, 'Yeah, no, you wouldn't be here if you weren't,' so I was like, 'Oh, okay, thanks.' And that, friend, is it."

Long, silent pause.

"I don't think the pills are working," I told him. "The lithium. I still have all these . . . unwanted thoughts. I'm tired all the time. Also look at my hands."

I held them out so he could see how badly they shook.

"Maybe we should try something else," I said.

"I don't prescribe pills," he said.

"Oh?"

This was news to me. I squinted at the framed degree on his wall. "I thought you were a doctor?"

"I am a doctor," he said. "But I don't prescribe pills."

"Oh."

I wasn't sure where to go from here. Was this the kind of doctor who wanted me to talk about my feelings and my mother? I glanced behind me and noticed the leather couch, although it was covered in loose papers, books, folders, envelopes. Another slob, a kindred spirit.

"When was the last time you stopped and focused solely on your breath?" he asked.

Well, this was not what I expected. The answer was never, really—not on purpose, anyway. In fact, sometimes as a kid I had stopped and noticed my breathing and it had terrified me. Because it never ended. It kept going. And if I started focusing on it it's all I could think about. I told Wolf this and he smiled.

"Sounds like you were a little Zen master without

realizing it," he said. "Essentially, you were practicing mind-fulness."

"I want to get away from my mind," I said. "Not get more full of it. Mindfulness sounds like a nightmare."

"But is it your mind that bothers you, or your thoughts?" he asked.

Hmm. I pondered this deeply. So deeply I swear my brain hurt. Or my mind? Or me? Where do my thoughts and big feelings end and where do I begin? Are we one thing, intertwined? Or am I a separate entity afflicted by my mind?

"You're a different doctor than the others," I said.

"I consider that a compliment," he said.

Now that I looked around, I noticed all the Buddhist books on his shelf, the Gandhi quote needlepointed and hung in a frame. It made sense why my dad was so excited about me going to *this* appointment today.

"I'm going to assign you homework," Wolf said. "You up for it?"

"Goody," I said. "Just what I need."

"What if I tell you it just requires you sitting with your eyes shut for ten minutes a day?"

"That sounds like some homework I can get behind."

So here I am, seated on my bed cross-legged, eyes shut, world dark, alone with my breath—that rhythm I always carry with me and never really stop to notice. That roar of ocean in me. That relentless heart throb. Inhale, exhale, up, down, in, out, full, empty, round, round again. A voice keeps trying to talk in my head—my voice. And it's annoying the crap out of me.

*This is dumb,* it says. *What's the point of this? What's the point of anything? I want to call Jonah. Why hasn't Jonah called? I hope we can get back together. I'm so sad. I'm so angry. I hate this homework. Nothing matters.*

But I do my best to drown it out by inhaling, exhaling, up, down, in, out, full, empty, round, round again. And for a short, blissful period of time—I don't know how long— that annoying voice in me shuts up. I only realize it after the moment has passed and it starts up again.

Dad's is easy. Just us and a lot of takeout and TV. But then the weekend comes, eight days post-suicide attempt, and it's time to face my mom, Levi, and my sisters.

Mom's cheerful—dare I say, too cheerful? She brings home fancy sandwiches for dinner. We eat around the table. "By the way," she whispered to me when I first came home today, "I haven't told the girls or Levi the full story yet." She told them all I had food poisoning last weekend because she thought it was a private thing I could share with people *in my own time.*

Um, no thanks.

Also . . . what?

I don't understand my mom's logic sometimes. She acts like mental illness and bipolar disorder and pills are totally acceptable, but then she wants to pretend the natural conclusion of it all never happened. I guess she's just really committing to this *everything is fine* schtick. Like right now, she sits at the dinner table and chatters on about her nemesis at work with the same name as her, Amanda, who looks eerily like her, too.

Apparently Amanda B. has been playing music with swear words in it in the café and flirting with customers. The *nerve*.

"Actually, Mom, Amanda B. sounds pretty cool," Ruby says.

Mom let Ruby dye her hair black, but only some crappy dye that washes out in six to eight washes, so Ruby's once-blond, then-black hair is now the color of a bruise. Her sandwich has been eaten, but all the vegetables remain untouched on her plate.

"She is not cool," Mom says. "Amanda B. is the bane of my existence."

"You're so dramatic, Mom," Stevie says.

Stevie's adult teeth still seem too big to fit in her mouth. She's at the stage where she can still wear pigtail braids without looking ridiculous. Consensus of the world is she's adorable.

"You're eating well for someone who had food poisoning this week," Levi says to me.

Oh, if only you knew, Levi.

"Right?" I say.

There is a balled-up sandwich wrapper on my plate, nothing more.

"That's how I do it," Levi says. "Get kicked off the horse and climb back up on the saddle again."

Levi is an embarrassing well of cowboy metaphors. Also he dresses like a cowboy. And he owns a boot store. He even has a twang to his voice. I was down with all that until I found out he grew up in Burbank. He's not mean or anything. He let us all move in with him in his big house up the hill. He gives us rides places. I just think my mom could do better. Mom swears up, down, and all around she and Levi didn't start seeing each other until after the separation with Dad. I'm not great at arithmetic, but that timeline seems dubious. The Levi thing happened as fast as my parents' breakup and stung as bad. Mom promised initially she would never date a man until us girls were ready, but when I called Levi a rebound and told her to slow down, she replied that she was happy now. A week into her new arrangement, she was ordering furniture and they were visiting dog shelters. I wasn't ready. I don't know if I'll ever be ready.

"What did you eat that made you sick?" Ruby asks me.

"I don't know," I say. "Taco Hell."

"You went to Taco Hell?" Ruby asks. "But you declared them dead to you after they gave you that smooshed seven-layer burrito."

Her eyes are little slits through her glasses. She studies me across the table.

She sees everything, that one.

After dinner, Mom and Levi go on their usual walk that

lasts so long I end up standing at the window staring out at the darkness wondering if they were eaten by bears. I go to my room at the end of the house, a tiny space that barely fits my twin bed and dresser, but has a window looking out onto an enormous, lovely oak tree hung with Levi's birdhouse collection. I lie on my bed. Ruby's music bleeds through the halls, bouncing off the wood floors. This house has high ceilings and was only half-furnished when we moved in. Levi's a man with money and a fine house but no taste and no things to fill it. That's where Mom stepped in.

The album Ruby's listening to is one I turned her on to, YesNoMaybe, a dark dance-pop band that I was super into last year. She is obsessed. It's all she listens to and, at this point, she has soured me on it. Tonight, though, the sound of it makes me more sad than annoyed. I feel like a failure of a sister, failure of a daughter, failure of a suicidal person, and here at Mom's I have to hide it and pretend everything is normal when really I'm falling apart. Or trying to put myself back together, I guess.

Ruby puts the album back to track one and I wipe my tears away, get up, and go down the hall to knock on her door. There's a sign on her door that says "DANGER! HIGH VOLTAGE." She can't hear me because she's cranked the music so loud. I open the door and she's on her laptop on her bed. Her hamper is overflowing with black clothes. She's drawn cartoons of sad-looking girl robots that cover the wall above her bed. Seventh grade has not been easy on her. Our parents split, she lost the county spelling bee championship, one of her best friends moved to Colorado.

"How many times are you going to listen to this album?" I ask from the doorway.

"I don't know, billions and billions." She doesn't look up from her computer. She's clearly playing a game. "So, you tried to kill yourself."

I close the door. Takes seconds for me to locate my tongue. "Mom told you?"

"Pffft. I knew she was lying about food poisoning. You have a stomach of steel. Remember when you drank all that expired eggnog?"

I sit next to her on her bed. "I thought it was supposed to be tangy."

"Plus all I had to do was go on Mom's laptop and read her history to find about a jillion Google searches all asking what to do when your daughter attempts suicide, and whether a bottle of Tylenol damages your liver, and what the chances are you'll try again, and yada yada yada."

"What are my chances?"

"Good."

"That's a relief."

"I mean, chances are good you'll try again. Suicide risk is thirty-seven percent higher for someone who attempted in the last year. Then again, nine out of ten people who attempt suicide don't ever end up actually dying by suicide, so you have that going for you."

"Sounds like Mom's not the only person who's been Googling."

She doesn't answer.

"So, you know. What do you think?" I ask.

"I think it's pretty stupid of you." I can hear the anger in her voice, even though she won't meet my eyes and keeps clicking her computer keys.

"You're right, it was stupid."

"I mean, what, you were just going to kill yourself? Without asking for help, or telling anyone, or explaining why? I don't get it. I mean, what's so terrible about *your* life?"

Ruby's right. There's nothing terrible about my life. I've thought this many, many times. And that almost makes it worse—that I'm this miserable, and I don't even deserve this kind of misery. I've got a good, fortunate life. I waste it.

"I don't, either, honestly," I answer. "I just felt—I felt alone. I felt like I was . . . in pain. I wanted it to stop."

"Dumb."

"I won't do it again."

"Yeah, okay, I'll be over here *not* holding my breath."

"Are you mad at me?"

"You were going to leave us," she says, finally looking up at me over her laptop screen. Her eyes are shiny. "You were just going to, like, leave us in the most selfish way possible. I looked up to you."

Looked. Past tense. I suck in a breath.

"I'm sorry," I tell her.

"You know what, it's fine." She goes back to her computer. "There are more bacteria in a centimeter of my intestines than people who have lived and died in the whole world."

"Is that supposed to be . . . comforting?"

She shrugs and puts her headphones on. Conversation over, I guess.

This thirteen-year-old girl used to be a shy brainiac who spent her time obsessed with her microscope and exploring nature and reading stacks of paperback books about little girls who solved mysteries. Now she's this angsty teen who blasts dark pop music and stares at her laptop. And doesn't look up to me anymore. I wish, for a moment, I had succeeded in my attempt, and then in the next moment, I wish I had never tried.

I leave her room quietly, my cheeks burning, and realize what I really want—more than anything—is for my little sister to be proud of me again.

Mom comes into my room that night after the girls and Levi are asleep. I spent almost an hour researching and ordering a stack of memoirs on bipolar disorder, and now I'm watching a show called *Is Love Blind?* about blindfolded people who get married to strangers. Marisol's watching the show at her house at the same time and we're texting back and forth about what a gorgeous train wreck the whole thing is. I put my phone down when Mom sits next to me on the bed.

"Let's talk about your future," Mom says.

I still have nine days before I return to school. Yes, I'm counting. I groan and pull my blanket over my head. She pulls my blanket off and flashes her tarot cards in the air.

"Oh, *that* talking about my future," I say, sitting up. "Okay, way better."

Mom sits next to me and shuffles the cards.

Late nights have always been our special time because we stay up later than everyone else. She wears men's flannel pajamas and her hair is in a giant bun on the top of her head, her makeup is faded and ready to be scrubbed off. I mute the episode. The sound of the shuffling cards is a purr.

This is our first time alone since I was in the hospital. I can't help but feel like I hurt her feelings by staying at Dad's instead of her house, even though she swore she understood. My mother's not one to ever show her wounds.

"I've missed you," she says.

"You too."

"I've worried."

"I know. I'm sorry."

"How are you feeling?" she asks.

"I mean, you can only watch so much reality TV before losing touch with your own reality."

"Maybe you'd consider going back to school earlier than we discussed?"

"I'd honestly rather light myself on fire."

She blinks extra long, visibly battling the urge to flinch. I feel bad. I've always expressed myself strongly, but she's sensitive to it now in a way she didn't used to be.

"You seem much better, and I'm worried about you passing—"

"I thought you talked to my teachers and the makeup work is fine."

"It is, I just . . . I want to give you the best shot I can."

"We said November first," I say, a little sharply.

"We did," she says. "November first is fine."

I exhale. It grips me with panic to imagine returning to school. I imagine myself a mess, bursting into tears for no reason, seeing Jonah and running in the opposite direction.

"How's that new therapist?" Mom asks.

"His name is Wolf and he's teaching me how to practice mindfulness and breathing exercises."

"Oh Lord. I knew if your dad referred us to him it had to be some hippie-dippie bullshit."

"It wasn't bad, really," I tell her, watching as she fans the cards down the bed in a long line. "I liked him."

"Hmmm," she says doubtfully, giving me a look.

My mother can raise one eyebrow in a way that says more than an entire lecture could.

"Sometimes I don't know about the whole bipolar thing," I tell her.

Her face now says *I am judging you.* "You're not messing with your medication."

"I'm taking my meds," I say. "But . . . think about it. I went off the deep end *after* I started taking medication, not before."

"You have to follow doctor's orders, baby doll."

"I am. But answer me something. Honestly. Do you really think I'm bipolar?"

"I trust the professionals. You know, I've learned a lot about bipolar disorder since joining The Forum."

The Forum is an online support group for moms with bipolar teens. Mom's super into it. Like I'm a little over hearing about *The Forum* and what the ladies on *The Forum* say.

"There are so many varying degrees and it looks so different on different people," she goes on.

"You tell me stories about those girls and they sound worlds beyond me, though. Like yeah, I like to stay up late and I can talk fast when I get excited and I've always been moody. But you told me about a girl who thought she was communicating telepathically with a prince."

"They're not all like that."

"When I was at the nutjob ward the other day—"

"Stop calling it that. It's stigmatizing."

"It's a joke," I say. "It's how I deal. I thought, I'm not like all these other people. There's been some mistake. My roommate tried to stab someone."

"*You* tried to kill yourself," Mom says.

She sits up straight and her gold eyes quiver, threatening to spill tears, and she does this twitchy thing with her mouth that happens when she's either trying not to yell at me or not to cry.

"You tried," she says again, slower. "To kill yourself."

My cheeks heat up. "Right."

"So . . . you have everything in common with those kids in the psychiatric unit."

She's right. Doesn't everyone think the same? We're *all* so different, *all* so special. It's bullshit.

"Someday, sure, you can maybe try coming off medication. But now? Not now. You cannot handle any more instability right now." Mom's voice lowers but also intensifies—it becomes a whisper-shout. "And neither can I."

I could argue with her. Past me would have argued with her. But frankly, I don't have it in me. And I'm not sure I know what's best for anyone anymore.

This is our ritual: pull one tarot card from the deck, look it up online together. I pull a card with a man hanging upside down from a tree. The Hanged Man, the card reads. Mom pulls in a sharp breath, like the sight of the card was a punch to the gut. My heart races and I get a queasy flutter. Because one of my suicidal fantasies and terrible brain loops has involved me hanging from a tree.

I would never tell my mother this. I would never tell anyone.

Mom consults her BFF, Google. Turns out the card has nothing to do with suicide. Look closely: there's a golden halo around his head, a slight smile on his lips. The Hanged

Man is a card that represents the need to turn your world upside down for a whole new perspective. The man first has to hang himself to achieve enlightenment.

"Profound," Wolf says when I tell him about the card the following Friday. There's a skeleton behind him, sitting on a table. I assume it's for Halloween, which is Sunday, but then quickly realize it's an anatomical skeleton that is a regular part of Wolf's mess.

He's leaning in, positively enraptured with this description of the Hanged Man. So much so that I scoff at him. "You don't actually believe in tarot cards, do you?"

"Like a good novel, or a vivid dream, it's not truth but points to truth."

I can't stop staring at Wolf's socks, by the way. Argyle. They don't match.

"And you brought it up here for a reason," Wolf says. "Clearly it meant something to you."

"I don't know," I say.

Which is what I say when I've been cornered and someone else is right. Wolf lets the silence go on long, so long I notice the sound of traffic, which I've never noticed before now. I fight the urge to look at my phone, crack a joke, anything to fill up the gap in conversation. Instead, I focus on my breathing.

"What were you looking for when you tried to kill yourself?" Wolf asks softly.

I study the dust floating in the air. I used to think dust in sunlight was so beautiful, magical snow that you only saw sparkle sometimes. Then I learned it was mostly just dead human skin that filled the air and it grossed me out. I close my eyes.

"I think I was just looking for . . . escape," I say. "'I'm going to kill myself' was this invisible black hole I could mentally hop into when real life and my feelings became too much."

"When you said the mantra, how did it make you feel?"

"Numb. Gorgeously numb. Like all the scared, confused, weird, uncomfortable feelings could just be shut off like a faucet. I wouldn't exist. I wouldn't feel anything. Problem solved."

"Did you think about the reality of this? Of what your death would look like, how it would affect everything?"

"No," I tell him. "I know that's selfish. But at first it was just a . . . a kind of inner conversation-ender. A problem-solver. I'd annoy Jonah by being melodramatic, or get a shitty grade at school, or freak out at my parents. Then I'd think, 'I'll just kill myself.' And it made me feel better."

Wolf nods.

"But then, just in the week or two before I tried, I started researching it online. People's experiences trying. Pictures of crime scenes with bodies, people hanging from trees." I go red admitting this, feeling gross, like I'm revealing some disgusting fetish or something. "I don't know why I kept doing it. I felt bad about it but I kept doing it. I told myself it's what I wanted, that life would go on without me. And then I tried, and I took all the pills, and as I blacked out I felt this desperate energy in me. Like a bird trapped in my chest, trying to fly. I wanted to live so badly."

I am now sniveling. Pathetic. I wipe my eyes with my shirtsleeves.

"I feel like such a coward admitting that," I go on.

"You're not," Wolf says, taking off his glasses and wiping his own eyes. Wiping his own eyes! How does he get through this job if my dumb story makes him cry? "You know, once I read a study on bridge jumpers who survived. All suicidal. And every single survivor said, the moment their feet left the bridge and the second they began plummeting through the air, they all thought the same thing. They all wanted to take it back. They all wanted to live."

I plant my face into my hands, letting the dam break. Lately I reserve my crying spells for the shower or late at night, places no one can see me. Like I'm trying to prove to the world I can be stable, and not too much. But I can't stop myself right now.

"What a stupid thing to put ourselves through, all for what?" I sob.

"Journey," Wolf says gently, pushing a box of tissues across the coffee table. Therapists must buy that stuff in bulk. "It's okay to want to live."

# PRESENT

My first week of college blazes by. The strangest part is how fast this new life, new routine, settles into normalcy. At family dinners, I share what I'm learning in my classes. For once in my life, I have science facts to share with Ruby rather than the other way around.

"If you were able to unravel your DNA, it would stretch to Pluto and back six times," I tell her.

"I don't know about that," Ruby says. "Did you fact-check that claim?"

"No, but you're welcome to."

She takes out her phone to look it up.

"No phones at the table," Dad tells her.

"It's for scientific purposes," Ruby says.

"Fine, look it up, then I want the phone off," Dad says.

After a moment of squinting at her phone, Ruby puts it away.

"And?" I ask her.

She says nothing, eating her dinner.

"Was I right?" I ask.

"Yes," she mutters.

"Ha ha!" Stevie says, pointing at Ruby.

I taught my sister a science fact. Now, that's a first.

I stay up late to study and actually get my homework done on time. Sunday night I turn down hanging out with Marisol to study for my first astronomy quiz. what have you become?!?! she texts. jk i'm proud of you.

Tonight is a level up—my first solo shift as an actual hotline volunteer, four to ten. No Davina by my side. I'm so nervous I'm one *boo* away from peeing my jeggings.

The room is a converted living room with mismatched paintings on the walls, one a watercolor violet, one a painted surfer, another a drawing of unhusked corn. The other volunteers sit at the long tables near the window, drapes parted. Outside, the maple is tacked with birdhouses and strung with lights.

"Hey," I say with a smile to the other people in the room when I take my seat, even though what I'm actually thinking is DON'T LOOK AT ME. These three are strangers. I'm the new girl in town and am convinced that I'm going to fail. Look at everyone else in the room. First of all, they've got a century on me between the three of them. There's a woman with a poodle puff of gray hair billowing out of a bandana, face wrinkled, eyes steely and judgmental, who crunches on something called "nutritional yeast puffs" in what can only be described as a menacing fashion. There's a twentysomething girl with a boy haircut, a babyish face, and sculpted eyebrows, who lounges back in a rolly chair next to a skateboard and says, "'Sup?" There's a woman with long black hair and a hippie skirt rolling a stress ball around in her hand who murmurs, "Welcome."

They are grown-ups, I'm a kid.

They are experienced, I'm a noob.

*Stop*, I whisper to my goddamn brain. *Enough already.*

I take a seat at the almost-empty desk, almost empty except for the antique phone, the headset, and the oh-so-familiar brick-heavy binder. I've come to know and love its comforting weight after fifty long hours doing my training here. In the binder, we have resources, like phone numbers to call for local police if someone wants to report a crime. Like nearby drug rehab centers and eating disorder clinics to refer someone to if they want help. We have scripts for suicidal callers, ways we can be supportive, dos and don'ts. We have rules outlined, like never offer explicit advice, only listen. Like if someone says they're going to kill themselves, you ask them questions, why and how, ask them to put it off, make a pact to stay alive just for tonight. You don't tell them not to, because we're not supposed to be there to give them orders or tell them how to feel. We're there to provide empathy, and to show them they're not alone. We have no authority. We are sounding boards. Faceless friends.

Although I'm nervous and awkward in this fusty room that smells like a window hasn't been opened in a thousand years, I'm convinced that there is a reason my life has come to this, and I feel about ten years older than the girl who swallowed a bottle of pills by the lakeside. I know now, after thinking my near death to death, that I didn't want to die. And I am wondering, after halfing my medication now for almost two months, and now letting myself skip a day here and there entirely, if I don't have a mental disorder. Maybe I'm just the same girl I always was, a girl with big feelings, one who filled out a survey with an aloof psychiatrist and ended up with a diagnosis I don't deserve.

The point is, I know who I am now in a way I didn't a month ago, and definitely didn't two months ago. I go days without thinking of Jonah. When the black hole presents itself, I roll my eyes at it, tell it to buzz off. Wanting to die is dumb, weak, immature. I want to return to the girl I was just two months ago and hold her hand and tell her to stay home that morning, write a poem, fake sick, take a bath, flush those pills down the toilet, eat some chocolate, cry into a pillow, but don't you dare try to die. Don't do something that will stamp you with a black ink you can never erase.

The point is, I am not her anymore. I am on a mission here; when I answer the phone, one of these days, I'm going to save somebody. Maybe, in some weird way, myself.

And holy shit: the phone is ringing.

First is a high-voiced man with a Southernish accent whose name I miss because he speaks so fast, plunging headfirst into a monologue about how he thinks someone's been stealing his mail and—*he thinks it's the mailman*. I wait for some kind of emergency to arise in his story . . . for, I don't know, the mailman to be harassing him somehow? But then his story changes. He hasn't been able to find his dang slipper in weeks now and the dang company stopped making them, so he can't reorder. He doesn't sound mentally ill. Why is he calling a hotline? At the end he's nearly weeping about how his sister didn't send him a card on baby Jesus's birthday. It's been almost twenty minutes of this. In training, Davina says if someone isn't in crisis, to gently try to end the call after twenty minutes. I tell him to hang in there and steer the conversation toward goodbye and hang up. Two of the other volunteers are on calls. I can tell, the way they lean in and press their headsets to their ears in listening mode. But the steely-eyed older woman—who introduced herself earlier as Lydia—stares at me, her crossword puzzle book open.

"You got Davis, didn't you," she says.

At first I think this has something to do with her half-filled crossword puzzle, D-A-V-I-S, 7 down, but she quickly corrects me.

"It's a rite of passage, getting Davis," Lydia tells me, holding her pen like a long cigarette. "He's one of our regulars."

"Regulars," I repeat.

I remember touching on this in training—that some people call in for no reason, just to have a warm voice on the other end of the line, just to vent, unleash, or even abuse.

"We have a bet going about whether or not he's real," Lydia says.

"Real?"

"Or a crank," she says. "Some kid. That accent, whatever it is, is hardly believable."

"Oh." I deflate, thinking I've just been made a fool of.

"That's just me being a cynical old hag, honey, don't listen to me, I'm full of shit. He's just a lonely old soul who likes the sound of his own voice."

I breathe a sigh of relief. "Okay."

"It's all about boundaries," Lydia says. "Davis calls, I say, 'Okay, buddy, I'm setting my timer here for ten and then that's it for you.' Otherwise he'll be on with you all night or calling, and then calling back."

"All night," I repeat.

"All motherfuckin' night," Lydia says, nodding her head with each word for emphasis.

We both bust up in a laugh, the first physical clue that Lydia has any joy inside her since I stepped foot in the room. She has a raspy cackle that makes me laugh a little extra hard. Her smile is wide and she's missing a back tooth. Then her face quickly resumes its serious, wrinkled state of rest and she answers her ringing phone.

"Crisis hotline, this is Lydia."

My phone rings again five minutes before I'm about to get off. It's a lot of heavy breathing.

"Are you safe?" I keep asking.

But then they hang up.

"I don't know if they were safe," I tell the other volunteers.

My heart, speed racer.

"Probably just a . . . self-soother," Beatriz tells me.

Beatriz is the hippie-skirt woman with the stress ball. Across her right wrist, the word *vida* is tattooed in black-blue ink.

"Well, that's a euphemism if I ever heard one," says JD, the girl with the boy haircut who I have now changed my mind about and wondered if he's actually a boy with femme features.

"Water off a duck's back, duckling," Lydia says without even looking over her reading glasses at me, concentrating on her crossword.

"Shouldn't we, like, report it?" I ask.

"Sure," Lydia says. "If shouting into the abyss is your kind of thing."

"You can report it," Beatriz says, nodding. "I have the number."

"To the abyss," Lydia says.

"Lydia," Beatriz says, shooting her a look with a story behind it. "Negativity."

"Oh, all right," Lydia says.

She gets up, puts her crossword on the table with a slap, and goes out to the front porch, where we can all hear her on her phone saying, "I love you, Camus. You're a good girl, Camus."

"Dog," JD tells me.

"She calls her dog?"

"FaceTimes," Beatriz says.

"Oh" is all I say.

I call the nonemergency police number Beatriz gives me and quickly understand why Lydia likened the experience to shouting into the abyss—the operator tells me that unless the person continues to call back, or says something threatening, they can't do anything. Thanks a bunch.

JD goes back to the smartphone game at hand, Beatriz continues leafing through a cooking magazine, and I stare at my philosophy reader. There's something easy and sweet about this silence I'm sharing with strangers.

I lean back in my chair and look at the skylight, a square of black crisscrossed with the white. When I don't blink, when I let my eyes relax and the room blur, stars appear.

I go home that night feeling older, even though I didn't do much of helping anyone. I listened, though. I tried something new.

I had an experience I wouldn't have had if I hadn't kept living.

# PAST

Our whole life we're told not to take candy from strangers, and then, every year, along comes Halloween.

It used to be my favorite holiday. The community centers that transformed into magical haunted houses; artificial spiderwebs veiling ordinary porches, fake tombstones on suburban lawns; the sweet, nutty smell of burning jack-o'-lanterns; "Monster Mash" rocking grocery store speakers. I swore I would dress up and trick-or-treat through adulthood, until last year, when I did, and everyone whose doorbell I rang told me I was too old. I ended up at Jonah's house that night in my bee costume, eating candy out of the bag, watching a movie about a masked murderer. It was okay, I told myself. Make way for new traditions. But secretly I wished I had known the year before that it was the last time. Why does no one ever tell you it's the last time? There should be a word for the special nostalgia you feel when you realize you already had your last time doing something and you didn't even know it.

Like when Jonah kissed me for the last time in the school halls, saying, "I hope you feel better." I was in a horrible mood that day.

Like last Christmas Eve, when my family fell asleep as a family under the same roof for the last time. I fell asleep early.

Like the night of the car crash, as the open window swept sweet summer air to my cheeks, when I had zero inkling that I'd never feel free and unafraid in a car on a freeway again.

Or like the day I tried to kill myself. That day, I told myself, "This is the last time you'll get dressed in the morning. This is the last dress you'll ever wear. This bowl of cereal is the last meal you'll ever eat. This is the last note you will write. This is the last walk to the lake you'll take. This is the last day of your life."

Lies.

I want to say that was the last time I'll try to kill myself. But who knows how believable I am.

This Halloween I agree to take my sisters trick-or-treating through our neighborhood. Dad's neighborhood, I mean. Ruby requested that I take them, as I'm "less embarrassing" than Mom and Dad. Thanks for the backhanded compliment, sis. Marisol comes over beforehand, not in costume, but in a blue fake-fur vest in which she could easily pass for a Muppet. As the girls get ready, Marisol and I eat so much fun-sized candy it becomes un-fun. Stevie and Ruby come downstairs in their costumes. Stevie is a unicorn, adorable in her fuzzy zip-up onesie with the silver horn on the head. Ruby is wearing her usual black jeans, black shirt, black Converse, with her bruise-colored hair. Takes me a moment to notice the fake blood coming out of the side of her mouth.

"Wow, really phoning it in this year," I say.

"I'm dead," she replies.

"You look like you always look," Stevie says. "I hope no one gives you candy."

"If they don't I'll go buy some at the store," Ruby says. "Halloween is dumb."

"What a little ray of sunshine you are," Marisol says, tousling Ruby's hair.

"Sunshine gives you cancer," Ruby says.

Stevie whips her pillowcase around like a helicopter. "I think she needs Zoloft."

"How do you know about Zoloft?" I ask, surprised.

"Commercial," Stevie says.

"Maybe I need *lithium*," Ruby says, finger-brushing her hair.

My neck prickles; heat hits my cheeks. I know she's talking about me. She's probably been peeking in my medicine cabinet. Ever since our chat when I stayed at Mom's, I get the feeling Ruby despises me.

"God, let's hope not," Marisol says. "Remember last year when you were a witch princess for Halloween? How fun that was? And you spent all that time on your costume?"

"No one knew what I was," Ruby reminds her. "The

costume ended up at the Goodwill."

"Just ignore her," I tell Marisol.

Dad snaps a picture of us before we depart. He's dressed in a button-up shirt and smells like cologne.

"Where are you going?" Ruby asks him.

"Meeting a friend," he says.

"You have friends?" Ruby asks.

"Ha ha," he says. "Have fun, girls. Be back by nine."

He leaves, his cologne lingering in the air. We all look at each other.

"I was being serious," Ruby says. "Who wants to be friends with someone who smells like that?"

"Man," Marisol says to her. "Thirteen has hit you hard."

We walk outside. The yard still looks so empty without the chokecherry tree. Sunset's smeared the sky with color; moon is high and waiting. It's windy and leaves scatter on the asphalt. Batman and a fairy ring a doorbell across the street. We walk from house to house and Marisol tells me everything that's been going on at school, how so-and-so broke up with so-and-so and another so-and-so got in trouble for having fireworks in his locker and there's a new so-and-so in her advanced French class who is totally hot. Some of the so-and-sos she talks about have messaged me or texted with well wishes.

I'm glad Marisol cares—good for her, that must be nice—but it's like listening to someone prattle on about a TV show I've never seen. I have to go back to school tomorrow, and I wish I never had to go back there again. I'm not even excited to see anyone at all. In fact—what's the opposite of excited? The circles we've floated in are circumstantial: fellow semi-punk music lovers we go to shows with on weekends sometimes, some folks from last year's failed poetry club. We're friendly, but I'm not sure we're really *friends*. Not in the "hey, let me tell you about my nervous breakdown" kind of way. The lie is, I have mono. Nobody but Marisol knows about the whole trying-to-kill-myself thing. I'd like to keep it that way. In fact, if I could move forward and never think or talk about the fact I tried to kill myself again, I could die happy. Or *not* die happy. What a weird phrase that is, now that I think about it: die happy.

We walk past the entrance to the lake, surrounded by eucalyptus trees, and I can't help but crane my neck to see if I can catch a glimpse of the top of the oak tree down the hillside where apparently a dog found me and saved my life. I say nothing, although I can feel Marisol tense up beside me. She must be aware of what we're walking past. Stevie and Ruby are steps ahead, arguing about the merits of Almond Joys versus Mounds bars.

"When will Halloween be fun again?" I ask Marisol.

"In college, when we get to go to parties and have an excuse to wear sexy costumes."

"Some of us aren't going to college."

"Stop talking like life is over when we're just getting started."

We've had this particular conversation before. Marisol refuses to accept I'm not university-eligible, and she certainly refuses to accept I don't care. Next year, she'll be somewhere cold and far away and full of tall buildings. I'll probably still be here. She thinks somehow some glorious opportunity is going to present itself for me, because she has so many to futures to choose from, she can't imagine what it's like to feel like you have none. And it probably makes her feel less guilty for leaving if she thinks somehow I'm going to leave, too.

"Marisol," I remind her, "I had straight Cs last semester."

She doesn't answer, shoves her hands in her Muppety (Muppetous?) pockets.

For the longest time, next year seemed so far away. But as I stand here, I realize . . . Halloween . . . end of October.

"Are you applying right now?" I ask.

"Yeah. I'm in the middle of my applications."

With that one simple sentence, it's like I've realized the world has turned beneath my feet. I've been stuck in this timeless, desperate place, a thing with feathers but broken wings. Meanwhile, my best friend plans to fly.

We stop in front of a house with a bougainvillea-tangled trellis and a birdbath. A white-haired man opens the door for my sisters and shouts, "A unicorn! Now I've seen it all."

"So you're really going to go to Seattle," I say.

Marisol's in love with Seattle. She went to camp there every summer, adores rain and gray skies, finds Southern

California and its relentless sunshine horrific.

"I hope so. Or Chicago," she says.

"Good for you." Man, I hope that didn't sound as bitter as it felt coming out of my mouth.

We go to the next house—a beige number with beige wood chips on the lawn and a beige woman in a beige dress answering the door for Stevie and Ruby. I hear Ruby say "I'm dead" again.

Marisol reaches out and gives me a half hug. A pity half hug. A my-friend's-a-loser-who-will-probably-never-leave-her-hometown half hug.

"It's going to be okay," she says.

I sigh and blink away tears. "I've been so down in this hole I forgot about school, deadlines, college, everything."

I kick a wood chip. We walk behind Stevie and Ruby as they pelt each other with candy-heavy pillowcases. I swear the only person who can evoke the kid in Ruby these days is Stevie. Ruby hates Stevie less than everyone in the world combined.

"Those new meds are kinda spacing you out, huh?" Marisol asks.

"It's like I'm half underwater."

"I know it's probably not the right thing to say . . . but I miss you, JoJo. I miss you even right now when we're together."

We stop in front of a house with an overgrown lawn covered with plastic toys. I look up at the moon. Same old moon. Crazy, not crazy, medicated, unmedicated, suicidal, ecstatic—moon doesn't care.

"I miss me, too, sometimes," I say. "Here I am, all Sylvia Plath, and I can't even write a freaking poem."

"Maybe it'll get better once they adjust your medication again."

"Do you think I'm bipolar?"

"I'm not the person to make that call."

"Your aunt is bipolar."

"She's a lot of things. Think of a disorder, she probably has it. Have I told you she's in group therapy now for shopaholics? Those American Girl dolls. Her house is, like, filled with them."

"We should try to get her on that TV show."

"That would be mortifying but also amazing." Marisol smiles. "Anyway, you're not like her. But she's not the singular representative for bipolar disorder. Neither are you. Neither is anyone."

We walk around a corner, across from my old elementary school, the one where Stevie goes now. Funny how miniature everything looks these days—like the whole place shrank to doll size and I stayed the same, when really it's me who became a giant. I know this street. I walk it in my dreams.

"I know what you're doing, Journey," Marisol says.

"Walking?" I ask, staring at my sparkly flats.

"Sometimes I think you're so convincing you even convince yourself."

"Of what?"

"You know exactly what," she says, flicking her gaze to the street sign.

I shrug. But she's so onto me. Damn best friends.

I was trying to shove it out of my mind, that we were headed his way, but deep down, I knew where the magnet of my unrequited love pulled me: right back to Jonah's doorstep. And now here we are, one house away. My heart races at the sight of his SUV in the driveway. He's probably home.

There should be a word for this mix of hope and dread that pricks my eyes with preemptive tears. It's not *Weltschmerz*, a German word meaning "world grief" that describes a romantic but gloomy outlook on life often specific to privileged young adults. Something more like *dor*, the Romanian word for sadly yearning for someone or something—but that's not quite it, either.

"Are you sure this is wise?" Marisol asks.

"We'll just say hi and let the girls trick-or-treat. What? It would be *more* awkward to skip his house."

Marisol pulls my sleeve. "JoJo . . ."

Stevie and Ruby seem blissfully unaware as they head up the walkway I've walked a thousand times, the one lined with rosebushes Jonah's dad cuts all weekend long, the one with the porch decorated with Jonah's mom's wind chime collection. As soon as they see the wind chimes, Ruby turns around with a look of doubt on her face.

"Wait, isn't this . . . ?" she asks.

But Stevie's already rung the doorbell. The door opens. And there he is, standing in his band shirt and adorable tight jeans with a bowl of candy.

"Happy—" he says, and then his stupid, beautiful eyes widen in surprise at the sight of us and he forgets to finish his festive greeting. He gives me a nod and meets my gaze like he hasn't been avoiding me since he texted asking for more space ten days ago. And come on. Ten days is *space*. "Hey."

"Hi," I say.

"Jonah!" Stevie says.

"Hey, kid," he answers, giving her a fist bump.

Stevie's always had a sorta obvious crush on Jonah. It's adorable. She almost cried when I broke the news that Jonah and I were no longer a thing.

"Nice costume," he says dryly to Ruby.

"I'm dead," she says.

Palpitations. My nose stings and I want to start bawling. The whole terrible night we were on the phone, the suicide attempt, everything rushes back to me in a tsunami of shame and pain.

"Can we talk?" I ask, throat tight. "Have I given you enough space?"

"Um," Jonah says, looking down at his socks.

There's a long silence.

"Well, this is awkward," Ruby says. "Can I at least have some candy?"

"Come on, girls," Marisol says, putting her arms around Stevie and Ruby and ushering them back to the sidewalk.

Now it's just me and Jonah and a bowl of peanut butter cups.

"Can I come in?" I ask.

"My parents are home, Journey," he whispers. "Can we talk soon?"

The humiliation burns my face, tears blur the scene. I can't help it. I spill over. "Why? Why are you ignoring me? You weren't just my boyfriend, you were my best friend. So much has happened, I—"

He comes out onto the porch and pulls the door shut behind him. "I know. I really wish I could invite you in, but . . . but my parents had a talk with me and they told me they think we should give each other a break."

Of course they did. All his parents care about is good grades—*appearances*. They've always thought I was too unstable, too wild.

"I've been so stressed out lately, Journey," he goes on, eyes shiny. "You have no idea because you're so worried about yourself all the time. But I don't know how to help you. And that hurts me so bad."

"You can help me," I say. "You make everything better."

"It's scary loving you," he tells me, fighting tears. "I just—I just want to be a normal guy, you know? School and guitar and . . . skateboarding."

"Who said you couldn't skateboard?"

"I don't want to have to worry that the person I love the most is going to kill herself," he says.

"This makes no sense," I tell him.

"I'm not saying this is forever, I'm just asking for space."

"Space," I repeat.

That word—that absence of a word, that nothing of a word. I hear the leaves skittering behind me and think *Waldeinsamkeit*, a German word for the feeling of being alone in the woods. Lately, it's like I have that feeling all the time. The whole world is deep, dark woods I am lost in.

"Can you give me that?" he asks.

"Don't talk to me like that."

"Like what?"

"Like I'm three."

This is one of those moments. I wish I were dead. I try to focus on my breath but it's useless. I want that hole to open up and swallow me. I want to not be here. I want to be gone, to hurt him with my gone-ness, I wish I never was.

"Journey," he says, all exasperated.

I walk away before I start screaming at him. What he's saying . . . I get it. I just wish he wanted to save me instead of saving himself.

I join Marisol and the girls at the next house. Marisol's got a worried look behind her glasses as I approach and the girls finish up their latest trick-or-treat. I'm trying to wipe my tears away but they come so fast.

"What's going on?" Stevie asks, her face a mirror of

sadness in the middle of her unicorn onesie. She's so pretty and perfect. She has no idea about things like heartbreaker boys and wanting to die.

I want to scream, run, light a fire. I'm dull all day, and then when I most need help, the medication does nothing. I still feel too much. A little Frankenstein's monster runs by, drawn-on crude stitches railroading along his forehead.

Where's my lobotomy?

I wipe my eyes quick, blame allergies, force myself to smile.

*Kill yourself,* the voice whispers.

But an ever so slightly louder voice says, *Shut the hell up. You're what got me into this mess.*

It's kinda startling, that louder voice.

"You okay?" Marisol asks.

I nod, suck in my breath, hold my sisters' hands, and keep on walking.

"Yeah. I think I am."

# PRESENT

It's February, second week of city college. I'm sitting in philosophy class. Our teacher is a bald guy with a monotone whose last name is Sacks. I text Marisol this fact and get an immediate !!! in response. He lectures about egoism versus altruism, chicken-scratch chalk on the board divided like a pros and cons list. I try to take notes but find myself staring out the window at the glowering gray clouds that hover over the green trees, the wind shaking them helpless.

Egoism would mean that everything I do is selfish, for me. Trying to off myself was the most selfish thing I've ever done. I'm sure if my parents or Marisol found out I stopped taking my meds they might call that selfish, too, even though it feels like the right decision for me. This is probably why I keep putting off sharing this info with anyone. But then there's altruism, or its possibility—like my volunteering at the crisis center. Helping people, just because. But what if it feels good to help people and that feeling good is why I do it? What if even being selfless is only something I do to help myself? There's something so hopelessly depressing about that thought.

Etta sits near me, scribbling notes all thirsty-brained. She bites her nails so close to the quick, betraying some kind of anxiety beneath her gregarious surface. Halfway through the class my pen dies and she whispers to me that she can loan me one. I get a peek at the inside of her backpack, a shockingly disorganized abyss of crumpled papers and travel-sized toiletries. She finds a pen and hands it to me, flashing me a red, red smile.

Since school started, I've found myself distracted, just a little. By Etta. I don't want to call it a crush. That sounds so dire. It's more like a . . . leaning. I'm leaning into her, the more I get to know her. At first I thought I envied her. Then I thought I wanted to be her friend. Now I wonder if it's more than that.

After class is done, she lets me share her umbrella and we walk to lunch together. The coconut smell of her mixes with the rain. We hurry across wet cement that reflects the world back up at us, blurry, wet smudges of shadow and color.

She makes a kaboom-like noise. "That class explodes my brain."

"That class is undoing months of therapy I've spent trying to learn how to stop thinking so much," I say.

She laughs heartily. I get a swell inside, a mix of relief

and the high of making her happy. Also gladness that she didn't skip a beat at the therapy comment.

"Also, Sacks kind of sucks."

"Don't be mean to Professor Sacks!" she says, batting my arm.

"He is so boring."

"He is kind and pensive," she says.

"And his name is Sacks."

"Do you know how hard that must be for him?" she asks. "I know, because my last name is Farthing. I'll let you connect the dots."

I'm not about to fill her in on the eighteen years of irritating puns about trips and classic rock I've had to put up with. "My condolences."

"Professor Sacks is a darling and a dear. He has a picture of his cat on the home screen of his phone and his cat's name is Harold."

Sometimes I truly think Etta's too nice. She never says anything mean about anyone. Everywhere she looks, she seems to only see the good in people. I wonder what she sees in me.

"Okay, egoist or altruist?" she asks.

I'd like to think I'm a good person. I try. But I tried to kill myself mere months ago. I can't reconcile that—the most selfish act imaginable—with being a truly good person.

"Probably an egoist who thinks I'm an altruist," I answer. "Wish there was a word for that."

Funny. I can tell you words for the way the moonlight can glow like a road on water (*mangata*, Swedish) and the wet ring a cold glass of water leaves upon a table (*culaccino*, Italian), but there is no word that I know of for a person who does right for all the wrong reasons.

# PAST

Today is the day. I'm finally going back to high school after two weeks "sick" with "mono," dolled up in my favorite dress printed with strawberries and matching lipstick, filled to the brim with fruit-flavored dread. Marisol picks me up and brings me a breakfast sandwich. She has my favorite playlist on her speakers.

"It's going to be just fine," she tells me as she drives us there.

I'd argue with her, but what would be the point.

As soon as she parks, Marisol has to rush off to go fix some transcript debacle in the administrative office, so I'm left alone walking back into the bustle of laughter, hand-painted signs for canned food drives, and our principal making unintelligible loudspeaker announcements. Nothing about the place has changed, but somehow it looks different to me now, the way my elementary school appears doll-sized. The light has changed. It's a movie set. That same feeling nags me, the one I've had since the year started—that I'm watching life happen around me instead of participating. I smile and wave, accept hugs and condolences about mono, yes, the rumors are true, Jonah and I broke up. It's amicable, it was mutual. Lie, lie, lie.

The truth is, I don't feel that bad besides the gross pit in my stomach whenever I think I see Jonah, but I'm utterly bored by school. I stare out the window at the windy day blowing oak leaves and trash through the empty halls, my class all repeating Spanish conjugations out loud together in chorus. Instead of imagining a hole opening up that I can jump into, I conjure a spaceship landing in the middle of the quad, me getting on it and ascending into the sky. Ta-ta, sayonara, so long, earthlings.

Finally, there Jonah is, in the lunch line, and it takes every ounce of willpower for my face to not break into a thousand pieces. He gives me a nod like I'm some passing bro. Seriously, screw him. I turn around and decide I'm not as hungry as I thought I was, go sit under a tree next to Marisol as she crams for an AP English test. I pen a letter into my composition book.

Dear future self,

I know depression has its treatments. But does unhappiness?

My nerves are calm but my brain burns, my heart screams. I'm sitting at school looking through the glass, life's lone audience member. Watching food fights and maniacal laughter and skateboarding tricks and make-out sessions on green grass. All these people seem to know where they're going—to jobs, colleges, families. But when I look forward to spy a future, I don't see anything. I'm stuck and I don't know how to move forward. I guess my question, future self, is—who the hell are you?

Marisol peeks over my shoulder and takes her earbud out. "*So* dramatic," she says, pointing to my letter.

I close my book, annoyed. "Maybe life is dramatic. Does that make you uncomfortable?"

"No, but the fact you tried to—" She makes a cutting-off-her-head motion with a *wheek* sound. "That makes me uncomfortable."

"I didn't try to sever my own head."

"You are like the most frustrating cocktail of drama and then joking so much you can't have a serious conversation about it."

And I'm not about to have a serious conversation about it now, in public, when I feel like I've been glued back together and am ready to fall apart again. Here is not the place to be a human wreck.

"So you're saying I'm a dramedy?" I ask.

Marisol puts her earbuds back in. "Goodbye."

"So dramatic," I tell her, elbowing her, which I know she despises.

"You asked for it." She pulls her earbuds out again, puts her books down, cracks her knuckles, and tickles me to the point where I'm writhing on the grass beneath her, begging her to stop.

"ASSAULT!" I scream, and she finally stops.

I sit up, wiping my eyes, which have been cried out from the tickle attack. Marisol looks very satisfied with herself.

"You feel better, though, don't you," she says.

"If by 'better' you mean my makeup is a mess and my sides hurt, sure."

"That should be a thing," she says. "Tickle therapy."

"It has to be a thing, right?" I ask. "In this big, weird world?"

I look it up on my phone. Sure enough, it exists. There are even "tickle spas" where you can pay people to tickle you with feathers in a dark room with incense. Well, I'll be jiggered.

"Maybe I should become a professional tickler," I say. "Maybe that's what I'll do after high school's over."

"You're going to do great things," Marisol says with a serious brown stare behind her red frames.

"Tickling people?"

"I'm serious. You say you don't see anything in your future," she says, pointing to my composition book on the ground. "I see so many amazing things for you."

The smile on my face disappears. Easy for her to say. Her life's shining ahead of her, filled with scholarships and school acceptances and new cities to explore. She's spending Thanksgiving weekend in Chicago to check out the university there with her mom. Soon she'll have a million new best friends. I'll be . . . superfluous.

Usually, this is where I would think of killing myself. *I don't matter, the world will go on without me,* yada yada. But instead, I focus on my breath.

"JoJo?" Marisol asks. "You with me?"

I nod.

"Promise me something," she says. "You're doing better, and I'm proud of you for getting through that suicide attempt."

"Don't say it so loud."

"Nobody can hear us. And you don't need to be ashamed."

I roll my eyes, because really? Anyone in my position would be ashamed after pulling a stunt like I did.

"I know holidays are hard," she goes on, "and I'm worried about you as they come up. I was reading that suicide attempts happen at an especially high rate this time of year."

"You're so good at cheering me up." I feel a pang, knowing she's been researching this, spending however many worried hours online.

Marisol pulls my book toward her, uncaps a pen. "Let me write down something for you." She opens it up and, in her big, bubbly eight-year-old-girl penmanship, jots down a local phone number I don't recognize.

"This is the number for the local crisis hotline," she says.

"They're available twenty-four hours a day, seven days a week."

"How do you know it by heart?" I ask.

"Well, the last four digits spell HELP. Also I almost volunteered there this school year, for community service. But ended up going for the tutoring gig instead."

We have a community service requirement at school. Last year I did shifts at the local library. It was so boring that time itself stopped while I was shelving books. I haven't even started on my requirement for this year. I look at the number she wrote down in purple pen and imagine all the people who call it every day. All the bizarre crap the hotline operators must listen to.

Must be fascinating, actually.

"Thanks," I tell Marisol.

The bell rings.

"Walk you to PE?" she asks, standing up.

Indoor PE: the bane of my existence. The stench of vinyl mats and sweatpants no one washes. The weight machines that resemble medieval torture devices.

"Lucky me, I have a counseling appointment," I tell her.

"With who?"

"Hooker."

Hooker is the chillest of guidance counselors at our school, responsible for students with surnames starting with $M$ through $Z$, with an unfortunate last name himself. To make matters worse, his first name is Richard. I've heard him referred to as "Rich Hooker" and of course "Dick Hook" by those who both hate and love him. He wears sandals and burns sage in his office, has old posters from hippie concerts all over his wall. He kind of reminds me of an even more extreme version of my dad. Due to my nosediving grades, I've unfortunately had enough sessions with him in the last year to get to know him all too well.

"Have fun," Marisol says, hugging me. "*My Secret Obsession*'s on later. Watch and text?"

"I wouldn't rather observe some weirdo make out with a finger puppet with anyone else," I tell her.

I go through the halls toward the admin building, feeling pretty good, actually. The sun is shining so bright I have to put on my cat-eyes. I can do this, I think. I can do this life thing.

Then I see Madison walking toward me, her damn perfect box-red hair up on top of her head. She's model-tall and dresses like some kind of stylish mom with her fringy scarves and long skirts.

"Hi," she says, smiling.

"Hi," I say.

When she utters that syllable it seems long, bouncy, uplifting. When I say it, it sounds like I threw a brick at her head.

I don't slow down. Keep walking, girl. But I am an elevator now, heading fast for the basement. My smile disappears and I keep reliving that dumb nothing and everything of a moment. I wonder if Jonah still talks to her, if *she's* the reason for the space—STOP IT, BRAIN. Brains ruin everything.

I head inside the admin building and concentrate on my breath as I sit in a chair in the waiting area. A photocopier whirs and squeals, repeating a mechanical cry for help. The air stinks like ink. There's an almost-empty water cooler, a wall covered in class photos from over the years that all look, from here, depressingly alike. A secretary keeps coughing into a tissue behind the desk. I remember I forgot to take my medication today.

"Journey Smith!" Hooker says when he opens the door, showing off the Grand Canyon gap between his top front teeth. "My favorite Journey!"

This guy's like four Red Bulls deep, all the time. I'm already exhausted just looking at him.

"I'm sure you've counseled a lot of Journeys," I say.

"That's the joke!"

I sit on a cushioned chair. On his wall hangs a giant framed pic of a stick figure with the words *Life is the dancer, and you are the dance.*

Hooker takes a seat at his desk, where he has one of those mini sand gardens, a couple cacti, and pic of him and I assume his wife person standing in front of a waterfall with big hiking backpacks on. He also has a hacky sack, which he picks up and starts squeezing as he leans back in his chair and swivels, studying me.

I'm sure this session is about my grades, the amount of

school I missed, how I should be thinking about some sad college somewhere that takes sad sacks like me. There's no way he knows that I tried to kill myself. But somehow it's like he does.

I shift in my chair.

"So, wow, you've had a lot of absences recently," he begins. "I'm a bit concerned you're falling behind."

"I had mono."

"Ugh, the *worst.*"

"Pretty much."

"Even before that, though, your midterm grades were . . . in need of some mojo."

"Yep, I suck" is all I can think to say.

"Hey, come on—you don't believe *that.*"

"Just stating the obvious. They don't call all-stars into the guidance counselor office multiple times a semester."

"Now that is bogus. I talk to everyone."

"Okay."

"What's going on?" he asks, leaning in. "Come on. Open up."

"I just . . ." I sigh.

I could say a million things right now. But I already have a therapist.

"I kind of hate school," I tell him.

"Hate's a strong word."

"Yeah. I feel strongly."

"What are you thinking in terms of college?"

"You've seen my grades. Kinda blew my chances at a four-year."

"Do you *want* to go to college?"

"I've thought about city college next year. Or maybe just working, saving up money and traveling."

"I look at you and I see a wonderful candidate for higher learning."

I laugh, because I think this must be a joke. But his lips don't twitch.

"I've actually thought about dropping out," I tell him.

Mainly just today. Just today that popped into my head, walking around—what's the point of even graduating? I have a terrible GPA and no hope of university life. And I don't ever want to see Jonah again.

"Come on, Journey," he says. "You know dropping out's not an option."

"I don't want to be here," I say, the words hurting my throat on the way out.

"Where do you want to be?"

"Nowhere."

"You're bored," he says, putting the hacky sack down with a *thwunk*. "What they offer here"—he gestures to his open window that looks onto the school's front lawn—"it's just not doing it for you."

I can't disagree, but hearing this coming from a guidance counselor's mouth is so unexpected that I'm not sure how to respond.

He leans in. "You and I have met a lot over the last year. And you know what I think? I think you're struggling because you're too smart for this place."

Now I know he's messing with me. Me? Smart? When people like Marisol with 1500 SATs and straight As wander these halls? When kids in my classes are applying to Harvard and other fancy-pants places? Come the hell on.

"Ever heard of middle college?" he asks.

"Is that college for screwups like me?"

"Not at all," he says. "It's a program that allows juniors and seniors to attend city college to get both high school and college credit. You'd go to city college early, get your diploma at the end of the year—win-win. I actually think you'd be perfect for it."

"If I can't even handle high school, how do you expect me to pass college classes?"

"Because you'll be engaged and interested in the material you're learning. You can take poetry classes, anthropology, improv."

"Huh," I say. "And I'd get credit for that . . . here?"

He nods. "Getting you on the path to middle college right now would mean we'd be able to transfer you to an interim program for the rest of the semester, get you into some makeup work you could do at home and salvage your grades. Because at this point, at least in government and English and precalculus, passing is starting to look . . . iffy."

I didn't realize how far behind I'd fallen. Also, is he really offering me an out right now? Like I'd never have to go back to high school again? Because that's looking pretty good from where I'm at . . . although what about Marisol? Could I really leave my best friend and go to school with a bunch of grown-up strangers?

Hooker pushes a city college catalog and a flier that explains the program toward me. "Think about it."

"Okay."

"And then come back and talk to me about it. I'm serious. I don't recommend this program to many people, especially nearly a quarter into their senior year. But I think you would really thrive in city college."

"Thanks," I say.

I take the catalog and flier and put them in my purse, tuck them in a half-read memoir about a celebrity with bipolar disorder. Hooker gives me a high five when I leave. And I hate to admit it—but his four-Red-Bulls-deep attitude is sort of infectious. I find myself enjoying the flutter of excitement in my belly as I walk away from his office. This glimmer of hope is shiny and it makes me nervous all at once.

Marisol's got some essay contest thing after school so I ride the bus home today. Probably for the best, because I imagine that she'd shoot down the middle college idea and beg me not to ditch her during senior year anyway.

Not that that's fair, I think, having an imaginary argument with her. *She's* going to be ditching *me* next year, isn't she? I'm probably the only senior on the bus and, golly, earplugs and a nose plug would be nice. I grab a seat toward the back and flip through the spring city college catalog. Human sexuality. Astronomy. Yoga. Improv. I imagine myself going to college, with adults. Why's that even weird anyway? I'm eighteen since August. Technically an adult.

It's strange, this lighter-than-air feeling I have when walking home, passing the lake, which, right now, twinkles like glass, surrounded by blond grasses, like some fancy painting on a wall. I can't see the oak tree from here. I just see the lake I spent my childhood riding bikes around and exploring.

For the first time since I did that stupid thing, I can imagine something ahead of me.

I can imagine a future.

"Absolutely not," Mom says.

It's Saturday. We're in a booth at the café where she works, waiting for Levi to come pick her up after her shift is over. She's still got her pink polo on with her name stitched on it. The ceiling fans reflect off silver spoons and vinyl seats.

"You haven't even read the flier," I say, trying not to raise my voice even though I want to scream. "You haven't even heard me out."

I knew this was going to be a tough sell on her, but she's not even letting one toe in the door here. Dad already knows about the program and thinks it'd be a good idea. Anything to get me on the college track and keep me from having a nervous breakdown.

She pinches her fingers together to show me what a millimeter looks like. "You are this close to graduating the right way."

A small fire of frustration burns in me. I'm trying so hard here. Trying so hard to find a solution that pleases everybody and looks like a life I want to live.

"You know, I'm eighteen," I tell her. "I technically don't even need my parents' permission to do anything anymore."

"Then why are you even asking me?"

"Because I want you to be on board with my plan."

"Have you been taking your medication?"

As if whether or not I've been chomping a pink pill is the end-all. The answer, in fact, besides a couple missed doses here and there, is yes. But I have been wondering what would happen if I stopped.

"What does that have to do with this?" I ask, pushing the flier forward. "Listen, I *would* graduate. That's the whole point of this. To get me on track to *actually graduate*. Because right now I wouldn't pass all my classes this semester. Next semester I would be going to city college and taking classes I'm challenged by and interested in: improv, poetry, anthropology."

"I'm sure if we explained the real circumstances of your absences this semester and made it clear to the administration you were hospitalized for a suicide attempt, they would make an exception."

"I don't want anyone knowing what I did," I say.

Even the words *suicide attempt* flood me with shame. It's like the farther we get from what I did, the more unreal and horrific it becomes. The more I want to hide it, hide from it.

"Honey, people would just want to help you," she says.

"I don't want people's help. I want to do it myself."

Mom's eyes dance for a moment, even as her lips form a frown. "You know, when you were tiny, you were the same stubborn thing. Buckling you into the car seat, you'd smack my hand. 'I do it myself.' Getting dressed in the morning, I'd try to help you pick out your clothes: 'I do it myself.' Of course you'd end up in a tutu and pajama pants and a witch hat, and couldn't be talked out of it. I couldn't help you tie your shoes. I couldn't do anything for you without a fight."

"I'm sorry."

She reaches out and touches my cheek, looks at me like I'm a little thing still wearing a tutu and a witch hat, not a grown person with faded purple hair and heavy eyeliner. "Don't be sorry you are the way you are."

Mom and I have had a lot of tension since the suicide attempt. She navigates around me like I'm a grenade with a pin missing. I fear, sometimes, that I lost her respect in a way that I don't with Dad. Hearing these words coming from her right now means a lot.

Her face softens. "What's your plan?" she says. "Pitch me."

I sit up straighter, turning the catalog and the flier around so they face her. "So ASAP I'd segue into this interim program where I'd do a bunch of makeup work at home until January, when next semester starts. That way I could salvage my grades this semester and knock out physics, which I got a D in last year. I'd take college classes next semester and maybe even get a job. Maybe by June I'd have money saved up and could move out on my own."

"That's ambitious. All that stress. Do you think you could handle it?"

"I'm ready for it," I say. "Mom, I want to move on so badly. I want to grow up."

"I have to wonder if this is mania talking."

I roll my eyes. "Everything I do shouldn't be reduced down to symptoms you WebMD'd. I'm sleeping fine. I'm eating fine. Taking care of myself better than I ever have, actually. Have you ever seen me exercising before? Enjoying fresh air? Meditating?"

She bites her lip. "I don't know."

"I made a huge mistake. I know that, and I'm trying to piece myself together again. You need to trust me. If I thought I was manic, I would tell you."

Outside, Levi pulls up into a disabled parking spot in his enormous white Suburban, honks the horn extra long.

"He is so obnoxious," I say. "Can't he text?"

"He's old-fashioned," she says.

We get up and go to Levi's gas guzzler. I get in the back, sitting next to Chewbacca, who pants and smiles even though he smells like halitosis and dirty laundry. Not his fault he stinks, though. I give him a hug and ask how his day went. He moans me a story. Chewie and I always have the best conversations. Levi is listening to Hank Williams, of course, who croons about being so lonesome he could cry. Talk about a depressive. The entire genre of country music could use a Prozac prescription.

"So," Mom says to Levi as we pull into the street. "Journey's going to go to college next semester. She's thinking of getting a job, too."

She says it like she's proud of me. Holy mother.

"We could use another pair of hands at the boot store," Levi says.

"I'll keep that in mind," I say, while thinking *hell to the no.*

"College already," Levi says. "You're pretty stellar."

"She really is," Mom says.

When I notice my reflection in the mirror, I sit up straighter, finger-comb my hair that's growing out. And I realize that at some point, while I was busy pining after a boy who hurt me, or thinking of dying or scared of dying or trying to die, I became a grown-up.

Roll with it, self. Keep breathing in.

There's no way to make what has happened un-happen.

Dear future self,

If I dared to have a dream for you, it would be this: that you go to college, even if you don't

*graduate; that you get a job and your own place,*
*even for just a little bit; that you fall in love again,*
*even if that person breaks your heart.*
*Dear future self, I hope you live.*

Wolf, who I've begun to think of as the Wolfman for no apparent reason, did some spring cleaning randomly in November, and today I actually get to both see and sit on his couch for the first time. Now that I am aware of just what a neon shade of orange it is, I can guess why he didn't exactly mind when it got buried in clutter last time. From here I can read the spines of the books in his library much better. Bunch of holy books from every denomination, beat-up and faded. He tells me he was a monk for thirteen years before he became a psychologist. I can imagine the charm of a monastery, the minimalist rooms and uniforms, the quiet solitude and early mornings, chanting and prayer. But I can also imagine my brain eating itself alive.

"I thought I went there to serve God," Wolf says, knocking on his leg like a door, which is a weird thing he seems to do when he's pondering something deeply. "But in the leaving, in the breaking away and realizing everything wasn't . . . what I thought it was—leaving the monastery is how I found myself."

He seems uncomfortable talking about himself. But fair's fair—I've been spilling my guts for weeks now.

"Soooooo, why did you leave?"

"I don't know what your beliefs are," he says quickly. "I'm just saying, for me, it didn't pan out. Once I unraveled a single thread in the story, it all seemed to unravel along with it. The teachings no longer made sense to me."

I'm not thinking about monks or the Wolfman. I'm thinking, of course, of myself, of the structures I live within. I'm thinking of the idea that everyone should graduate high school and go away to college. I'm thinking that if you have big feelings a pill will fix it, that if you try to kill yourself you're crazy. All the things the world tells me that I feel doubt about. There's so much passion inside me, a fire I don't know what to do with. I, too, want to "find myself"—a phrase said so much it lost its meaning.

Wolf agrees the middle college idea looks promising.

"Should I do it?" I ask him.

"Do you want to?"

"I mean, *can* I?"

"Are you asking my permission?"

"I'm asking your professional opinion."

"I think you should do what makes you fulfilled."

"I won't know if it fulfills me until I do it, though."

He cleans his glasses with his plaid shirtsleeve. In the silence, my own words ring in my ears. I hear the word *fulfilled*. I hear the words *do it*.

"I'm going to do it," I say.

"I think that's wonderful," he tells me.

He puts his glasses back on and smiles at me like this is what he hoped to hear.

I've been avoiding telling Marisol about my new academic plan because I know it's going to involve some ugly tears and possibly even bitterness. The best course seems to be to tell her at school, a public place, where she's more likely to keep composed. Same goes for me. Bestie tears are contagious.

However, the time and place make little difference. Marisol is so devastated when I tell her about middle college it's as if I'm dying of a rare disease.

"No you're not," she just keeps saying.

This during lunch break, when we are eating soggy tacos. The middle college paperwork has been filed in the guidance office. Hooker just signed his final autograph. I break the news that tomorrow will be my last day at school.

"No it's not," she says.

This is why I have waited. This is why I loathed the idea of telling Marisol about my plans.

"My best friend is *not* leaving me *in the middle of our senior year*," she says, her voice rising.

"I need to start over," I say.

"That's what next year is for!" she almost shouts.

"For *you*," I say. "For me, my next year starts right now."

"You are messing with me," she says, shutting her taco box and wrapping her long scarf around her neck. She wraps it so many times it swallows the bottom half of her head.

"What are you doing?" I laugh.

She pulls it off. "How can you seriously be laughing right now?"

"You should've seen yourself—"

"You are such a *diva*," she says, voice shaking. "Why can't you make an exit like a normal person?"

I sit up straighter, cock my chin. "Because I am not a normal person."

She gets up with her bag and walks away, leaving me alone on the lawn with tacos hardly appetizing enough for a hungry dog. My cheeks go hot and I wonder if I'm making a huge mistake. Or if something is wrong with me for not caring that this is it, I am really going. There's a rush about it—the dare of starting over—a spontaneity that I can only compare to joyriding in a car, or skinny-dipping in a cold ocean, or staying out past curfew.

*Or wrecking something,* a voice whispers. *Or taking a bottle of pills.*

It's not like that, though, right? It's not like that.

I get up to toss my things in the garbage and am tackled from behind by a warm hug and sniffling sounds. I turn around and embrace Marisol.

"And you tell me I'm dramatic," I say.

"Shut up," she says. "I'm going to miss you."

"I'm going to miss you, too."

"We'll still see each other?"

"All the time."

"You're going to get your license and come have lunch with me sometimes here?"

"Sure I will. And you can have lunch with me on campus."

"I don't want to lose you, JoJo," she says, pulling back, raccoon-eyed from smeary mascara.

"I'm literally going to school in the same city. You're the one moving states away."

"I almost lost you already this fall," she says.

"City college does not equal attempted suicide."

"Can't you just stick it out?"

"Marisol," I say, tired of arguing—with her, with myself. Tired of the fight that is life. "I need this, okay? I need this to keep going and have something to look forward to. Otherwise, I don't know what the hell I'm going to do."

"Okay," she says.

The bell rings and we walk.

"Congratulations," she says brightly as we part ways outside my fifth-period class.

The next day, I get in Marisol's car in the morning for a ride to school and am swallowed by about half a dozen balloons. She baked me a pie. She made me a card and somehow, in the past half day since I saw her, she bought me a sequin-covered bookbag, a binder with a unicorn on it, and a bag of my favorite pens.

And that's when it finally becomes real, and I get a piercing feeling in my gut and pinpricks in my eyes.

They can be slow burns, goodbyes.

Levi picks us girls up the next day, Saturday, for our weekly migration from Dad's to Mom's. He has a mannequin sitting in the front seat strapped in with a seat belt. She's wearing a "GIMME THE BOOT" shirt from his store.

"Sorry, you'll have to climb in back with the squirts," he says.

"You are a weird man," I say, obliging.

As soon as he heads up the pass, we drive into heavy fog. I hardly recognize where we are until we turn onto the main road that connects to ours. I have this weird feeling, like everything is changing and I want to be sad about it, and I should be sad, but for once, I'm not; instead I'm just mildly excited. It's still surreal that I won't have high school on Monday. Life happens so excruciatingly slowly until suddenly it happens so fast. Levi pulls into the gravel driveway. I'm relieved at the sight of his house—now our house, my house, too—my mother's shape in the kitchen window looking for our arrival. This place used to be new. Now, after all our time living together, the sight of it has become a comfort the same way my dad's house is.

The glow of the gold kitchen window illuminates the front yard, oak leaves shivering above. Something rectangular shines in the gravel of the driveway and I lean down to pick it up. It's a phone. The cat ears of the phone case tell me right away it's Ruby's. Without thinking, I press the home button. Her phone is locked but I see a message from a phone number that illuminates on the lock screen, no name attached to it, only a number.

Smrtass tattletale bitch watch yer back, it says.

I stop my feet in the gravel, my belly sinking.

What the hell?

I press the home button again, rereading it, trying to make sense of it. Inside, Levi goes straight to my mom and gives her the world's longest, most passionate peck, and the dinner she's cooking suddenly seems so much less appetizing. I follow Ruby back to her room and stick my foot in the doorway before she has a chance to shut her door in my face.

"You dropped something," I tell her, holding the phone out to her.

"Oh, thanks," she says.

I step inside her room after her and pull the door closed. She has one of those foldable science fair boards on her bed with a bunch of construction paper.

"Um, come in, I guess?" she says, giving me a death stare.

"What are you working on there?" I ask.

"You wouldn't care."

"I care!" I say, sitting on her swivel chair and doing a swivel.

"I'm studying the effects of aeration on yeast metabolism."

"I understood the word *yeast*," I tell her.

"Told you you don't care."

"Hey, just because I don't understand doesn't mean I don't care."

Ruby heaves a sigh and throws her backpack on the ground. "So . . . what do you want?"

"Nothing," I say innocently.

Ruby gives me a look, takes off her glasses, wipes them with her black shirtsleeve, returns them to her face.

"I accidentally touched the home screen button on your phone and saw a text," I tell her. "Look at it."

"Why are you creeping?"

"I wasn't. Just look at the text."

She presses the home button, types in her password, and gazes at her screen. Her eyes don't flicker. Her expression doesn't change. She shrugs. "Probably a wrong number."

"I hope so," I say. "Ruby, if you ever need anything, you know I'm here, right?"

"For now," she mutters.

"What?"

"Nothing."

"What did you say?"

"I said okay, okay?" she almost yells.

But she didn't. I watch her sadly, realizing this thing that opened up between us, whatever it is—whether it's my fault, or Mom and Dad's fault, or stupid time's fault for making us all unrecognizable—it's gotten big. So big, I don't know if there's any going back. So big nothing, not even light, can escape it.

I don't show up at high school again except to get packets of makeup work. I spend whole days in my pajamas at home, work my ass off without moving a muscle, take quizzes, write papers. The days go gray, gray as they get in this beach town. The fog rolls in thick and sweet-cold in the mornings. You know when the cold is almost sweet in your nose?

One morning I go to take my pills and notice I have only half a dozen left. I should call the pharmacist. But I don't yet. Instead, I decide to skip my dose on purpose for the first time. It gives me a rush to go against the rules, the print on the side of the orange bottle that yells at me in all caps to TAKE ONE IN THE MORNING AND ONE IN THE EVENING PREFERABLY WITH FOOD. Every morning after that I skip them, only taking my night dose. A week passes. Another week passes. I wait for someone to notice, or for the suicidal thoughts to return, but instead they lurk there in my mind's shadows. I don't even think I am bipolar. And if I am, I don't need medication. But I'm too afraid to argue with my parents about it. I have to prove I've truly got my shit together before telling anybody.

This year we decorate two trees at two houses, buy a new set of stockings for Mom's, and Levi sets up a blow-up, light-up nativity set in the front yard that slowly deflates throughout the season. During a windy night, baby Jesus blows away completely. It's fine that we celebrate holidays twice now. More presents, right? I spend Christmas afternoon in my room at Dad's watching movies, trying not to think about last year. Dad makes Ethiopian food for Christmas dinner and leaves early to go meet a friend. I'm alone in the house. For the first time since I tried to off myself, I've been trusted to be by myself. Gold star for me.

If only he knew I was taking half my meds. And look at me—no outbursts, no theatrics, no suicidal tendencies.

*Aren't you proud, world?*

Then I have that feeling of shame. What a low, low bar I need to clear to experience what passes for pride these days. That needs a word of its own, too. I'm starting to think I, Journey Smith, could write my own dictionary.

I go to city college to sign up for classes, overwhelmed by the number of buildings, fascinated by the grown-up life here. The parking lot, glimmering full as the ocean behind it. The people, from my age to grandparents', bustling in ones, twos, threes. I feel small here, in the best way; I feel new here. Alive. The last thing I have to do is find a community service gig to sign up for. A job, too, would be nice. On campus with my packet of info on my new classes, late afternoon, I read the bulletin board outside the cafeteria. One flyer has a message shaped like a poem.

**EVER THINK**
**OF COUNSELING?**
**LOOKING FOR**
**CRISIS HOTLINE VOLUNTEERS.**
**WILL TRAIN!**

Is it the words that make it a poem? Or the shape of them? My chest swells, because not that not long ago, I *was* the crisis. I wish I could go back to my past—change what happened. I can't. But I could help someone else who is where I was then.

# PART
*two*

# PRESENT

At my next appointment with Wolf, I have so many updates to share. My first week at city college, my first hotline shift. I'm breathless relaying the details to him, but the details don't seem to concern him.

"You've been busy since the year started," he says. "Tell me how you pause and care for yourself when you're this busy."

"Does eating corn dogs count? I ate three corn dogs late last night in bed."

He smiles. "We all unwind in our own ways."

"My mom's been watching me like a hawk for manic symptoms this whole month."

"Do you feel manic?"

"I never felt manic, even when other people thought I was manic."

"This medication seems to be working much better for you," he says.

I smile, not answering.

"Am I wrong?" he asks.

"Dumbo's feather," I say, thinking of the movie I loved as a kid. The one where an elephant believed he could fly so hard he actually flew.

"Pardon?"

"Dumbo's feather," I say. "It wasn't real. It gave him confidence to fly, but there was nothing magic about it."

"You're likening your medication to Dumbo's feather?"

"Wolf, you're not going to tell my parents, right?"

"No. This is between us, here, always. But tell them what?"

"I haven't been taking my meds," I tell him proudly.

I sit back and smile, expecting him to be amazed. Expecting him to say, wow! This is all you? Congratulations, Journey! Not only are you cured, there was nothing really wrong with you to begin with!

But instead he gets that look on his face where his eyebrows furrow and his mouth draws into a little zero.

"Journey, that's very irresponsible," he says.

"I mean, regularly," I say, backtracking a little. "I take a couple a week."

"This is not good," he tells me.

"You don't even prescribe meds!" I say, taken aback. I can't even look at his face. I look instead at a statue with a bunch of arms serving as a makeshift tie rack that sits on a crate in a corner.

"That doesn't mean I don't believe in their power," he says.

"God, make up your mind," I say, irritated. "First you tell me exercise and then you say meditation and talking will fix everything, now you're acting just like every other pill-pushing doctor I've ever met. *What if I don't even need them?*"

"The world isn't black and white," he says. "And I believe you're smart enough to know that. It's *all* important, every remedy."

"If pills are so great, maybe you should prescribe them," I mutter.

"Patients with bipolar disorder often need medication, but very often think they don't."

"So you're saying I can't trust myself."

"That is not what I'm saying, but I would like you to consider that it's a common theme among bipolar patients."

"Fine. Considered."

"Let's discuss the risks here, at the very least," Wolf says, pushing his glasses up his nose. "First, there are serious withdrawal symptoms that can occur if you stop your lithium dosage without medical supervision. You should consult with a doctor before tapering off any medication. Lithium's not a joke."

"I'm not treating it like one."

"You've made impulsive decisions before—how is this any different?"

I feel berated right now. Lectured. Spoken down to. Which is something that's never happened with Wolf before. I cross my arms in front of my chest and wish I could go back about five minutes and eat my confession up. Whether I take pills or not is none of his or anyone else's business.

"Have you told your parents?" he asks.

"No, and you said you wouldn't—"

"Journey, *I'm* not going to tell them."

I breathe a sigh of relief.

"Have you told anyone else?" he asks.

"Just you. And gee, look how this is going."

"You should discuss with your doctor at the *very* least," he goes on. "It's reckless to do this yourself. You're doing so well—why throw a potential bomb into this new life you're building?"

"Because it's not a bomb, it's *me*," I tell him.

"I'm sorry if that sounded insensitive," he answers. "But I'm worried about you. Your parents, your friends, and I all care about you and want to see you healthy. So I just want us to discuss this fully. Let's say, hypothetically, you stay off medication. What happens if your symptoms return?"

"Then I'll tell you."

He sits for a long moment, watching me, probably trying to figure out a way to change my mind. Maybe he's realizing he can't. "My professional opinion is you should not go off your medication. But I know I can't force you to do anything. So I would like to ask you to please contact your doctor. And I want us to work on something together."

He gets out a piece of paper and turns this whole thing into something like a homework assignment for my broken brain. We write down a list of warning signs to look out for, in case I get a bipolar disorder relapse. Things like needing less sleep, extreme irritability, racing thoughts, making big plans—and then other symptoms on the other side of the scale. Needing too much sleep, feeling unmotivated, sadness. We write down a list of what I'll do if those symptoms return: text Marisol, talk to my parents, reach out to Wolf, or go to the ER if it's really bad.

I spend the last five minutes of our session staring at this paper in my hands and giving Wolf something like the silent treatment. I burn on the bus ride home, thinking of his disapproving face. There's something about authority that just makes me want to do the opposite of anything they force on me. It's primal. Maybe this is why, when I get home, I throw my last half-empty (half-full?) bottle of pills in the garbage. I look at them there and think, I know I'm being immature. I hear Wolf saying the word *reckless* in my mind. But I leave the pills there and don't look at them again. I guess I still have some growing up to do.


At Saturday sushi lunch with Dad, right before he's about to hand us back over to Mom for the weekly switcheroo, I tell Dad about my first paper I have to start researching this weekend about utilitarianism.

"John Stuart Mill!" he says. "I wrote my graduate thesis on Mill."

This first month of school, Dad is *so* into talking about

everything I'm learning. It's the college counselor in him, I guess. He's also very interested in discussing my prerequisites and whether or not I should pursue an associate's degree, and UC requirements versus state schools, and I kind of wish I had never started this conversation now. And I can tell, by my sisters' glassy stares, that they feel the same.

Thankfully, a woman walks up and stops my impromptu college advisory session. A pretty woman, eerily ageless with her so-blond-it-could-be-white hair, her relentless smile that hides wrinkles or the lack thereof. I notice exactly three things right away, in this order:

She is wearing a purple sweatshirt.

She is not wearing any ring on the fourth finger of her left hand.

She is clearly flirting with my dad.

They talk about boring things like meetings, caseloads, students, trainings. They must work together. Ruby gives me a look, raising her eyebrows, which she recently decided to try to dye black as her hair (she's stepped up to semipermanent, twenty-four washes). Her brows are now kinda Groucho Marxy. Makes the raising of them even more intense. Stevie, of course, has no idea, dunking a tempura shrimp daintily into her sauce.

"Bye, Gary," Dad calls after the woman when she leaves.

*Gary.*

He looks happier and pinker than I can remember ever seeing him.

The whole ride home after that, my soul is sour. Don't know why. Is it the night creeping in so early, the snowless Southern Californian winter air? Life is good. I rest my forehead against the passenger window, watching the plotted poplars and garish glows of grocery stores sail by. The heat blasting hurts my eyes. I close them as we head toward home, the home we all used to live in together, where now my dad lives alone, with us sometimes. I know I shouldn't be bothered. Mom found someone else. Dad deserves to find someone else. It was hard when Levi came along, but I got over it. Sometimes I just wish life would pause for a period of time, not throw any new changes my way, give me some time to breathe.

*Gary.*

I ride the bus everywhere because, while I've made strides in wearing my big girl pants lately, I'm still terrified of the prospect of being on the freeway or driving a car. At night, I'm still occasionally jolted awake with the fiery orange flames heating my lids from the recurring car crash nightmare. The bus isn't the worst. On the long rides, I catch up with Marisol, texting back and forth about school, or I do my homework. Near the bus stop that lands a few blocks from my house, a pizza place with lit gold windows emanating the smell of sweet crust and tomato sauce has a sandwich board outside that has, for two weeks, said "HIRING: INQUIRE WITHIN." One brave early evening two weeks into school, on the walk home, I tell myself I should, indeed, inquire within.

The place is typical old-school family pizza parlor, with dizzying carpets, the cacophony of arcade games and Top-40 radio, wooden booths and fluorescent lights. A dude in a backward cap greets me with the enthusiasm of an evangelist. A pizzavangelist. I tell him I'm looking for a job and he introduces himself.

"Full name? Timothy," he says, pointing to his badge to verify this info. "But you can call me Tim-Tim. And eff yeah, we're hiring. I got an application right back here and check it—I like your 'look.'" Finger quotes and all. "I like the shock thing, you know, bright hair, look at me, I'm young, I'm hip. I dig. So fill out that application and guess what? Chicken butt. Kidding! You're hired. Come back here tomorrow three to eight and you got yourself a job."

"Three to eight," I repeat as he hands me a pen, one with a big black feather on it.

"That work for you?" Tim-Tim asks.

At first I think he's asking about the feather pen, which does seem a bit much. But no, he's asking about a job. A job he's offering me.

I am getting offered a job right now. I was just walking down the street, walked into a pizza parlor, and now I have a job.

Change doesn't need time to do its business.

I fill out the application and I come back in the next day. Tim-Tim's behind the counter, singing along with the music with enthusiasm while he wipes the counter down. No one else working shares his enthusiasm. After showing me how to clock in, and having me fill out a couple pieces of paperwork, Tim-Tim goes to the back to show me my uniform.

Here's what I'm expecting: a black apron, perhaps a polo shirt like the one he's wearing with the pizza stitched on the breast. Here's what I'm not expecting: a giant costume that is a person-sized slice of pepperoni pizza.

The laughter that rolls out of my throat and into the air between us in this fusty back room with a wall of lockers and another wall of cleaning supplies is not something I can stop. Tim-Tim just stares at me. He has very nice eyebrows. People pay to have his eyebrows. They get theirs waxed or whatever. One of them is twitching.

"You're not serious," I say.

"Serious as gingivitis," he almost shouts.

I stop laughing because Tim-Tim is really fucking serious right now, holding the pizza costume, and I'm seeing my immediate future ahead of me, which involves donning a pizza costume and also humiliation.

"I thought I was getting a waitressing job," I say.

He scoffs at me as if I just told him I expected to be a brain surgeon.

"You don't have waitressing experience," he says.

"I don't have . . . pizza costume experience, either."

"Look," he says. "With no job experience, you've got to start somewhere."

"Yeah, but . . . here?" I ask, pointing at the costume, which, up close, is not even that clean.

"Here," he says, handing me the costume, backing out to give me my horrible privacy.

The costume smells like a wrestling mat mixed with pizza mixed with traces of various body odors. I stare at the long, spotted mirror, a human slice of pizza, a round hole cut up at the top where my head sticks out. My eyes well up. I wish I were dead. No, I just wish I weren't dressed in a super-gross pizza costume. There is a difference. Then the absurdity hits me. I take a selfie and send it to Marisol.

WHAT?! I get in immediate response.

No time to respond.

Tim-Tim gives me the Crusty's Pizza sign and walks me out to the corner. He does a bunch of dances as "inspiration" for what I might do. Let's just say Tim-Tim's as comfortable doing the Charleston as he is twerking. He can helicopter his ponytail and he can almost do the splits.

"I started as a slice of pizza," he tells me, shouting over the traffic. "Years ago. And now I'm manager. It could be you next. Show me your moves."

This is the stupidest moment of my life.

"Okay," I say. "I call this one 'The Statue.'"

"You're not . . . doing anything."

"And I do it so well."

"Can you at least, I don't know . . . march?"

So I do a march back and forth for him.

"Sick marching," he says, giving me a high five.

I despise his enthusiasm.

"This is a new rock bottom," I tell him. "And I tried to kill myself a few months ago."

"Wow, now that is . . . a dark sense of humor you got right there," he tells me, laughing uneasily, *he he he.* "See? Probably for the best you don't work with customers."

He leaves me out in the dark to march back and forth on the street corner in a pizza costume. I would be lying if I told you I don't contemplate death. Not that I want to die really. I wish I could just die for the rest of this shift. I wish I could die *temporarily.*

I go home that night after marching for hours in a pizza costume in a weird daze. Honestly, the shame kind of stunned itself into disbelief halfway through my shift and now I'm simply confused. My legs hurt like I actually tried hard in PE. I can't tell you how many random strangers honked at me. I don't know if I'm ever going to go back there again.

I stumble upon an article online late one night that I read and then reread and then spend an hour in the dark thinking through. "Kids Can't Be Put in Boxes or Fixed with Bottles," it's titled. It's an opinion piece about children being pre-scribed ADHD medication sometimes when it's not neces-sary and how it is, effectively, not the kids who have anything wrong with them, but it's the parents' impatience, or schools expecting children to all learn with the same methods, at the same paces. How if the country had better public education in place that encouraged different methods of teaching, or if we didn't desire children to behave in certain ways and taught them better avenues of self-expression, we wouldn't need to medicate them. The author of the article clearly has an anti-Western-medicine agenda that gives me pause, but I largely agree with her. She brings up true points. I know nothing about ADHD except people take Adderall for it and some kids at school get more time to take tests and stuff because of it.

But the article makes me think about my bipolar diagnosis and the medication I took. About my big feelings. About what it's like to live in a world where you're too much to be normal, but too normal to be ill, a girl in between sanity and insanity. I think about that nether place where I exist. There should be a word for it. But of course there isn't. Not in this world.

"Journey," my dad tells me the next morning as I shuffle into the kitchen in my pajamas and open the fridge door. "Your mom is on her way over here. We're having a family meeting."

The words *family meeting* snag my breath. I shut the fridge. "What fresh hell is this?" I ask him.

His face is somber, his eyes glassy and concerned.

I scour my mind for what this could be about. "Look, the last time you called a 'family meeting,' you and Mom broke up, so this is freaking me out."

Dad points to the table, where a half-full orange prescription bottle sits. A bottle with my name on it.

"Spectacular," I say flatly.

"Kiddo, this is serious."

I would like to scream. This, here, is *exactly* why I didn't want to tell my parents about going off my medication. The look on his face is like I tried to off myself again. I'm so tired of everyone around me thinking they know what's best for me.

My mom arrives shortly thereafter. At least my sisters aren't here to witness the inevitable disaster this conversation will be. Apparently Levi took them to a petting zoo, which is kind of hilarious to think about, but I'm not in the mood to laugh. Mom has a steely expression and won't take her jacket or purse off as she sits in the chair, like she's ready to up and leave at any second. Three thoughts occur to me as we sit around the table: this is the first time I have been with both my parents in the same room since I tried to kill myself last year; this is the first time I've sat at this old family dinner table with them since they were still together; and I do not want to have this fucking conversation.

"I was going through the garbage when I found your pills," Dad says.

"Why were you . . . going through the garbage?" I ask.

"To make sure we're properly recycling." He points to the pill bottle. "Which clearly you're not. This is recyclable, you know."

"Okay, Seth, stay on script," Mom says.

*On script.* Like they practiced beforehand.

"Journey, you clearly haven't been taking your medication," Dad says.

"How long has this been going on?" Mom asks.

I sigh. "Weeks. I don't know. On and off. Listen, I tapered off, I didn't stop all at once—"

"Did you talk to a doctor?" Mom asks.

"No."

"Did you talk to your therapist?" Dad asks.

"Yes."

"And what did he say?" Mom asks.

They're both sitting across from me, interrogation style.

"He said . . . that it was fine." The lie sounds so unbelievable once it leaves my mouth, I sigh and put my head in my hands. "He said that it wasn't a good idea and that I should tell you."

Mom looks like she is strangling her purse. "And so why are you not following his *advice*?"

"Because look at what happens when you find out," I say. "This is so dramatic right now. You're both acting like I killed someone."

"You *tried* to kill someone," Mom says, her voice climbing in pitch. "A few months ago. Remember?"

"Yes, I remember, because nobody will ever let me forget!" I almost yell.

Dad holds his hand up like some kind of referee.

"Part of the trick of mental illness is that when medication is working, you don't notice it," Dad says. "When it's working at its best, it feels like nothing is happening."

"This coming from the person who originally tried to tell me Saint-John's-wort would fix my chemical imbalance," I say.

"That was before you were hospitalized," Dad says.

"Seth! Saint John's wort can be *incredibly* dangerous," Mom interjects. "I read on The Forum that it can have life-threatening interactions with other medications. It's a supplement that does a *lot* more harm than good."

"It's natural—"

"*Hemlock* is natural."

"Okay, enough," I say, my voice cracking. I hate how desperate I sound. How badly I want them to understand, suddenly. "Haven't I been doing well? Besides this, haven't I been doing everything right?"

"Yes, but that's partly *because* of the treatment you're getting," Mom cuts in.

"Mom," I say, meeting her cold stare. "I've been getting off my meds for a while now. And you know when I was most diligent about taking my medication? Last fall. When I had a nervous breakdown."

There's a pause in the kitchen between us, a long one; shockingly, they are listening to me. They are considering that what I'm saying is true. Perhaps even more importantly, I'm convincing myself of something that has been percolating inside me for some time.

"I know myself," I tell them. "I know I'm not 'normal.' I do probably need treatment. But that doesn't mean medication is the only answer right now. And I'm an adult. Technically, I can make my own decisions."

"An adult still living under our roofs," Mom reminds me, corkscrewing a fingernail in the air.

"At some point, you're going to have to trust me that I can make decisions for myself," I say.

"If you had come to us and told us this is what you wanted, we could have helped you," Dad says. "We could have done this responsibly, gotten you an appointment to talk to your doctor about it. The fact you just threw your pills away and did this secretly—that's the disturbing part."

"Yes," Mom says. "Exactly."

It's the first time they've agreed on something in longer than I can remember. For a moment, I'm sort of stunned at the mellowness of this conversation. I came in expecting a fight.

"Okay," I say. "What if I'm telling you now? What if I'm asking for your help now?"

Mom closes her eyes and exhales for a moment. Dad puts his hand on her hand for a second, and she opens her eyes. They exchange a look. I don't know what the look says, but it softens me to see it.

"I've been thinking a lot about this, actually," I say. "It might look to you like I'm being irresponsible. And yes, I could have handled this better. But I don't think anything is as simple as bipolar disorder, take a pill, problem fixed. I read this article about how a lot of people, especially teenagers, are overprescribed medication. And we're not given a lot of coping mechanisms besides pharmaceuticals. The world isn't built for girls with big feelings, you know?"

"That's true," Dad agrees.

Mom is biting the inside of her cheek, deep in thought. "I'm glad you've been good about going to therapy, at least."

Dad picks up the pill bottle and turns it around as he thinks. "How long have you been off?"

"Completely off for a few weeks," I say, a little flutter in my chest as the air in the room changes, as I feel them becoming convinced I might be safe to be trusted with myself again. "Tapering off for a couple months. I tried not to do it all at once."

"Lithium is serious business. You're supposed to be getting regular blood tests. Have you been at least doing that?" Mom asks.

"Um . . . no," I admit. The robots have left me messages on my phone telling me I need to come in, but I haven't obeyed them. "I'm sorry. I keep meaning to, but . . . I haven't."

"*Journey*," my mom says, with enough emphasis that my own name sounds like a curse word.

Dad puts the pill bottle down. "We have to go forward

with open communication."

"I want you to call your doctor *today*," Mom says.

"Okay," I say. "I can do that."

"I want to *see* you do it," Mom goes on. "I want you to call your doctor *right now* and make an appointment, and your dad and I will take you."

"Geez, Mom, seriously?" I ask. "I said I'd do it."

"Yes, Journey, *seriously*."

I look at my dad, who often backs me up, but right now he's just nodding like a bobblehead.

Mom gives me the phone number and my medical card. They sit there watching me like a rapt two-person audience as I call and make an appointment for the next day.

"There," I say, putting my phone on the table when I'm done. "Happy?"

"I wouldn't go that far," Mom says.

"I'm going to be fine," I say.

"I'll feel better after your appointment tomorrow," she says.

"No more secrets," Dad says, leaning over the table and squeezing my hand.

"Yes, message received," I say.

"I will be watching your every move," Mom says.

"And that's not creepy at all," I joke.

They are not laughing.

"That's fine, Mom. I'm used to it by now."

"And if the doctor advises you get back on your meds, I

want you to listen," Mom says. "You understand?"

"I will," I say.

"I have to be able to trust you. I cannot live with the fear of you . . . hurting yourself again," Mom says.

I hate that she has that fear now. I hate that I did that to her.

The next day, I have to go into the lab first and get a bunch of blood tests because apparently the DIY approach when it comes to getting off lithium is a very bad idea for your bloodstream. Even though my levels are okay, I get another lecture, this time from my doctor. She sounds like the end of a pharmaceutical commercial on TV, the disclaimer part listing off all the unwanted side effects. *Mood instability, flu-like symptoms, headaches, pain, insomnia, and even seizures.*

Seizures. I mean, that's not nothing.

My parents sit there nodding in agreement with her, a trio of stern faces watching me as I listen.

Okay, okay, I get it. Congratulations, you've all really hammered this one home. It was dumb, getting off my pills without medical supervision. I shouldn't have done it. But my doctor goes on to say that as long as my blood levels are monitored over the next couple of weeks and I take a few doses as prescribed to taper off, as long as I am getting support in therapy, and as long as I promise to come back in if I have any symptoms, I can try getting off the medication for a while to see how it goes. She orders more lab tests over the next few weeks, because you know how doctors are—they can't pass up a chance to prick you with a needle. Seriously, though, I had braced myself for more of an argument today, and I'm shocked I didn't have to make much of one. I have to suppress the urge to jump in the air and yell *hooray*.

Instead, I get up and hug them, one by one—even the doctor, who emits a weird "oh!" as I embrace her in her white coat. I'm lightened momentarily by my own relief. Now they know. There's nothing to hide. They *trust* me. But there's an equal and opposite weight to their trust; now I know that if my inner weather does change, if the depression comes back, I have to tell them all. And I really don't like the thought of that.

When I next get together with Marisol, it's Galentine's Day. As is our tradition, we thrift in old town Goleta, wandering about a maze of secondhand clothes and mannequins, and try on the worst clothes we can possibly find. She is in an oversized shirt with boobs painted on it and I am in a sweatshirt with a horrific amateur-puff-painted dog face. She takes a selfie of us on her phone and texts it to me. When she looks at her phone she ends up laughing so hard she almost collapses on the floor next to the racks of ladies' boots.

"That good?" I ask.

"No, I just remembered the last picture you sent me."

She shows me the picture of me in the pizza uniform.

"You're . . . a slice of pizza," she says, wiping the laugh tears from her eye corners. If you can make Marisol laugh, you can make her cry.

"I can't help but question my life choices when I look at this," I agree, looking at the photo of myself, a human joke in bizarre costume.

But as she and I weave around the store, stopping to gab about the latest *Obsession* show, which involves a man hoarding stuffed teddy bears, she and I next to the Christmas decorations glimmering red-green-gold in plastic bags, in the back of my mind, I wonder about Marisol. I wonder about her laughing at the picture in an *at* and not *with* kind of way. Because Marisol lives up on a hill in a house so big I get lost in it. Marisol's never had a job. Marisol will be moving away soon, living in a dorm, and I'll be her loser ex-bestie who dons a pizza costume and goes to city college.

Is that why she laughs?

Weird how, since I left school for makeup paperwork and junior college classes, I went through a door and I didn't look back. Marisol's back there in another world, one with a different set of doors. Now my life is different. As we grab lunch at the grocery next door, eating deli sandwiches at plastic tables outside, Marisol sporting a new hat with a fake rose in the rim, listening to her gush about scholarships, I can't tell if I feel more or less grown-up than her. I just know I feel the gap.

This is Marisol I'm talking about. Marisol who befriended me the first day of fourth grade, taking my arm at recess, teaching me the rules of handball. "I picked you," she's always said. Marisol of the constant sleepovers, the movie marathons, the living room manicures, bathroom dye jobs and haircuts. Marisol of late-night whispered conversations and texting marathons and shared soundtracks. Marisol who stayed my bestie even when she veered Ivy League and I veered deep into trouble. If there was anything steady, anything unloseable, her name was Marisol. But now we sit in silence, chewing food, thinking of our dissimilar presents, our even differenter futures.

In my chest, there is a stone, cold, unmoving, realizing for the first time that next year is now and Seattle or Chicago is a planet away and she's already drifting and if she's not already lost . . . I'm going to lose her.

I'd be lying if I said the thought of death didn't cross my mind as I ride the bus home. The lights of so many apartment buildings stare back like gold eyes. Liar brain. I don't want to die. My mind just goes to that place, that desolate place, when I'm alone and out of ideas. But I carry a new tool in my box now. I close my eyes and count my breath. I locate where the fear dwells, a bird in my chest. And I know that dumb death wish is nothing but a lie. I just miss Marisol already.

I run full speed toward change, and still, change scares me terribly.

I still feel the cracks in the places Jonah broke my heart. It's been four months plus. I try not to think of him, but in trying, I think of him.

One cold night in late February, I wear his sweatshirt as I walk around the neighborhood, standing outside his house and staring at the warm hint of light behind the curtained windows. I smell the sleeves of the sweatshirt and inhale just the tiniest hint of him. I want to cry and I hate myself for it. I take the sweatshirt off and fold it up and put it in his mailbox. It's the last thing of his I still had. But after walking just two houses down the block, I turn back again, open his mailbox with a squeak, and put the sweatshirt back on. It's just so cold. I'll do it in the spring.

I wear it to bed that night.

And the next. And the next.

I'm not proud of the hole he carved out in me, of the fact I am still stinging, insulted by his need for space. I used to think space had edges, space had an end. At some point he would call me and want that space to close. But besides a couple hollow texts that could have been written by cheerleading robots (Merry Christmas! Hope your well! around the holidays, hey, Marisol told me your at college now! good luck nerd! when the semester started), he has shown no interest in me, in my life, in my progress, and that hurts if I let myself think of it. So I try very, very hard not to think of it.

There are lots of rules at the hotline, and I try my best to follow every one of them. The mother of all rules is, the binder is your bestie. Do not pick up the phone without it. Always ask if people are safe if they are calling about abuse;

ask if they have taken anything, and what they have taken, if they're suicidal; never give anyone your last name; if you think you know the person on the end of the line, place them on hold and ask another volunteer to take it. Even the small house where the crisis center is located is full of rules. Rules in the kitchen: *Please rinse your own dishes, NONE IN THE SINK!* Rules in the bathroom: *No flushing feminine products, even so-called "flushables"!* All written in the same pretty cursive, clearly a red pen faded to brown after so many years.

I break a rule, though, on my second shift.

Not on my first call of the evening. First call is Davis. *Le sigh.* He talks to me so long my ear starts going numb. He names off everything on his Amazon Wish List. He tells me, in meandering detail, that his next-door neighbor—he's pretty doggone sure—has a ferret. *Can you fathom?* Davis ponders whether or not it's his responsibility to alert the proper 'thoritays. I find myself zoning out on the binder on my table, my reflection peering back up from the plastic cover, as I wonder if this crisis hotline gig is going to end up being this right here. I mean, I came here to help people. I thought I was going to be a lifesaver, not be a sounding board for socially awkward humans and/or prank callers.

My second call is a girl named Coco. She's seventeen. She has a soft, velvety voice, a looseness in it that makes me wonder if she had a drink before she picked up the phone.

She thinks she's dead.

"I've got this switch inside of me," she says. "This . . .

there's no other way to describe it. I'm here, I'm living, I'm laughing, I'm holding my boyfriend's hand—and then, bam. The tunnel hits. Everything around me becomes weird. I think, I don't exist. I'm already dead. None of this is real. The feeling—it swallows everything. Even talking about it right now, I get scared it's going to happen."

"How long does it last?" I ask.

"Sometimes just a few seconds, sometimes hours."

I lean in, concerned, and put my hand on the binder page I have open titled *Teens and suicidal ideation*. There's no exact entry for this, no resource center or 1-800 number I have here for girls who think they don't exist.

"Does anything . . . trigger it?" I ask.

"Um, my brain?" She gives a single nervous giggle. "But no. Nothing happened today . . . I went to school . . . went to song practice. Erica Nunez is talking to everyone about how the state championships are coming up and I find myself staring at her, thinking, 'This isn't really happening. I'm not really here.'"

At the name Erica Nunez, my brain grinds to a halt. Erica Nunez goes to my high school. And at my high school, the lead cheerleading squad is called the song team—they do highly choreographed dances and acrobatics and have won awards. So whoever this girl is on the end of my line, I could know her.

"Hello?" she asks. "Did I bore you so much you fell asleep?"

"Not at all," I say.

But which girl is it on the song team? Which glimmering,

gorgeous, female-perfection-incarnated specimen on the song team—walks around thinking she's dead? Nicola Albierti, with a waterfall of dark hair that reaches her waist? Emma Wong, the peppiest, ever-grinning gymnast who can do a double backflip? Eva Barnes, the athletic captain with a booming voice? I don't know them all, but I've seen them, gliding through the halls in their maroon bodysuits and gold cheerleading skirts, their pantyhosed legs flawless, their heaven-white never-scuffed sneakers. Girls like that don't worry about anything except what lip gloss to wear that day. But the ethical thing is to pass the call to someone else, because it's not fair to talk to someone who I might know in real life.

Thing is, I really want to stay on the line. Out of curiosity, yes, but also because I feel like out of everyone here, I should be able to help a girl my age best of all.

"I think I should maybe hand this call over to one of my colleagues," I say.

"Why? Oh my God, did I totally freak you out?"

"Not at all—"

"I can't believe I'm such a reject that even the crisis hotline people won't talk to me."

"It's not that," I tell her. "I actually—I understand. It's just . . ."

Now I can't tell her I went to the same high school, because then I'm outing myself.

"You understand?" she asks brightly.

I don't know what to do right now. The binder can't help

me. Lydia, JD, and Beatriz are all on calls. If I put Coco (which must be a fake name, I know no Cocos at my school) on hold, I risk losing her trust and patience, her hanging up and never calling again. What if she feels so alone and rejected she kills herself?

"Yeah, I do understand," I tell her, leaning onto my elbows on the tabletop, pushing the headset closer to my ears, making the conversation feel more intimate. "I mean, not completely." I recall the out-of-touch feeling I had when I was attending my high school earlier this year, like I was on a movie set and not in real life. "But I do know what it's like to be somewhere and feel a million miles away from what everyone else around you is experiencing."

"I'm so glad you said that," she says. "Because—this is the first time I've ever talked to anyone about it and I was afraid you were going to tell me I lost my mind. I was sobbing last night looking up diseases on WebMD. Do you think I'm paranoid schizophrenic? Are these psychotic episodes?"

"Rule number one in life is never, ever Google your symptoms," I tell her. "Do you know how many times I Google a common cold and end up thinking I'm dying of lung cancer?"

"True," she says, laughing.

Strange she can laugh when she feels nothing. Is she faking it? Or is laughing when someone makes a joke just a physical response to her, like when a doctor knocks your knee bone and you kick?

"You're right," she goes on. "No more WebMD. I'm cutting myself off."

"Have you thought about talking to someone?"

"Like who? My boyfriend, who has about three brain cells in his head? God, I'm so mean. I don't mean that. He's sweet as a teddy bear. He's just—you know, he's a football player. He's a *dude*. He's not into talking about . . . deep stuff."

"He might surprise you," I tell her.

"Or what? My mom, who is so zonked out on Xanax half the time, nodding off? I'm sure her answer would be pills. That's the last thing I want."

"Maybe a therapist," I suggest.

"So you *do* think I'm crazy," she says accusingly.

"Not at all. Therapy can help everyone—"

"You don't understand. In my family, no one goes to therapy. They go to the doctor and get pills, but we don't . . . 'air our business,' as my dad would say. That's for weak people."

"Is that what you think?"

"I don't know what I think. I'm so tired of thinking," she says, her voice cracking. "I don't know how I'm going to keep going sometimes. I'm supposed to be so excited right now, waiting to hear from schools, getting ready for the championship—it all feels surreal. Like I'm watching a TV show I don't even care about."

"A trick I learned that helped me a lot is to practice breathing," I tell her. "When you get overwhelmed, just concentrate on your breath for a bit. Let all the other thoughts pass by, like little boats on running water. Watch them go, but don't dwell on them. Instead, count your breath as you inhale, exhale."

She breathes in. I can hear her. The sound of it—of a real-life person hearing my advice, of someone possibly feeling better because of me—is something I'm still getting used to.

"Thank you. What did you say your name is?"

I pause. "Journey."

"Thanks, Journey," she says, not skipping a beat. Clearly she isn't familiar with me. Not surprising. I'm not popular. Nor have I ever cared to be. "I'll try that breathing thing—I'm sure I'll be fine. I feel better already. Just talking to you made me feel better."

We say goodbye and I hang up. By the time I'm off, JD and Lydia are also off their calls, gabbing about some zombie TV show I've never watched. Lydia is knitting a pink beanie.

"That's really cool," I tell her.

"It's for my grandson. He's going to hate it." She cackles. "I can't wait to see him have to wear it every time I come over."

"You're so evil, Lyd," says JD.

"Need to decompress?" Lydia asks without looking up.

Decompressing is something we do after calls, especially if the calls have been hard in any way. We discuss them together and offer support. I've found it really helpful, actually, even though I thought it was a bit much at first. Lydia, JD, and Beatriz have volunteered here long enough to have all sorts of calls, and their advice is super helpful.

"I just got a call from a girl who reminds me of me," I tell them. "Except she has these moments where she . . . she thinks she's already dead. Like nothing is real. Like she doesn't exist."

"Derealization," JD says, looking up from an iPad. "Or depersonalization. Or disassociation? Shit, I should know this."

"JD's chasing an advanced psych degree," Lydia tells me.

I Google these terms on my phone, fascinated yet horrified by these new additions to my mental dictionary. *Derealization* is "an alteration in the perception or experience of the external world so that is seems unreal." *Depersonalization* is a "state in which one's thoughts or feelings seem unreal." *Disassociation* is "disconnecting from one's thoughts, feelings, memories or sense of identity." All of it sounds similar to what the caller described, and it all sounds like hell.

A while later, Beatriz hangs up her headset, wipes her eyes, and looks at us. "God, that was a hard one."

"Bring it in, chica," JD says, with open arms.

Beatriz scoots over in her rolly chair and JD embraces her. Beatriz breathes deeply. Lydia puts her knitting down and breathes deeply, too, from across the room. The silence, besides everyone's audible breaths, is so intimate.

"The woman was assaulted last year," Beatriz says quietly.

"She wouldn't stop crying. No matter what I offered, she cried harder. Finally she just said, 'You can't help me,' and hung up."

"Rough," JD says, rubbing Beatriz's arm.

"It's hard feeling like I can't help," Beatriz says, wiping tears away.

"Helplessness is worse than pain," Lydia agrees.

She takes a swig from the jar of green on her desk—some kind of disgusting-looking homemade wellness drink—and puts her headset down, goes outside, sits on the porch. I can see her figure through the window, rocking back and forth on the swing.

"Be back," Beatriz says. "I'm going out there with her."

Beatriz, too, puts down her headset and gently opens and shuts the door behind her, sits on the porch. She puts her arm around Lydia and Lydia rests her head on Beatriz's shoulders. This is the first time I realize that these three have a special relationship, that being plunged into this intense experience of answering calls with strangers makes you more than strangers, closer than friends.

"Lydia had someone die on the phone with her once," JD says, looking at me. "A year or two ago. Right when I started. Someone shot themselves on a call. She heard the whole thing, *bang*, the person moaning and dying slowly, the police showing up, everything."

"Oh my God," I say, my heart dropping so intensely I

actually clutch my chest as if I could lose it.

"Yeah. This shit ain't for the fainthearted."

Usually my instinct would be to find some terrible dark joke to fill the uncomfortable emotional canyon that is our silence, but now's so not the time.

"Why'd you start volunteering here?" I ask JD.

"'Cause I used to call hotlines growing up, and that's why I'm still alive, my friend," JD says. "You know what it's like being nonbinary and growing up in rural Oklahoma? I thought I wasn't going to make it past fifteen."

"Nonbinary?"

"Not all masculine and not all feminine. I go by 'they, them' pronouns."

I've heard that term, just never met anyone who explained it to me. It's exactly JD, who sometimes looks like the butchest femme or femme-ist butch, who is so beautiful and so handsome simultaneously. I'm super glad I was careful with my pronouns and didn't assume they were female or male.

"You were bullied?" I ask.

"Verbally abused, ostracized at school, depressed as fuck. Jumped out the window of the highest building I could find and tried to end my life."

"Holy crap," I say.

"I landed in some bushes and broke my leg instead," JD says. "Because in rural Oklahoma the highest building I could find was three stories. I can laugh about it now."

I imagine JD at fifteen, alone, thinking their world

was done as they leapt from a window. And here they are, grown-up, eyes twinkling, a graduate student getting their master's, a volunteer, so confident it edges on endearingly cocky.

"I tried to kill myself, too," I say.

It feels weird to say it, the weirdest part being how normal it comes out, the way JD just nods and pops some cinnamon gum in their mouth, then offers me a piece sticking out from the pack.

"Well, glad you stuck around," JD says.

I smile and take the gum. "Same to you."

Etta and I usually eat lunch Tuesdays and Thursdays after our philosophy class. We get plates of hot food from the cafeteria and sit on the same sunny spot of grass over an ocean so pretty it could make a postcard jealous. Etta's lunch is some eggs, two strawberries, and ten slices of bacon.

"Heart attack special," I say.

"Basically. I'm so despondent after reading about existentialism this morning I require bacon."

"The Germans have a word called *Kummerspeck* that literally means 'grief bacon.' Like, you're so depressed you stuff your face."

"What? That is the best word in the universe. My whole life is grief bacon."

"My whole life is grief bacon," I repeat in a German accent.

Etta falls back on the lawn, clutching her stomach. When she laughs super hard, there is no sound. It's completely silent.

She sits back up. "You are the goofiest weirdo. It's amazing."

"Nothing compared to you," I say.

"True. No one can compete with the master." She does a nonsensical upper-body dance. "Sorry. I had a quadruple espresso with seven packets of sugar. I think a heart attack's next, followed by a coma."

And I thought I was a spaz. "Get it under control, woman," I say, laughing.

"I know, I'm a mess!"

Etta and I have hung out enough at this point that I know her sense of humor is practically pathological. I always thought I was the jokester, but hanging out with her makes me feel like Queen of the Feels.

"So, you play guitar?" I ask her.

"How did you know that?" she asks, giving me the side-eye.

"That first day I met you at the hotline, you had it with you."

"Oh, that's right. Well, I don't really play. I want to learn. I signed up for intro to guitar but I . . . I chickened out the first day."

I'm shocked. "You don't strike me as the shy type."

"I'm a clown," she corrects me. "I'm in it for cheap laughs. I can't be serious."

"Huh," I say, looking at her in this new way. Her vulnerability. The more I know her, the more I like her.

I really like her.

Not that Etta and I will, in any shape or form, be a thing. It's impossible. Let me count the ways.

She might only be a year older than me, but she is a bona fide grown-up who lives in a studio apartment.

I am a human pizza slice who lives with her parents.

She is rainbow-flag-bumper-sticker-sporting queer and I am a quasi-closeted bi girl who has only had boyfriends.

When I mentioned to my parents I was attracted to girls as well as boys, my mother kind of rolled her eyes at me like it was a phase, and my dad just nodded and smiled and I could tell he didn't really understand. I'm not confident about that part of myself. A part of me feels like, because I've only had boyfriends—one serious boyfriend, really—it's not even true that I'm bi. What I'm trying to say is, my sexuality is complicated.

Etta asks me what I'm doing tonight.

"Hotline shift."

Her eyes are this mesmerizing golden brown. "How's that going?"

"I love it. You should really do it when you have the time."

"What are the people like who call? I'm so curious. Has anyone been suicidal?"

"Not really. They're just people who need to talk to someone for the most part."

"I used to volunteer at a children's hospital," Etta says. "Holding sick babies."

I wait for a punch line. But there is none.

"Yeah, because, you know, a lot of babies in the NICU—baby intensive care—their moms have to work all day, or live far away, or some of them are addicts, or just not around," she goes on. "So I would come in every Thursday after school senior year last year and hold babies."

"How sweet," I say.

It's strange that between class and our lunch, I've spent hours with this stranger. So much so that she doesn't feel like a stranger anymore. Her hair is electric, blowing everywhere as a sea-damp wind breathes over campus.

"Yeah, my brother had cancer when he was a kid," she says. "Those babies I saw on the ward, the ones the nurses held because there was no one there for them—they shook me."

"I'm sorry your brother had cancer," I say.

"He lived," she says. "He's a big old pain in my ass now."

"That's good."

"But holding those babies was pretty much the best thing ever," she says, gazing across the lawn, where some dudes play Frisbee. "It feels good to do good, don't it."

This is something that has bothered me for weeks, ever since I learned about egoism and altruism. I can't tell if there's ever anything in life that isn't inherently selfish.

"Is it just a self-serving thing, to serve others?" I ask.

"Even holding sick babies gives you an oxytocin rush," Etta says. "So basically I held babies for drugs."

A woman walking by does a double take, apparently having heard just the last sentence Etta said, then continues on her way, shaking her head.

"That's right! I held babies for drugs! And don't you forget it, lady!" Etta yells after her.

As we walk to the edge of campus, down a long-sloped path, I let myself pretend for just a second she is my girlfriend. I imagine introducing her to some nameless so-and-so: "This is my girlfriend, Etta." But then she says, "Well, bye, little buddy," and hops on her baby-blue moped with cherry-red streamers and I am left at the bus stop with my heavy backpack, staring into the clouds blocking the sun, heart sinking back to earth.

The whole bus ride home I think about what Etta said. I look up *oxytocin* on my phone—the cuddle hormone—a chemical—and wonder if love is just as much a lie as lithium.

Since I last saw Marisol, just two weeks ago at Galentine's, she pierced her nose and got new glasses. It makes me feel like we've been apart a year. We meet up for breakfast at our favorite diner on a Sunday.

"Two coffees," she tells the waiter, who remembers us from last summer when we used to brunch every weekend.

"Where you been?" he asks us.

"Having a nervous breakdown," I say.

He laughs and laughs.

Some joke! So funny!

It occurs to me the last time I was here, Sunday brunching, it was the weekend before I tried to off myself. I was miserable, failing at faking it. Marisol asked *what's wrong* over and over like a broken robot and I couldn't find the words to tell her. I stared out the window. The cars looked like toys. I longed for earthquakes. I fought tears and wished I had died in the car wreck.

I get a jolt remembering, like I stepped too close to the edge of a very tall building.

"Remember last time we were here?" Marisol asks.

"I was just remembering."

"That was when I actually thought Hobart was sexy," she says.

Oh, right. Yeah. Marisol had the hots for her tennis instructor, Hobart. I forgot about Hobart. I forgot about how she was into tennis for ten seconds. Honestly, all I remember about that day is me.

"Hobart," I say, looking out the window wistfully.

She cracks up. "Hobart," she imitates, with wide-eyed naivete.

I kick her under the table.

Marisol's wearing, by the way, the most ridiculous black shirt that has the shoulders and boob area cut out. Underneath, a neon-green camisole blares out her tit area like a stoplight.

"You okay? For reals?"

I dislike the way she asks this, dripping with such concern, like I'm *not* okay and she knows it and I don't.

"I'm dazzling and wondrous and sensational and tremendous," I tell her.

She smiles. "Okay, human thesaurus."

"Ever notice how a thesaurus sounds like a dinosaur name?"

"I have not. But you make a good point."

We order the usual, chicken-fried steak split on two plates, and I tell her about Etta.

"Cool, cool," Marisol says. "As long as you're not trying to replace me."

Marisol has a jealous streak that is, frankly, quite flattering.

"I'm hoping this is a pretty gay thing going on between us."

"I'm glad you're finally exploring the gay in you," she says. "Took long enough. Plus, anyone who isn't Jonah is a ten in my book right now."

I sigh.

"Yuck, really?" she says.

Because she's that good at reading my sighs.

"I'm trying really, really hard to forget him," I say. "But if I let myself remember him, I start thinking there's still a chance."

"There is not, and you must stop."

"Is he with someone else?"

"Not playing this sick game again, JoJo."

Marisol refuses me any updates on Jonah these days. Believe me, I've tried.

"You'd tell me if he was," I say.

"The obsession must stop."

"You'd at least—"

"No," Marisol says, banging a spoon on the table. "No, no, no, no, no."

"But—"

"*No.*"

Our chicken-fried steak comes and I tell her about the hotline, about my shift buddies ("Oh my God I want to meet Lydia I love her so much already") and Davis ("That is so wrong that he abuses the line like that, come the hell on").

Marisol signs the credit card receipt with a flourish. Marisol always pays. She is some kind of ninja at intercepting the waitress before I can and accepts no "splitsies," as she calls it. If I do manage to pay, she'll find a way to slip money in my pocket before we say goodbye. She is a lot better off than I am and I know she's just being generous. But sometimes I wish she wasn't so eager to pay all the time, like I'm a charity case.

She seems to be thinking hard, biting her lip.

"Good seeing you," I say as we linger out in the parking lot near her Beetle. "Do this again soon?"

"What are we, business associates? Have your people call my people?" Marisol smiles, tight-lipped. "I have some news to share with you."

"Oh God. Is it about Jonah?"

"*No.* I'm going to kick you if you say his name again."

"That was the last time."

"This is serious. I got into Chicago."

She delivers the news like a death, and it feels like one. I suck in air. "Chicago."

"They're the first I've heard from. They have the best funding, though, and I think that's where I want to go."

"Congrats."

"Thank you."

"Chicago," I say, graver, the entire scene shifting with that one word repeated.

"You've already moved on anyway," Marisol says.

She's so despondent, she looks like a child. Then she bursts into tears and I hug her. That's how it is with Marisol: the storms only last a minute, and then they blow through.

"Sorry, I'm so periody and emotional right now," she says. "But you have. You're, like, suddenly a grown-up. Chasing girls and going to college and working and volunteering. I feel as if our friendship is over. You don't even wonder how I am anymore. Or how anyone at school is. You marched forward and never even bothered to look behind you."

"If I looked behind me, I thought I might . . . lose my

balance. Fall flat on my face."

"You have to at some point," she says. "It's not healthy to just forget."

Talk to me about that when you're in Chicago, sweetie.

We still text on a regular basis, but I know what she's talking about. It's hard to be close and discuss real things in text messages. It's not the same as when we saw each other every day.

"I stopped taking my meds," I tell her.

"Oh geez."

"It's okay. I'm *fine*."

I hate how insistent my voice sounds. I want to be fine. I am fine, right? I hate that I live my life constantly doubting if fine is truly fine.

Marisol shakes her head. "I admit, I worry."

"I talked to a doctor, okay? And my parents are worried about me enough, you really don't need to take that on. I'm good."

I can tell she wants to press on, but instead she asks, "You want a ride?"

"I'd love nothing more."

She drives in her usual careless way, running red lights, almost clipping corners; she talks about the dorms, how cold Chicago winters are, and all the famous people who went to the same university. I nod, eyeing the side-view mirror, my hair way past my ears and heading for my shoulders, now a steely platinum blue with two inches of dark brown roots, palm trees and the blue sky passing behind me.

I don't look back.

I must be a masochist, because I show up to my job as a human pizza slice on time every shift and stand out in the heat or darkness with diligence, holding a Crusty's sign. Today is my fourth shift. I plug through it the way I plugged through the psych unit: with an end goal in sight, knowing I deserve better than this, and I will live through it, as humiliating as each honk and each expletive shouted from a random stranger's window is.

"Dance, pizza girl, dance!"

"Pizzaaaaaaa!"

"Lemme get a bite!"

"Hey, pizza! OLIVE YOU!"

"You want some of *this* pepperoni?"

It's weird to say, but standing on the corner during traffic long enough to trace the sun's movement across the open sky, long enough to watch the Taco Bell and McDonald's lights blink on, the gas station glow, the sky settle from periwinkle to ink blue to simply black, the nip of the SoCal winter on my exposed hands and face, my arms burning from holding up the godforsaken sign—all this, after the loathing and questioning of life choices passes, reaches a certain point where it's nothing more than counting my own breaths again. I am not Journey. I am not pizza. I simply *am*. My soul leads me peacefully through my five-hour shift.

"Our last pizza slice needed to pee all the time, leaving gaps in coverage, so I truly appreciate your bladder control," Tim-Tim tells me when I go inside to change from my pizza costume to my human girl costume.

Tim-Tim is grossly, relentlessly positive, to the point where I often wonder how long he had to rack his poor brain for a compliment.

"Maybe just think about a little . . . inspiration," he says. Then he moonwalks in and out of the walk-in, freezer fog surrounding him in a puff that instantaneously disappears. "You know."

"Yeah, listen, paying someone minimum wage to wear this crusty-ass costume and wave at strangers on street corners, eradicating any hope they ever had of human dignity, shouldn't be, like, a thing you expect people to care about."

Tim-Tim seems genuinely sad, stroking his soul patch. "I thought I saw a spark in you." He backs up to go out to the floor, where a server is freaking out because the receipt tape has been eaten by the receipt machine. "My bad."

I leave that night still smelling like the fug of the never-washed pizza costume that is my life two nights a week. I have regret. Tim-Tim has made me feel regretful. What is wrong with me that I even give a crap?

Truth be told, irritability is a symptom of getting off medication. But I can't tell what's my irritability and what is . . . entry-level fatigue. I hate that I don't know what emotions *I* experience and what are pharmaceutical lies. I know my parents want me to keep them updated, but I don't even know what is worth sharing and what is worth keeping to myself anymore.

*Someday I'll be gone*, I think, passing the lake on my walk home, the dark, quiet lake full of ducks, crickets, secrets.

I don't think it in a morbid way—it's me thinking, surprisingly, for the first time I can remember, that someday I will not be here anymore. I'll be elsewhere. Another city, maybe. Another job, for sure. Another person entirely. Because that's what time makes of us.

Dear future self,

My therapist gave me homework this week (I know, paying someone for more homework, what horror is this?) and it's to outline some goals. Which made me think there are so many future selves there. They're lined up like paper dolls. They're mashed together like a loud crowd. They're two steps and/or a galaxy away from one another. None of them are real, though. There's something scary about that, when I let myself think of you: you're a ghost, a maybe, a thing I could lose if I lost myself again.

Is surviving not enough of a goal?

What is the difference, really, between surviving and living?

◆ ◆ ◆

Wolf is an interesting human. He seems to have stepped out of an old-school film, from black and white to the shades of tan/beige/brown he is today. His office, as I've mentioned, is a hot mess. And his answer to everything is basically to ask more questions or urge me to pay attention to my body, be mindful. Isn't that strange? That when we're asked to pay attention to our bodies, that's called being mindful? Shouldn't it be called being bodiful? My mind races, and I don't know if it's a symptom of bipolar disorder or the human condition.

I wonder.

"I think I have a thinking problem," I tell him.

He sits there, chin in hand, knee over knee, hunched like a judgmental man pretzel.

"Do you think I'm bipolar?" I ask.

"I think you have a big engine," he replies.

A big engine that never turns off.

In my bed—the hard twin at Dad's, with a black open window above me in the good-night darkness, the sound of wind hissing through the leafy wigs of trees—I have much to think about. My heart hurts with its drumming. I remember this intensity that lives in my chest. Has the medication fully worn off? Is this a reaction? Is this withdrawal? Is this *me*? Am I always like this? Big engine. Big feelings. But do I propel them, or do they propel me?

◆ ◆ ◆

Tonight's hotline shift is my sixth, and it's the busiest yet: three phone calls in the first hour. I sit at my usual spot at the scuffed table, my schoolbooks sitting in a stack in front of me, untouched.

I get one high school sophomore who cries about a recent abortion.

An entire shift flies by where our phones never even ring, hours spent playing hearts with a set of feminist playing cards Lydia keeps in her purse.

An older woman who feels guilty about not feeling sad her dad died.

A man who just keeps whispering, "Terrible. I did something terrible," before I hear a click.

Shivers.

"Hey," I say to the hotline three I share a shift with. "Decompress?"

And they always make me feel better. We've become total shift buddies.

"You're a pro," Lydia tells me as she crushes some vitamins on the desk with a paperweight. I half expect her to snort them but then she sprinkles them on her doughnut. Which is somehow way weirder. "You've got a career in counseling."

Honestly, I've thought this myself lately. I never feel saner than when I'm here on the line with a stranger. Here, I'm my best self—I'm good advice and patience and forgiveness. I leave the Journey with big feelings behind me. This hotline is all kinds of magic.

"You do have a talent," Beatriz agrees, folding origami.

"When I was your age, I was working at Arby's," JD says.

JD likes to talk about the seven years between us like it's the difference between now and the Victorian era.

"I moonlight as a pizza slice," I respond.

I make them laugh with this comment. I don't think they realize I'm serious.

But a couple weeks later, I get my second call from Coco.

"Hey," she says, surprised to hear my voice. "We talked last time I called, right?"

"Yep, we did," I tell her.

"I'm glad I got you, actually, because it's *your* advice that made my life fall apart." She sounds broken up. My stomach drops. I lean into my headset, close my eyes. "I told my boyfriend about my . . . problem. And now he thinks I'm a basket case."

"I'm so sorry."

"He told me I should go to a psychiatrist and then he told my team captain I'm losing my mind and they should keep an eye on me. Then he dumped me—in front of his friends. Laughed at me. Got up and walked away from me."

I am flotsam. I remember, in a wordless flash, the pain of Jonah needing *space*. The word *space* opening up inside me like a sickening chasm.

"It's going to be okay," I insist. "You're going to move on from him."

"It's not just him, it's everything," she says. "Because even feeling that humiliation—it was better than how I feel normally. Like nothing. Like I've always been nothing, will always be nothing."

"What you were talking about last time," I say.

"You remember," she says, softer.

Her voice is bittersweet. Again, I wonder if she's been drinking. And this time I'm bold enough to ask.

"You been drinking, Coco?"

"So what if I have been?"

"It's okay," I tell her. "Just want to make sure you're safe."

"You know what, right now, Journey—that is your name, yeah? Journey?"

"It is," I tell her, touched she remembered.

"When I drink, I don't care if I'm dead or not."

Must be nice, I think, to not care if she's dead or not. I care far too much if I'm dead or not—oscillating between fear of death in speeding cars or desire for it at dark moments where I dream up black holes. Unfortunately alcohol has the opposite effect on me. It just turns me into a weepy sentimental mess with even bigger feelings than usual.

She's quiet, breathing in, out, in, out. "I don't care that Clayton dumped me in front of everyone."

Clayton? I rack my brain. Big guy, redhead, goofy grin.

He was in my math class last year. Who's he with again? For-give me, but who is this girl? Stop, Journey. *Focus.*

Her voice climbs up a key. "Thank you for listening."

"I'm so sorry you're going through this," I tell her. "I hope—have you thought a little more about seeing some-one?"

"I don't want to go to some psychotherapist or whatever. What if they lock me up in a psycho ward?"

"They won't."

"How do you know?"

"Because I've been locked up in a psycho ward," I say, quicker than I can stop to realize it's probably out of bounds to say that.

Coco is quiet. Then her voice curls up, curious. "What'd you do, Journey?" she asks. The way she keeps saying my name is strange, this stranger so familiar. "What's wrong with you?"

"This isn't about me," I say.

"I'm glad we talked again," Coco says, (I think?) giggling. She must be at least somewhat drunk. "You know what? For a few minutes here, I forgot. I actually, totally, completely, utterly forgot."

"Forgot what?"

"That I'm already dead."

The click that meets my ears might as well be a gun's safety releasing. I sit stunned for a moment at the silence in my headset.

She's gone. Hung up.

"Decompress?" Beatriz asks as soon as I'm off the phone. The other two are hunched into their desks, murmuring softly to callers.

I roll over and accept Beatriz's hug, surprised at the shake in my breath.

"She hung up. I didn't really help her," I say.

"You don't know," Beatriz says, patting my back. She smells stiflingly earthy, patchouli something. How bizarre to be suddenly this close to a person I've never actually even exchanged a handshake with.

I pull back and wipe my eyes on my sweater cuff.

"I heard you tell the caller you were hospitalized?" Beatriz asks.

"Yeah, was that—shouldn't I have—I tried to kill myself," I stutter.

Mouth, stop! Why do you have to say it like that, just lay the ugly truth out there for strangers to gape at and see? I want to take the words from the air and cram them back in.

"I was, too, once," Beatriz says with a half nod, the way someone might say you shared an astrological sign or an alma mater.

"Really?" I ask.

"I was twenty," she says. "My mom had just died. My mom was everything. I went through a grief spell that—well, it consumed me. I wanted to be nowhere."

Nowhere. She says it like it's a place, the same place Coco lives, the same place I dreamed of when I wanted out. Beatriz tells me this without blinking. As she adjusts her hands, folded on the lap of her broomstick skirt, her bangles jingle. She doesn't ask me why I tried to kill myself. Maybe it's not appropriate to ask.

"I only brought it up—you mentioning it on the call—" she starts.

"I shouldn't have said anything," I interrupt. "I know."

"It's not that," she says. "It's just, in this work, you have to ask yourself how much of yourself you're willing to give."

She puts her hand on mine—bracelets clanging—and I nod.

"Yeah," I say.

"You're going to want to save people," she says. "That's not what this is about. It's just about being here."

I take the bus home, straight shot down Santa Barbara's main drag of fancy restaurants and boutiques, State Street; it passes the Mission, the dark relic surrounded by gardens and lush lawns, through neighborhoods lit with bungalows and streetlamps, till it becomes Hollister Avenue and the houses shrink, and the lights get fewer and farther between, and the shopping centers, and the churches, and my dark hush of a neighborhood with cars parked and curtains drawn. As I walk past Crusty's, which is closed, Tim-Tim dancing with a mop through the window, I wonder about Beatriz and her dark days in the mental hospital when she was barely older than me. How close does she still feel to that girl? Like an older sister? Like a stranger? Does the darkness live on in her, like a flame? Or does it go away?

Dear future self,
   Some days you scare me. Some days the blankness where you live makes me flutter with fear. Dear future self, you've got to be there, and that's got to be enough. Breathe in. Out.

Freshman year, there was this girl named MacKenzie. She moved in from North Carolina, blew into school like a girl hurricane with her spiky strawberry hair, her raggedy jeans cut off below the knees, her eyeliner charcoal smudges. She was so pretty and yet so hard. We had bio together and I sat next to her, side-eyeing the anarchy signs she drew in the margins of her textbook. I found myself preoccupied with her in random moments throughout the day, chewing my lunch, maybe, or lying in bed at night, my brow furrowed, thinking, why does she think she's such a badass? She thinks she's, what—punk rock? What does that even *mean*? I found myself mentally outlining, in detail, her glossy scowl. Once, I caught myself drawing a picture of her on a napkin. My dumb pencil couldn't capture what it was about her that enraptured me, though. Honestly, I didn't know what to do with my preoccupation with MacKenzie. I thought I hated her.

This thing I felt for MacKenzie (who, by the way, never knew me, blew out of town as quickly and unexpectedly as she blew in, back to North Carolina or wherever) had no history within me; thus, it had no name. Maybe I envied her—maybe I wanted to give zero fucks like her. Maybe I wanted hair that strawberry, eyeliner that thick. Or maybe, just maybe—this thought sucked the breath from me— maybe I had a crush on her.

At the time, this thought was so foreign I shut it down. Me like girls? What? I'd loved boys all my life. Ridiculous. Me like MacKenzie? Pffft. No way.

One night, Jonah and I hung out in our neighborhood park. It was the same park with the horse swings we rode as kids. The twisty slide, the picnic bench maze where a million birthdays had been squandered. But now we wandered it in the dark, as teenagers, with phone flashlights and hushed conversations and a delicious sense of danger chirping in the background like cricket symphonies. I was talking some shit about MacKenzie for no reason.

This was before I made the dumb move of falling in love with him, back when we were buddies and life was simple.

Jonah turned to me, his long hair haloed by moonlight. "Can you just shut up and accept it already?"

"Accept what?" I asked, a little stunned by the interruption.

"You have a big fat crush on MacKenzie," he said.

Then he just kept walking and I stood there in the dark, his statement washing over me. Like whoa. Like tsunami. Oh my shit. What if . . .

What if he was right?

What if this weird twisted obsession I had with a girl who sat next to me in bio, who I hardly even knew, was all because I had a crush?

How she smelled, how soft her skin would be, her lips. I mean, her *lips*.

What they would feel like, practically edible, probably incredible.

I still remember how the moon appeared that night, almost full, shining up there in its color that is silver, that is blue, that is yellow all at once.

It took me a few minutes to catch up with Jonah. I had to search all the benches in the dark and finally I found him there, lying back on one of them like a bed. He was gazing up through the thatched tree branches at the showy moonbeams.

"I think I'm bisexual," I told him.

"You're just now realizing this?" he asked.

Jonah had known me so long, he knew me better than I knew myself.

Sometimes I miss him like an amputee must miss a limb.

Sometimes I ache so bad I have to grind my teeth or get

in an all-hot shower till my skin scalds or pull my hair to think about anything except him.

He can't possibly be actually, forever gone.

*A heart blown apart*
*Then glued together*
*Is never the same.*
*But maybe a heart*
*Blown apart*
*Will be bigger*
*From the scars*
*That form it together again.*

Etta invites me to her apartment to study for midterms.

"Sure," I say with a shrug as we part ways outside the cafeteria. "That'd be cool."

Inside, though, I am confetti, I am uncorked champagne. Is this, like, a date? Or are we study buddies? Also, please note that I'm a secret high school student and I've never kissed a girl in my life, just dreamed about it. The point here is: I don't know what she thinks of me, or if she even thinks of me, but I have the MacKenzies for this girl and the fact she invited me over is sunshine to my queer little soul. And a welcome respite from me torturing myself with Jonah again another night. (If you looked at my web history, you'd see *Jonah Patterson* social media profiles all the way down. Of this, I am not proud.)

I go to Etta's on March 13. I take the bus a short distance—she lives on the edge of Isla Vista, near UCSB—and think to myself, if Etta and I got together today, our anniversary would be 3/13. It has a ring to it. Jonah's and my anniversary was 5/15. Isn't that something. Ha ha. Totally kidding. I know she'd never like me.

STOP!

Out the window, it's drizzling on golf courses. It's drizzling on shopping centers. The bus stops and I follow my GPS under an umbrella printed with cupcakes. I get to the gate, where I punch in her number and do a little nervous dance in my rain boots while I wait for her to answer, and it strikes me why this bread-colored box-shaped apartment complex looks so familiar: this is where I snuck in to skinny-dip in the Jacuzzi that night we saw Girl Cheese. This was the last place I was before the first time I almost died.

This was, essentially, the last place I felt invincible.

Before I started unraveling and became unlovable.

My brain is a telegram.

STOP!

"Well, you look as adorable as the Morton Salt Girl," Etta says, opening the gate for me. "With your li'l pigtails and your dress and your umbrella."

"Gracias," I say.

She's in slippers, with a bag over her puff of kinky ginger hair like a plastic babushka. She doesn't seem dressed up. SO, this does not seem like a date.

That's fine. Everything's fine.

We go inside to her studio and she takes off her babushka, puts a pot on for tea in the corner that is her kitchenette. Because Etta is a year older than me and miles ahead, she rents her own studio, and lives on her own. In fact, she moved to Santa Barbara from Oregon to go to city college and learn to surf, realizing a month in that the ocean was too cold and surfing was boring and grueling. Her apartment walls have more framed pictures and postcards on them than white space. All people—street artists, toothless elderly folk, babies, family portraits. There's a series of black-and-white photographs of all sorts of eccentric-looking strangers at a bar, laughing, clutching drinks, a woman braiding her long hair, a guy with a brass instrument and a needle-thin mustache.

"My brother took those," she says. "He can do everything and do it so well. He's basically a genius."

"Where is this?"

"A place my parents own. Want to hear something so cute you'll barf a little? They now own the bar they fell in love in. 'So an Irishwoman and a Jamaican man walk into a bar . . .' that's not a joke. That's my origin story."

"Your parents are still together?"

She nods.

"I did barf a little," I say.

She pats my back. "Good."

Christmas lights strung along the ceilings and paper

lanterns hung from the walls give the tiny space a warm glow. There's a large queen bed covered with a woven blanket with Prince's face on it. It's decorated with brightly colored throw pillows that transform it into something sofa-like. There's a glass bowl with an angelfish in it on a desk. Her closet is open, and she separates her clothes by color; she lines up her shoes.

She would be horrified at my room—either one of them—the chaos, the ankle-deep mess.

We take out our books and drink chai and quiz each other about philosophy. I can't help imagining whether Jonah would be jealous, if he were able to see us. (STOP!) We sit on her floor and make flash cards about existentialism and utilitarianism and a blur of other -isms. Soon she's sitting there shuffling the cards and our conversation has meandered away from schoolwork and into a gossip about our classmates—the endearing stutter of a woman who sits in the front row, the guy who wears a suit every day and raises his hand so much the professor pretends to ignore him.

"The Russians have a word for him," I say. "*Pochemuchka*. A child who asks too many questions."

"You speak Russian?" Etta asks.

"No, I just collect words with no English translation."

"How gorgeous is that? Share them all with me!"

"In time, grasshopper."

Etta's like that. She sees people's knowledge and aims to soak it up. I love her thirst. It's so different than my own cynicism—the dark thoughts I battle that tell me people are unreachable, life is boring, and other mean lies. I am closed. Etta is . . . open.

After the rain lets up and we've guzzled multiple chais and quizzed the crap out of our flash cards, it gets dark outside. Etta convinces me to Lyft to get burritos in Isla Vista. We share a quiet ride with a driver blasting radio commercials and there's a voice whispering in my head, *Hey, look at Journey acting like a grown-up, acting like she's really a college student and not a high school student, acting like she's a girl who knows how to like girls, acting like a sane person when she's really on the edge of crazy. Look at Journey pretending to be pretty and lovable.*

*How long,* it asks, *till she finds out who you really are?*

We order burritos, and Etta holds hers like a baby when she gets it, commending its size, saying that she doesn't want to eat her baby but it smells so dang good. I eat mine and joke around with her, but really, I'm stiff. When she clutches my forearm to emphasize a point she's making, when she brushes a fly out of my bangs for me, when she tells me how lovely my lipstick looks, I like it so much it almost makes me sick. I'm scared that she likes me. I'm crushed that she doesn't. I want to know what Jonah would think of this; his imaginary hurt is so satisfying. OH MY GOD, PLEASE STOP ALREADY. Why do I carry that boy around in my bones like a living ghost?

We walk around a bit, students whizzing by on bikes or scooters, shouting in small groups. Students hanging out on apartment balconies, students toting twelvers back to their homes. I dig my heels into my goals. Yes, I think. I'm going to save my dollars. I'm going to move out on my own. Someday, maybe, I'll even go to a four-year university like all these smarty-pants, either here or elsewhere.

There's a coffee shop with people singing karaoke and Etta pulls me inside, linking my arm, daring me to sign up.

"Karaoke!" she says.

"Okeydokey," I say, shrugging.

I sign up for a Patsy Cline number my mom's been singing since I was a kid called "I Fall to Pieces." Etta signs up for Journey's "Don't Stop Believin'," apparently just to troll me. We order more chais and find a table near the back and watch as people go up and sing. There is a guy who just recites lyrics like a robot. There is a girl on the edge of crying who cannot get the timing of her song right. There is a ballad sung between a couple so off-key I'm pretty sure they didn't hit one note between them.

"I'm in love with them," Etta whispers to me.

"I think you're alone there, friend."

More than once, Etta clutches my hand across the table and makes her eyes enormous.

"You nervous?" she teases me between songs. "Peeing yourself a li'l tiny bit?"

"Yeah, I'm peeing right now," I tell her. "All over the place."

I mean, there are fifteen strangers here that I will never

see again. There is a barista who has a look on their face not unlike the look on my face when I am in dancing pizza mode.

"What? Not even a little?" she asks, surprised.

"No, are you?"

"Honestly?" she says, with wide, lovely eyes. "I'm terrified."

They call my name after we sit through four or five songs. I get up, grab the mic, close my eyes, and sing my heart out to "I Fall to Pieces." I pretend I'm alone. I pretend I'm in front of a million people. Big feelings, take it away. I know every lyric of this song from so many years of my mother singing it. The hurt of Jonah, the longing for Etta, it runs through me thick like honey.

When I open my eyes, everyone is hooting and clapping. Etta is standing up. I swear her eyes are shining. She must be joking. She's always joking. She comes and takes the mic from me and we switch places, me back in my seat.

Up there, Etta is shockingly pretty. The lights give a golden glow to her brown skin, to her explosive ginger hair. But I see something new in her as the cheesy karaoke background song plays and her voice shakes. She struggles to hit the notes, half smiling, no humor in her performance, lyrics about strangers waiting and streetlight people. It goes on and on and on and on. She's new, this girl, but I recognize her. I see something soft. A rare glimpse of what a shell usually covers.

"I was terrible," she says, coming back to the table, her

shaking hand with its bitten fingernails. "You were amazing."

Amazing. Jonah used to call me amazing. More than once, I sang that song to him. One night his parents were out of town and I snuck out of my room in the middle of the night and snuck into his and I slept with him in his bed. I sang him Patsy Cline songs in his ear and gave him shivers. We planned our future, our wedding on the beach, the countries we'd visit on our honeymoon, we brainstormed baby names. He held me all night long. That night felt like forever.

STOP.

I take the bus home, watching the cars.

I get my first prank call at the hotline.

"Hi, my butt hurts," a pipsqueak tween says into the hotline, trying to deepen his voice and failing miserably. I can hear another kid snickering in the background. "Can you help me . . . with my butt?"

"Sure," I say super cheerfully. "What's your address? I'll be right over."

"Uh . . ."

Both boys bust up laughing. They hang up.

When Marisol and I were in junior high, we made some prank calls from my mom's cell phone, pretending to be UPS trying to deliver a pony. The people on the other end of the line were totally convinced it was real and got super pissed, until they called back and realized it was my mom's phone, and then I got in huge trouble. I was grounded for three weeks, then went on a forty-eight-hour hunger strike. Then my parents called a truce and my sentence was reduced to three days. At the time, it was a tragic battle of wills, a melodrama so intense I packed a bag and contemplated running away. But now I sit here at the hotline, stifling a laugh.

Davis calls again. Davis, for the love of God, I do not care about your lifelong fear of chickens. I do not care about your lack of special soap, or your eczema, or your elimination diet. Your trip to the dentist does not need to be described to me in vivid detail. You do not need to name every dog you ever remember meeting in life—"Well, there was Wally, he was my friend Dougie's dog, fleabag, that one, fluffy as a footstool; and then there was Sheriff, he belonged to the preacher from our church and used to bring up the communion bread on Sundays in this little sack in his mouth, holy little thing he was; oh, and then there was Ms. Nelson's dog, she was our landlord, and she bit everyone in the ankles—the dog, I mean, not the landlord . . ."

DAVIS. DO YOU HEAR YOURSELF. DO YOU HEAR YOURSELF, DAVIS. This is what I scream inside. And yes, I realize I am going to hell. Don't worry, I'd never say these things. It's just so hard to take him seriously when he calls every night and talks about nothing at all for half the night. Instead I offer monosyllabic, not-friendly, not-unfriendly responses.

"Hmmm. Sssss. Flarg."

And I've learned to set my alarm, thanks to Lydia. Once we hit ten minutes, Davis is done. "We've reached the end of our time together tonight, Davis. Toodles and fare thee well."

Now that I've been here two months, I'm much more confident. No matter who I've gotten, I've found an answer, and had to refer to the binder less and less. There have been a couple crises—a teenager freaking out about a positive pregnancy test who I convinced to call Planned Parenthood. A guy who said he wanted to bomb his school and I had to call the police to report it. But mostly it's been people who, more or less, when it comes down to it, are just like Davis: lonely.

It's been weeks since Coco called. When each shift ends, I find myself disappointed. I wonder if she's okay. I wonder what she's doing when the moon comes up over the hills and the flat town beneath lights up like a crowd of candles. She's somewhere out there, not that far away from me, someone oddly close, a girl I maybe shared a class with, or brushed arms with in the hallways.

What are you doing, dead-feeling girl? Who are you? Where are you now?

Gary is now my dad's girlfriend and she comes to dinner at our house to meet us. She requires a "grain- and animal-free" dinner, due to allergies and annoyingness. That's strike one. Strike two? She's wearing a parody version of a Yale sweatshirt that is a Kale sweatshirt.

"Watch out, I've heard kale accumulates high levels of

thallium, not to mention aluminum and arsenic," Ruby tells her as we all sit around the table, eating African peanut stew. Actually, Ruby's not eating anything. She's been stirring for five minutes straight. I was skeptical because I've never had a nut stew before, but this is actually really good.

"I had no idea," Gary says, with her eternal smile.

"Also it tastes bad," Stevie says.

"You haven't tried my kale chips," Gary says.

"I've tried your kale chips," Dad says, raising his eyebrows. "And they are *de*-licious."

Somehow, he's made a comment about kale chips almost . . . gag . . . sexual.

I hurry up and eat my stew as fast as possible. As I'm washing my bowl, Gary comes up beside me and pats my back like she knows me. She's so short and so youthful, even if she isn't all that young. She's the kind of person who will always seem small and young.

"Your dad says you've been volunteering at a hotline?" she asks.

"Yeah." I take her dish and rinse it. She keeps standing there, arms crossed, beaming up at me. Besides her weak kale sweatshirt, she wears jeans and sandals, her feet tan like she's out in the sun all the time. She probably does yoga, like, on the beach.

"That is really amazing," she says. "What a special person you are, to do that."

I shrug. "Not really. I had to do community service."

Which is true in a very tiny way. I did have to do community service in order to graduate this year. I'm not about to tell her the rest of my story.

"I called a hotline once," she says. "Many moons ago."

I turn around. "Really?"

"Yes. I was depressed, because my boyfriend at the time—well, anyway, it's a long story. I spoke to this lady. She was very nice. I still remember her name: Martha."

Gary. What kind of name is that for a girlfriend, anyway? *Gary* is basically a stranger. I know nothing about her except she works with my dad and makes him act like a moron. She has a sense of style I won't pretend to understand, and a smile so constant you'd guess it was surgical. But even she's called the hotline. It zings to know I know nothing about the extent of other people's suffering.

This should be comforting, but I go to my room and fight tears. Who knows where these feelings come from? I've stopped trying to pretend they are logical. They are ugly, unpredictable, a storm that rocks me recklessly. But at least I know they're me.

Even though I don't go to our high school anymore, I still get the senior email newsletters in my in-box on the first of every month. Whoever it is who puts the email together really enjoys shouty all caps. And April Fools' jokes, apparently. I about crap my pants when I read ATTENTION: YOU ARE NOT ELIGIBLE TO GRADUATE!!! in the subject line.

Then I shout many loud swear words when I see the email opens with *April Fools, seniors!!!*

I'm about to reply and ask to be removed from the list because I don't think I care anymore about prom, graduation activities, or who made it to the Ivies. But a quick scan of the page snags my attention, right there under Student News— Marisol's name in bold all caps.

MARISOL CRUZ has received first prize in the state-wide Judith Bloomberg personal essay contest, receiving a $5,000 scholarship award for her entry, "My Best Friend's Suicide Attempt."

I'm lying in my bed on my phone reading this early in the morning, scrolling through with bleary just-woke eyes, and the title of her essay is like a kick to the head. I gasp, sitting up. The room suddenly does not have enough air.

*My Best Friend's Suicide Attempt.*

Stunned, I keep rereading those five words, thinking, *Every student in our class got this email.* Everyone who knows Marisol knows I'm her best friend. That means everyone now knows I tried to kill myself.

Marisol never asked my permission. She never even told me she was entering an essay contest, let alone writing about my experience. Now she has shouted my secret to the world, and for what? For $5,000 she didn't even need. Her parents started her college fund when she was still in the womb. They could probably afford to buy a goddamn building at an Ivy League.

Marisol is supposed to be my best friend. How could she do this to me?

I lie back down, staring at the ceiling.

After an expletive-filled shower rehearsing what I'm going to say to Marisol, I go downstairs. Dad took the girls to some kids event at the Santa Barbara Zoo. Poor Ruby looked like she had been sentenced to death as they left, Dad assuring her, "It'll be a blast!" *So* glad I'm old enough no one bothers to invite me to crap like that anymore, and I get the house to myself for the afternoon. Of course, Dad looked nervous about leaving me here alone.

"You going to be okay?" he asked at least three times before he left.

At both houses, my parents still keep all the painkillers stowed away somewhere out of reach. Every time I mention moving out of the house they nod and give me a tight-lipped smile.

I sit on Dad's living room couch, wrap myself in an afghan, and dial Marisol's number.

"Hello?" she asks suspiciously.

"Hey."

"Is this some kind of emergency?" she asks. "First off, we strictly text. Secondly, you never respond lately."

"Marisol, I need to talk to you about something," I say. "Have you seen our monthly class email?"

"No, why?"

"Well . . ." I swallow, digging my fingers into my palms,

closing my eyes. "You were mentioned in it."

"Yeah?"

"The essay content you won? For your entry, 'My Best Friend's Suicide Attempt'?"

"Oh," she says.

The silence is long.

"I—I didn't mean for that to go in the newsletter," she says. "My mom probably sent an email to the school or something. You know what a braggart she is."

"You wrote about me?" I ask. "Why didn't you ask me if I was okay with that? You submitted an essay about my suicide attempt . . . to a bunch of strangers! And now everyone in school will know what I did."

"It's not like the essay had your name in it," she says, raising her voice. "And no one reads those emails anyway."

"So what? I don't even want *one person* to see it! And what about the people who read the entries? The judges?"

"They all live in Sacramento and don't even know us."

"I think you're missing the point," I say, my anger swelling, my voice shaking with it. "It's not your story to tell."

"It *was* my story." She's audibly fighting tears. "It was my story about how helpless I felt in being able to comfort you or empathize or see the warning signs. It was about how suicide—even when it's just an attempt—has a ripple effect and transforms friendships and support networks. About how hard it is to watch someone you know suffer."

"So if it was so not a big deal, then why didn't you mention it?" I ask. "You usually tell me everything."

"Because you haven't exactly been accessible lately," she says. "You rarely answer my texts. I invite you over all the time and you always have some excuse."

My temperature has risen. I can't sit still anymore. I spring up from the couch and pace the room. "You outed me as a crazy person to our entire school!"

"Our class," she corrects me. "And I didn't 'out' you. Was the essay called 'Journey Smith Tried to Kill Herself'?"

"Everyone will know it's me."

"You haven't even read the essay. It's not about what happened to you. I don't go into detail. It's about me."

"Yeah, big surprise. It's about you. It's all about you."

"Listen, do you want to read it?" she asks, sniffling a little. "I think you'll feel better once you read it. I have no problem sharing it with you."

"Oh, how generous," I say. "Thanks for sharing the story of the biggest shame of my life with me after you've already shared it with a bunch of strangers."

"I'm emailing it to you right now," she says, her voice shaking. "I didn't realize what a big deal this would be. I think you'll change your mind when you read it."

"I don't want to read it," I say. "Ever. Good luck with your final."

I hang up and burst into tears. Loudly. Like a toddler

who's had a toy snatched away. I'm glad the windows are shut or the neighbors would worry. The tears turn to rage. Rage at myself.

Because, why? Why am I so upset? Marisol's probably right, hardly anyone cares about the stupid newsletter, and it didn't say my name. It could have been another friend of hers. Why isn't she allowed to write about her life? I told JD and Beatriz that I tried to kill myself. I joked about it with Tim-Tim. Why does this feel like such a violation, then? An inner argument commences.

*Because it's mine. My story to tell.*

*But you're not even telling it. You basically pretend it never happened.*

*That's my decision to make. Nobody can force me to tell my story if I don't want to.*

*And it's Marisol's decision to tell* her *story. Like it or not, your suicide attempt is part of her story, too.*

Maybe that's what makes me so upset: I hate that my suicide attempt happened. I hate how it hurt, but I hate most how much it hurt everyone around me. My parents, who still hesitate before leaving me alone in the house and raise their eyebrows when I tell them I'm planning to move out. Marisol, our friendship now irrevocably different. And Ruby, who scorns me like a microbe. Scratch that—if I were a microbe, I'd be much more interesting to her.

I don't respond to Marisol's email that says "the essay"

in the title line, instead archiving without clicking, nor do I respond when she texts me later that afternoon saying she's really sorry. I'm glad she's leaving the state soon for college. It's just the amount of space I need from her.

A couple weeks later, Saturday night, Levi picks up what he calls "a feast" from the grocery store—a bucket of fried chicken, potato salad, rolls. It's about as gourmet as he gets. On the sixth chair at the dinner table sits an enormous panda bear with a heart that says "I LUV U BEARY MUCH!" Ruby is sitting directly across from it, eating her third dinner roll, watching the bear like a nemesis.

"Why is 'love' misspelled?" Ruby asks.

"Because it's cute, Rube," Mom says.

Mom has picked all the deliciousness off the fried chicken and is eating the meat underneath. Yet one of a million things that make her the polar opposite of Levi: her aversion to fried food.

"Being wrong is cute?" Ruby asks. "How dumb."

"I like it," Stevie says, smiling. "It's romantic."

"What's the occasion?" I ask.

"Just a little ol' thing called L-U-V," Levi says, winking at Mom.

Ruby makes gagging noises.

"What has gotten into you?" Mom asks Levi, blushing.

"I've been bitten by the love bug," he tells her.

"There actually is a Central American fly called the lovebug," Ruby says, lighting up momentarily. "The mating pairs remain fused together for *days*."

"Mom, Ruby's going to talk about bugs and I'm eating," Stevie whines.

"Ruby," Mom says, raising her voice.

"Since when do you like stuffed bears anyway?" Ruby asks Mom. "Didn't you give that crap up when you were five like the rest of us?"

"You're such a hot poker," Levi laughs, grabbing another chicken leg and biting into it with a crunch. "Just you wait a few years. You'll be bitten by the love bug, too."

"Doubtful," Ruby says. "Microbiology is my one true love. I could never love a human being the way I love single-celled organisms."

"Even single-celled organisms need other single-celled organisms," Levi says.

"Actually they don't. They reproduce by binary fission," Ruby says.

"No sex talk at the dinner table," Mom says.

"Binary fission isn't sex. It's asexual reproduction, by definition—"

"No *a*sexual talk, either," Mom says loudly.

We finish dinner, not talking about sex or asex, just chewing and crunching and, in Stevie and Ruby's case, kicking each other under the table. After dinner, Levi brings a cupcake with pink frosting out of the refrigerator and sets it on my mom's empty plate.

"My love," he says, kissing Mom's head.

"What is this?" she asks, laughing.

Ruby gets up to rinse her dishes. "Vomit."

"You didn't get any cupcakes for us?" Stevie asks, stung.

But Mom and Levi are embracing and kissing—lost in their own gross old people world.

"You can't buy just *one* cupcake," Stevie says.

"Yeah, what kind of monster are you?" Ruby chimes in, coming back for Stevie's dish.

In one second, Chewbacca gets up from the floor, stands up on his hind legs, and swipes the cupcake off the table. Ruby tries to shoo him, but it's too late—all Chewbacca left was a trail of crumbs on the floor.

"You damn dog!" Levi yells, running after him.

"Levi!" Mom yells after him. "He didn't mean to!"

"Yes he damn did!" Levi yells from the other room. "If you all didn't feed him from the table all the damn time . . ."

"Oh, so it's our fault," Mom says, rolling her eyes, looking at us.

"Maybe if you bought more than one *damn* cupcake, it wouldn't matter," Ruby says, not loud enough for him to hear.

Levi comes back out, his hair askew, leading Chewbacca by his collar.

"Lock that dog door down," Levi says. "I had a special something baked in that cupcake. Now I'm gonna have to wait for it to come out his other end."

"What?" Mom, Ruby, Stevie, and I reply.

"It'll get washed and be good as new," he says, getting on one knee. "For now, you've just got to imagine." He opens an invisible box. "Amanda, will you marry me?"

I'm standing here, realizing a diamond ring is in Chewbacca's stomach. I envision its wayward journey through his gastrointestinal system and out his rear end. I realize, perhaps more importantly, that this means that my mother is going to *marry* this weird poseur cowboy man from Burbank whose idea of romance is fried chicken in a bucket and a stupid stuffed bear who can't even spell a four-letter word. I don't know whether to laugh or cry. By the way my throat hurts when I swallow, I can tell I'm veering toward the latter.

I spring up from the chair and go to my room, quasi-accidentally slamming the door. I lie on my bed and turn my face into my pillow. I imagine screaming that he's not good enough for her. I imagine slashing the tires on Levi's truck. I imagine burning his cowboy hat in the fireplace. I know these are mean things. I don't like being the person who imagines them. I am so filled with fire right now and I can't do anything except close my eyes and breathe.

Everything comes back to me, big dumb feelings. My heart aches. I regret the suicide attempt, I fear death and its fiery crashes, I'm angry my parents split and dare to even think of remarrying, I am falling back into the abyss. It's as if I haven't grown at all.

I think of Coco, for some reason, walking around like

a zombie in a cheerleader's body. The people who call the hotline, they have real problems. Here I am, venomous, melodramatic, when I should be grateful and lucky. My mother was unhappy. Levi makes her happy. I should be celebrating.

This makes me feel worse. I have my whole life ahead of me and I want to shrink backward into childhood, or shrink back even farther, to a time when I was nothing at all.

Later, out in the kitchen, Mom's sitting at the table by herself, drinking tea, flipping through junk mail like it's interesting.

"Feeling better after storming off earlier?" she asks.

"Sorry about that," I say.

"Have something you want to say to me?"

Yeah, Mom, I do. I want to say, *How can you get married so fast? How can you be so sure that Levi's the right man for you? He's nice, but is "nice" enough? He snores so loud I need earplugs and I sleep across the hall. When I asked him where he would visit if he could go anywhere in the world, he said, "Arizona." Mom, if this is it, if this is true love, I don't know what to tell my future self anymore.*

Instead I say, "Congratulations. I'm sure you two will be very happy."

# PART
## three

# PRESENT

I never feel like I play the role of "normal human" better than at my hotline shifts, and I adore my co-operators at the crisis center. Beatriz is empathy personified and thinks deeply before offering responses to people. Between calls, I've gotten to learn about how she rescues animals from kill shelters and helps find them homes. She lives in a house on the Mesa with four dogs, six cats, and three chickens. And for a living, she works for a program for homeless youth. I'm kind of in awe of her. She's basically Jesus. And Lydia is a hilarious cynic who it turns out has spent decades protesting wars and writing books on pacifism and even has her own Wikipedia entry. She's had chronic back pain her whole adult life, since a gnarly car accident (which we bonded over), which is why sometimes, on nights like tonight, she skips shifts.

JD, though, has fast become my favorite. I am capable of getting along with most people, but when you meet someone who is one of *your* people, with whom you have friend chemistry, it's a step above. That's how it was with Jonah,

Marisol, even Etta. JD treats me like a younger sibling, giving me advice I never asked for, and lets me in on all the inside info. Like tonight, for example. After Beatriz goes for a short walk to take a break after a call with Davis that lasted several lifetimes, JD whispers, "Hey."

JD is dressed damn sharp right now in a black dress shirt and purple tie because they just came back from giving some speech to junior high kids because that's how JD rolls. They publish articles online, give speeches, accept awards, get their masters, work full-time as a personal trainer, have three girlfriends (they're poly), and volunteer here. JD makes me feel like a total slacker in the best way.

"Hey hey," I say back.

"I have . . . the most amazing gift to share with you," they say.

Rolling up on a chair, JD pulls up a website on their iPad and shows it to me.

*NOBODY Keeps a Carpet Clean as DAVIS DUNCAN!*

An almost elderly man, bald on top, ponytail on the bottom, with one gold earring, grins a yellow grin and gives two thumbs up to the camera. It has his contact info on there, a coupon for 10 percent off our first shampoo.

"Oh my God," I say, closing my astronomy notes on multiverses to come look at the screen. "Is that . . . is it . . . ?"

"I know the hotline is anonymous, and we're not supposed to do this," JD says, laughing. "But come on, haven't you wondered who he is?"

"How'd you find him?" I ask.

"He told me his last name a couple times. You know, when reading me his spam email."

"Oh, Davis," I say, taking in his on-screen magnificence. "Your hair . . ."

"Your lack of hair."

"But then too much hair."

"Both too much and not enough hair," JD says.

We crack up.

*Too much and not enough*, I think as JD rolls their chair back to their desk. That could basically describe my life.

I should be studying for finals in this downtime in my shift. I have my philosophy flash cards in front of me with every -ism known to humankind scrawled in permanent marker. But instead I keep going back to my phone to scroll through social media, where the end of senior year is in full swing. We're deep enough into May now, with June within squinting distance, that all my "friends" are shopping for prom dresses, or getting college acceptances; I tell myself I don't care, that was my old life, it might as well be a million miles away, but then why do I keep coming back to peek into it? Mom texts a picture of some long gowns with bell sleeves to Stevie, Ruby, and me, saying, Bridesmaids. You like???

I'm trying to figure out a nice way ask my mom if she's kidding when Ruby texts back, I would rather be eaten alive by rabid wolves at the same time that Stevie texts back sure!

Mom sends three more pics, all of them atrocious, and I just can't right now.

Sometimes I feel like my entire life is being a guest at other people's celebrations.

I turn back to my flash cards. I flip them over again and again. Last year, less than twelve months ago, I was sure I was going to go to prom with Jonah, and I knew exactly what I was going to wear: a bright purple lace dress I found at a thrift store. It still hangs in my closet in a bag. I was going to wear it with my combat boots. We were never even going to go to actual prom. We were going to spend the night on the beach, just the two of us.

The phone finally rings.

"I just swallowed a bottle of hand lotion," a tween-sounding girl with a shaky voice tells me. "I—I don't know why I did it, I don't know what's wrong with me . . ."

"I'm so glad you called," I say, flipping to a page near the back of the binder that says TOXIC SUBSTANCES. My heartbeat flutters from the lovely adrenaline boost of being useful in an emergency. All of a sudden, prom dresses and bridesmaid dresses vanish like ghosts. "Okay, have you reached out to poison control?"

"Should I call them? Is that what I should do? Oh my God, I don't want to die!"

"You're not going to die," I assure her. "Take a deep breath and grab a pen . . ."

◆ ◆ ◆

Tuesdays are my longest school day and one of the days I see Etta, so I doll up in my cutest dresses, bright tights, and boots. I am old, I am old, I wear my lipstick bold.

Etta and I sit on the lawn. I only saw her last Thursday and yet the sight of her, when I first walked into philosophy this morning, made it slightly hard to breathe. She wears a sundress printed with ice cream cones, her blinding red lipstick curling into a smile.

She throws chips for a wily seagull flock. I pick at my pizza.

"I don't know whether it's adorable or gross, watching you maim that pizza."

"Why did I even order this?" I say. "I work at a pizza place."

"Riiiight! I forgot about that! Please tell me you wear a little uniform."

In my mind, I can smell the pizza slice costume for a moment. I suppress a dry heave.

"Yeah" is all I say.

She sips her soda so loud I give her a playful push. She gives me one back. Is this flirting? Anyone else, I'd say yes. But Etta's so dang nice to everybody I just never know.

"Can I ask you something? Is it weird listening to people tell you their secrets on the hotline?" she asks.

"At first it was," I say. "But now I don't think twice."

"You know what my favorite part about you is, Journey?"

"What's that?"

"Your unflinching spirit."

As soon as it sinks in she is not kidding, I am touched by this, although I don't know if I can trust her word on me, since I haven't gotten around to showing her all my ugly parts. I'm about to tell her my favorite part about her is she's so kind to other people I sometimes can't believe she's real, but then a sassy seagull gang basically attacks us. They became real assholes since Etta fed them chips. We get up and shoo the seagulls. She walks me to the bus stop, which is near where she parks her moped. We hug goodbye. But Etta hugs everyone. She hugged the cafeteria cashier today.

"So, I'm probably sounding all gushy and lame," Etta says, her face serious, her eyes wider than usual. It's the face she often gets before she cracks a major joke. "But you kinda sorta inspired me."

"Uh-huh," I say, rolling my eyes playfully.

"Yeah. To start volunteering again."

"Oh," I say. "Really? Holding babies?"

"Opposite end of the spectrum this time . . . there's an old folks' home near my apartment. I have orientation for it tonight."

"Oh. That's sweet."

"Anyway, thanks for, like, being such a good human." She switches to a German accent, for no apparent reason. "Das ist good human."

I'm not a good human, I want to tell her. I'm a selfish person who lost and is trying to find her way back.

"I'm only in it for the compliments," I joke.

"Oh, of course. Of course you are." She grins. "Want a ride home?"

"On a moped?" I ask. "I kind of want to live another day, so I'm going to have to say no."

"Pffft. Scaredy-cat."

I could tell her I almost died on the freeway in a ball of fire, but now—in the sunshine—such a downer of a truth bomb seems out of place.

"Nah, but thanks," I say.

"Are you really that scared of mopeds?"

A shadow passes over my soul. It's as if I've been caught in the act of pretending to be a normal person. I'm not normal. I can't do things like ride on the back of mopeds. I can't bring her to my house, because I'm not a real grown-up. I can't even flirt properly because I've never kissed a girl, so I'm not even a real bisexual.

I'm faking my way through life, through everything, too much to be ordinary, but not enough to be extraordinary.

"I have issues," I say.

How else to say it?

"No worries at all," Etta says. "Did I just make everything awkward? Of course I did. Etta's gonna Etta." She laughs. "See you Thursday."

She gets on her moped and rides away.

I go over the conversation again in my mind. I could eat my own words. How would it have felt, my arms around her waist, my chest pressed up against her back, the speed loud in our ears, the wind a taste in my mouth?

Those three words form a feedback loop in my brain: *I have issues, I have issues, I have issues.* That special horror of hearing your own words on repeat.

The excitement of the conversation sinks into doubt and, looking out the window of the bus, my chest swells. It's hard to control my own breath. The black hole whispers, *I'm still here.*

My nemesis. My friend. The electric fence around every gift.

Wolf's whole office is in boxes. Towers of boxes. Walls of boxes. On the sofa, on the desk, on other boxes. He has to move a box for me to sit in my favorite swivel chair. The bookshelves, the walls, are bare. To be honest, I've never seen the place so clean.

"You're moving?" I ask, swallowing.

"The building is shutting down for earthquake retrofitting and I'm supposedly getting new floors and paint in the meantime," he says. "I'll be shutting down for a month or so."

I swivel once and put my sneaker on the floor. "And what happens if I lose my mind in that month?"

"I can still do phone appointments. But if you're feeling like a risk to yourself, please dial 9-1-1."

Sometimes, since I told Wolf I got off my meds, it seems as if he's become stricter with me. His responses—like that one, like a message a robot might tell you while you're on the Kaiser psychiatric phone line—make me think he no longer trusts me.

"A risk to myself," I repeat.

It strikes me the biggest risk to myself has always been—myself. In other places in the world, people have actual problems. There's no clean water, or there are wars, or diseases. But me? I'm just a risk to myself.

"How's the hotline?" he asks.

"I'm actually good at it. The other people I work with tell me I have a gift. Maybe I want to be a . . . therapist."

He raises an eyebrow.

"Is it true therapists are all converted nutjobs?" I ask.

"Where did you hear that?"

"It seems a general consensus. Are you a nutjob? Were you once a nutjob?"

"My grandpa owned a cashew farm, and I worked there in the summers, so I suppose I once did *have* a nut job."

Wolf's smiling again, and I'm thankful I've broken him. He's human again, not a robot.

I groan. "That's, like, beyond a dad joke."

"Have you been in contact with Jonah?" he asks. "Had any closure there?"

"Is sleeping in his sweatshirt every night closure?"

Wolf shakes his head at me. "You know the answer to that."

"It's a very nice sweatshirt."

"Why would you do that to yourself?"

I think about it, staring at the window, where a bunch of sunlit fronds dance wildly in the palm tree outside. "It's the last part of him I have."

"What would happen if you let it go?"

"I'd be cold at night."

Wolf sighs.

"It's just a sweatshirt," I say, maybe too loudly.

"Is it," Wolf says.

In the silence, his point sinks in, and I'm irritated this man is always so right.

Every therapy session is a story you tell someone about your life. That's all it is. Sometimes I omit things that maybe would change his perspective—the fact my mom is getting married and there's nothing I can do about it except smile and say congratulations. Or how Marisol and I are in a fight now for the first time in I can't remember how long, because I tried to die and she dared tell the world. Or how I like a girl so bad I ache and yet when I'm with her I am plagued by a creeping sense of doom that this can't happen, I'm too crazy, nothing will be right.

The story I want to tell today is this: I rocked school this semester. I'm saving money, I'm working toward my goals of moving out and going to school. I'm learning to drive. I'm well. So that's the one I give him.

Wolf shakes my hand when I stand up to leave and I agree to call him in a couple weeks to make an appointment when his office is done. He says I can call him sooner if I need him. I don't like that he said that, like he could sense something was off about me.

Is it? Did I not tell the right story to him today?

Today was supposed to be my two-year anniversary with Jonah. I woke up in tears. I thought of the lake. Of lying in the grass. And for a split second, I got sucked into that stupid lie of a suicidal fantasy. Then I remembered what it was actually like—lying in the bushes in panicked regret, stomach twisting in agony.

Then I pushed it from my head. I wiped the tears away. I changed out of his sweatshirt, put on regular person clothes. Then I went out in the world like I did every day, faking like I wasn't falling apart. If I let myself stop—if I let myself feel—

I couldn't do that.

This afternoon Etta texted and invited me over. She didn't say to study. I didn't bring my books. It's Saturday, and evening's rolling in on the horizon, barely darkening the sky. Is this a date? Ha ha. No, really, is it?? I'm nervous, which is dumb, and I hate being dumb and I WISH I COULD STOP. I get dropped off by my Lyft driver, a long-haired dude who seems mighty high. The apartment building has a placard out front that says Manzanita Meadows. There are no manzanitas. There are no meadows. Six months ago I skinny-dip hot-tubbed here on that night a car almost killed me on the freeway. Reminding myself of this fact is like telling myself a story. It's amusing but meaningless. It's unreal.

Two years ago I kissed Jonah for the first time by the oak tree near the lake.

That's just as meaningless.

Just as meaningless now.

STOP.

Etta's apartment looks like a dozen other apartments, a brown cluster of buildings I would get lost in if Etta didn't meet me at the entrance. Tonight she waits for me there in a neon shirt and cutoff shorts in the twilight, jiggling her long brown legs with restless energy, her hair piled atop her head in a crazy bun the size and color of a small pumpkin.

"Hey!" she says, smiling.

She opens the gate for me and hugs me. Just one second of her body being pressed up against me fills me with something even more electric than hope. And I forget about Jonah. She leads me through the maze of the courtyard, plotted trees all exactly the same distance apart. Every balcony the same, except decorated with different stuff—a mess of bicycles, a neat row of plants, a bunch of hanging beach towels.

"I hope you're hungry, and I hope you like Chinese food," Etta says. "Because I was starving and you took forever to get here, so I ordered us dinner."

I was trying on clothes for almost an hour. Putting on makeup. Bursting into tears while looking at pictures on my phone of Jonah and me. Taking my makeup off. Contemplating canceling this date. Deleting Jonah's pictures off my phone, freaking out and Googling how to recover deleted photos, putting makeup back on again. Rubbing it off. Then I show up makeupless, in jeans. Typical me.

We serve up some kung pao shrimp in the kitchenette. As I stand with the steaming meal in my hand, I'm momentarily spooked by what I now realize is a teased-high white-blond wig hanging on a nearby chair.

"Oh, it's my Dolly wig," she tells me, sitting on the chair next to it and petting it like a cat. "You like?"

"Wh-wh-wh-wh . . . why?"

"For the old folks' home."

The silence is so long I hear a distant train.

"Why?" I repeat.

"Because I've been playing music for the old folks."

"Really? But I thought you sucked *sooo* bad at playing guitar and singing. I thought you quit guitar lessons."

"Yeah, captive audience. It's elder abuse, really."

I roll my eyes. She can't be that bad.

"Anyway, I've discovered they're way more into me if I come in character. Check out my outfit," Etta says, gesturing toward her closet door, where a sparkling cowgirl dress hangs, an abomination of glitter, white leather and fringe.

"Did you spend money on that atrocity?" I ask, sitting on the edge of her bed and eating.

"You don't even want to know," she says.

"This food is so spicy—"

"God, yes. My mouth is burning," she says, putting her

plate down. "Thank you. I thought I was being a total wuss but this is, like, undoable."

"Can I have some water?" I ask.

"Water," she sputters. "I'm about to pull the fire alarm." She heads to the kitchenette.

She comes back with a glass of water. We chuck the food that burned our tongues so bad. She makes us hot dogs and hot cocoa for dinner, serves it on mismatching plastic plates. We eat it sitting on a futon/love seat thing covered in a floral sheet. For a second, I think, this grown-up thing is perfectly achievable. I could do this.

"Hot dogs and cocoa, what a combo," I say.

"I know, right? This is a little special I like to call 'the Etta.'"

"You have impeccable taste."

"My parents raised me a sugar-free vegan," she says. "This is my revenge."

We decide to watch an old musical on her laptop. We get on her bed together, pull Prince over our legs to keep warm. Even though I've hung out with Etta many times now, many lunches, many long walks across campus, even hung out here studying and did karaoke—tonight feels different. I can't explain it. I am sure she really likes me. And here we are, in this intimate space, the space she lives in, that smells like her, where she sleeps at night. We are sharing a Prince blanket. She invited me for no reason at all. And what if she wants to kiss me? What if I fall totally in love with her and it makes me a crazy person? And isn't it wrong to do this on my would-have-been-iversary? Like what if we do get together and we have the same anniversary as Jonah and me?

Why can't I stop my brain? Why am I so much??

I will channel Wolf and his breathing exercises.

Be here with Etta, appreciating the smell of the pear candles she lit and the lighter-than-air wonder of Gene Kelly tap-dancing down rainy lamplit streets on-screen. She's so near I can feel the warmth of her. I can see, out of the corner of my eye, her neon-red lips glistening in the movie-lit darkness.

It should be easy to be here now with Etta. Desire can keep you focused.

"You have any ChapStick?" I ask her.

"I don't believe in ChapStick. I have lipstick, though." Etta pulls it out of her pocket and hands it to me. "Who needs boring ChapStick when you can have moisturization *and* color?"

I put it on, giving her a look. "So in the middle of the night, you put red lipstick on when your lips are dry."

"A lady always has to look her best," Etta says, in some kind of old movie star voice. "Even in the dark."

"Weirdo," I tell her, handing her the tube of lipstick.

She takes it from my hand, but I don't let go, looking at Etta's flickering eyes and glistening lips.

There's a word for this in Yaghan, *mamihlapinatapei*, a look two people exchange when they both want to start something but don't know how to, exactly—an expressive shared quiet moment that means everything. All the want rises up in me and I am here now. I am being all the way here right now. The song is ending, Debbie Reynolds and the boys collapsing in laughter on a golden couch. Etta pulls the lipstick harder and I don't let go again; instead, she pulls me in, all of me, and then my red lips are on her red lips, my hands are in her hair, her hands are around my neck, pulling me down on her bed as the movie goes on without us.

The lipstick rolls off the bed and to the floor.

Nothing has felt this good in a very long time, possibly since last fall, when Jonah and I last kissed. (Stop thinking of Jonah. Get out of my brain, Jonah.) Etta. I am kissing Etta. And it's nothing short of perfect. For whole moments, with my eyes closed, I am only my body. I am not my thoughts or my brain.

I am red lips and warmth and tangled hair and soft skin.

I'm not sure where she ends and I begin.

I am not sure I want to know.

After a minute, we open our eyes and sit up and catch our breath.

"Journey," she says, so sweetly, touching my cheek. And then she starts laughing. As the movie changes scenes and the lighting changes, I see Etta's face, her clownish mouth smeared with red, and laugh, too. I look over at the mirror in her vanity and see us both there, faces coated, and we double over and can't stop laughing to the point of crying, of practically sobbing with laughter.

"This is why ChapStick is better," I finally manage.

"Touché," Etta manages between gasping fits. "Touché."

We get up together and wash our faces in the bathroom, pausing the movie. No matter how much I scrub, I still look oddly pink. I moan into the mirror.

"It's okay," Etta says. "You just look sunburned. All around your mouth."

"Comforting," I say, fixing my hair.

She puts her arms around me. "Is this okay?"

I see us there in the reflection, my heartbeat wild. Her chin rests on my shoulder. I reach backward and put my arms around her back. This is real. I am with her, she could love me, I could love her.

Dear past self, I'm happy.

Dear future self, I'm scared.

"So much okay," I say.

"Let us celebrate our make-out session with ice cream," Etta announces after we go back to her room.

"Sounds delightful."

"Bowl or cone?"

"Bowl *and* cone."

"I should've known," she says, shaking her head, and goes back to the kitchenette.

My lips are still buzzing as I sit and stare at the bright screen paused on Gene Kelly's overjoyed face. I consider writing Marisol a text gushing the news that I made out with Etta, but I need to get used to life without Marisol just like I need to get used to life without Jonah.

"You look so sad," Etta says, putting the bowl in my lap.

"Not at all," I say.

She climbs under the blanket with me.

"You're a little hard to read," she says. "I thought you liked me but I really couldn't tell for sure sometimes."

She probably doesn't mean it as an insult, but I take it as one. *Hard to read.* Probably because if I showed her who I really was, this whole movie we're making would be ruined. And in that one second, all the sweet guts and gush of our kissing is erased.

I smile. It's forced. I can tell she can tell it's forced.

Hello, shadows. Missed me, didn't you?

There's a sudden tension in the air. It's all my fault. My moods come in and turn a bright day black. It's happening right now and I have no control over it. The most exquisite girl is in front of me—she kissed me, she likes me, I should be overjoyed. But instead I hollow out.

"I haven't kissed anyone in a while," I say. "I was with this guy who broke up with me and . . . I've had a hard time putting myself together again."

"I haven't kissed anyone since my ex in Oregon," Etta says.

"Seriously?"

"That girl mind-fucked me good," she says.

I feel a little better hearing this, like we have something in common. I take a bite of ice cream. Rocky road. So good, except for the nuts.

"She threatened to kill herself if I broke up with her,"

Etta says. "So . . . I had that fun sword dangling over my head. Honestly, she's half the reason I up and moved so quick. I needed a fresh start away from her."

That better feeling I said I had? Gone now, thanks.

"Did she . . . try to kill herself?" I ask.

"Thank God no. She wasn't *that* crazy."

"That's good," I say, dying inside. *Oh, not* that *crazy. Not like me.*

I can't ever tell her what I did.

We finish the musical, holding hands under the blanket. I'm some kind of fraud. She's going to find out what a mess I am at some point and she'll be gone, just like Jonah.

I'm always too much. There is no such thing as unconditional love.

My mom and Levi are set to get married in less than a month: the first Saturday in June. They're doing it at Stow House, this historic Victorian tucked around the other side of the lake where I tried to off myself. The ceremony is small and a fake Elvis is officiating.

This is what compromise will look like in this household, because my mom was hoping for a traditional ceremony and Levi wanted to elope in Vegas. I consider inviting Etta, but haven't yet. Today Ruby, Stevie, and I are getting fitted at a tailor's. Since none of us could agree on bridesmaid dresses (I wanted violet, Ruby wanted to wear black, Stevie wanted floral print) Mom chose the fabric, which I like to refer to as "velvet vomit," as it's a somewhat atrocious coral pink.

"Good God, you're thin," Mom says as the tailor writes down my measurements. "I thought your clothes looked loose. Are you eating?"

"Isn't she fun?" I ask the tailor, Jean, who (somewhat appropriately) is dressed in a long denim dress with a thousand pockets on it. She has frizzy gray hair and pins in her mouth.

"Mmm," she offers in response.

"What do you weigh?" Mom asks me.

"That's a personal question," I tell her. "How old are you again? How much money's in your bank account?"

She gives me a look that could wither a sunflower.

Honestly, I have lost a couple pounds. Not intentionally. I'm not that hungry lately and forget to eat breakfast sometimes. But Mom is being so obnoxious about it and blowing it into some Thing right now, and I can tell it's because she's anxious about her wedding. She's been biting her lip nonstop for the entire last month.

"You know what's interesting about tapeworms?" Ruby asks, looking up from her phone.

Stevie, my mom, and I all groan in response, because this is not the first nor will it be the last time Ruby offers this prompt.

"They don't even have mouths. They don't eat at all. Technically, they absorb your nutrients through their skin," Ruby says.

"Gross," says Stevie.

"It's not gross, it's smart," Ruby says. "Then they can dedicate most of their energy to creating more eggs."

"Gross," Mom and I say in response.

After the fitting, Mom takes us to In-N-Out and I get a Double-Double and fries and eat the whole thing, just to prove to Mom I'm not starving myself. She checks the trash before throwing it away, like she thought I'd hidden something or tried to trick her.

"Your dad says you stayed up all night the other night," she says to me as she drives us home.

"Finals," I mutter.

I go on my phone and check my email to busy myself. Glory, glory, hallelujah—a landlord wrote me back about seeing an apartment next week. Couldn't have better timing.

"Everyone needs sleep," Mom tells me, as if this is some revelation.

"Technically, bullfrogs don't need sleep," Ruby says, chiming in from the back. "They remain alert when they shut their eyes, and only truly sleep for hibernation purposes—"

"Ruby, enough," Mom shouts. "I don't care about bullfrogs."

"You should," Ruby says. "Because they play a vital role in terrestrial and aquatic nutrient cycling and are key to the ecosystem—"

"Can everyone just shut up?" Stevie says, annoyed.

"Mom, stop picking on Journey. Ruby, shut up about science, nobody cares."

I look back at Stevie, surprised. She's usually the sweet one. And if there was a way to hurt Ruby's feelings, attacking science would be it. Ruby crosses her arms and puts in her earbuds. Mom turns up the classic rock station and drives a little extra hard. Stevie gazes out the cracked window, her hair blowing back from the breeze coming in. She appears older with her hair down like that. It makes me sad for a second, the sight of my youngest sister looking like a teenager. As I obsess about my life and plot my getaway, here my dear little sisters are, growing up. And I've hardly noticed.

When Mom pulls into Dad's driveway, she asks me to stay and talk with her a minute and the girls go inside without me. Goody. Swell. This'll be fun.

"Do you think Ruby's been doing okay?" she asks.

I'd braced myself for a "you're crazy so take your crazy pills" lecture, so I'm a bit shocked by this turn.

"She's the same bitter nerd I know and love," I say.

"I don't know. Something seems off lately. I've been trying to get it out of her. She stopped going to Cindy's and said they're not friends anymore."

Cindy has been Ruby's bestie since grade school. They used wander around our backyard with magnifying glasses and worked on a comic book together for years about a heroic shape-shifting vapor named Misty. I haven't seen her in a long while, now that I think about it.

"Mona said she eats lunch by herself in the library," she says.

Mona is Mom's bestie, who happens to be a math teacher at our junior high, which is rather annoying because she is the nosiest and she tells Mom everything.

"I'll keep an eye out," I say.

I reach for the door.

"And Journey . . . are you really okay?"

"Mom," I say, my door on the handle of the car, just in case I need to flee, because I can feel her anxiety in the air right now, choking as carbon monoxide. "I am doing fine."

"But are you? Your meds—"

I pinch the bridge of my nose between my fingers and sigh. Bipolar I, bipolar II, rate your sadness and happiness on a scale of one to ten, take this many milligrams for your pain. I truly hate the way the world looks at people sometimes, like something entirely inhuman, a problem with an answer, an equation to be solved.

"I just pulled off straight Bs my first semester at college, I'm due to walk with my class at graduation, and my boss said I'm ready for a promotion because of my most excellent pizza dancing skills," I say. "I wish you were proud of me instead of nitpicking. Instead of looking for a black hole for me to fall into."

"You're right," she says. "I'm sorry. I worry."

I've sprung into a state of defensiveness during this conversation, every muscle tense, my heart ready to fly. It takes a moment of silence for her words to sink in. I relax. She's been looking at me the whole time. I finally let myself look back.

"Thank you," I say.

I hug her.

"I *am* proud of you," she says, squeezing tight.

How long, I wonder, does it take to win back trust? How long until the suicide attempt is a thing so far in my past nobody ever thinks it will happen again? How long until it's no longer a part of me?

In late May the fog burns off in the mornings; the days are long and golden and sunny. The eucalyptuses and the oaks and the palm trees glow a particularly shocking shade of green. Santa Barbara is rich with open, pretty space, with long stretches of driving with nothing but nature to interrupt the mess of Spanish-style houses, beach bungalows, and mid-century homes. I've lived here so long I'm blind to it. I ride through it, my mind elsewhere, a buzzing like brown noise playing underneath the gorgeousness.

Why do I hurt? Is hurting just a part of me? Is it my Journey-ness, or my humanity?

Earlier today I washed Jonah's sweatshirt—disgusting to admit, but for the first time since he gave it to me—and the fabric felt stiff and different when I took it out of the dryer. It smelled of detergent. I panicked, wanting to undo it, like I'd killed something dear. And I burst into tears in the laundry room.

I still don't understand why Jonah asked for space when really he wanted infinity. I've been waiting for months for him to call me and for that chance to happen. Remember? He said there was a chance. I've waited here. I've been denying I'm waiting. Feeling guilty and immature, sleeping in Jonah's sweatshirt.

Tonight is prom. Not that I care, I tell myself as I look at my phone and scroll through dim-lit pictures of people all dressed up and sparkling on social media. Marisol sends me a selfie as she gets ready and tells me she misses me. I try to think of a reply, but what to say? I'm a terrible friend. I can't drum up a response. I'm still angry and embarrassed she told the world what a basket case I am. It seems simpler to say nothing for now.

Scroll, scroll, scroll.

I know what I'm looking for, and I hate myself for it: pictures of Jonah. What do I care about prom and the "Night of a Thousand Stars" decorated with tinfoil planets and twinkling lights at the ballroom of a local hotel? I mean, really. I'm in college now. None of this matters to me. Please explain to me why, then, my throat burns as I sit alone in a quiet house with nothing but the sound of the dishwasher running. I would have been miserable had I gone. I don't care about this. I don't care so much I want to scream.

I put on my sneakers, grab Jonah's sweatshirt, and leave the house, biting the inside of my cheek. I concentrate on my breath even though I want to leap out of my skin.

Tonight is prom and I don't care.

It's dark outside. My dad is barbecuing tofu outside because that's what Gary has done to our household: she has inflicted tofu upon us. I fold up the sweatshirt and head out the door before I think too hard and chicken out. I jog to Jonah's in two minutes. It's going to be simple, me opening his mailbox and depositing this article of clothing inside, a transaction.

I know Jonah's house like I know my own. I have played here since I was a child. I know what his parents' cars look like, and know they park them in the driveway unless they're both teaching late that night, which is how I know that now, they're not home.

I know what Jonah's car looks like, and am surprised to see it there, and a little satisfied, even, knowing he might have skipped prom, too. I know how to open the gate on the side of his house from the outside, with a reach and pop over and a *click*. I know where Jonah's room is, in the back near the fig tree, and that he keeps his window propped open with a mildewed copy of Shakespeare's complete works. I know this is probably all kinds of crazy and illegal, but I used to do this all the time when we were together. Late at night, sometimes, I would come and sneak into his room and lie in his bed with him. Or I'd leave him notes or little gifts on his desk to greet him when he woke up. Looking into the sliver I can see between his curtains, everything's the same as it ever was. Same posters in the same places on the walls, same row of cacti on his desk, even the same copy of *Infinite Jest* on his desk with the bookmark, swear to God, in the same place. He's such a poseur, I think through tears. *Infinite Jest*. He never even liked reading all that much, unless you count biographies on bands.

The only difference is the other girl lying with him on the bed.

They're watching something on his laptop, the flickering light illuminating them blue. Her head rests on his chest and they are under a blanket, eyes transfixed on the screen. The girl? It's Madison James. I want to scream a series of swear words but realize that I've already crossed enough of a line here that I should probably just leave and keep my shame-tainted rage to myself. And I do. But not before picking up a palm-sized rock and throwing it at his window. By the time he is probably able to get up and investigate, I've slipped out the side gate quietly, the latch clicking into place. Before I even realize it I'm up the street back home, sputtering tears all over the place, with nowhere to bury my face but this stupid sweatshirt that smells inhumanely clean.

Fuck. It's fine; I knew this would happen. In fact, I knew this was happening, months ago. I've already kissed another girl, so why does it feel like someone is stepping on my heart with a cleat?

I do not go into my house. I walk back along Calle Real, a main drag that runs along the fenced-off freeway on one side and the lake I live near on the other. I walk up the overpass and look down at the cars, full of people who all know where they're going at full speed. The sky is so endless and star-scattered—real stars, not tinfoil ones—and all I can think is, my astronomy professor was right: knowing how immense the universe is, how most of it is unexplained dark matter, it does threaten my sense of self-importance. On a night like this, though, when my brain sits ready to eat me alive, a threat to my self-importance is not only deserved, it is welcomed. I am not that important. Whether I go to prom or I don't, we are just stardust in a sea of so much black.

For a second, my feet itch to jump. It would take one second, one tiny second.

There's a French phrase *l'appel du vide*, "the call of the void"—the instinctive desire to leap from tall places. I press my body against the railing and look down at the headlights zooming by, the sucking noise of each passing car. The sight holds a violent allure.

In an impulsive moment—all feeling, no thought—I throw the sweatshirt over the side and watch it fall near the median. Goodbye, Jonah. For real. Heart racing, I turn my back to the void and head home.

When I do slip into the house, I'm surprised to see the light of my room is on. Dad sits there, on my bed, head in his hands. And why, hello, feeling of violation. Not because I have anything to hide, but because no one needs to be sitting among my dirty underwear and chip bags and dead cacti buried under a pile of wigs I never wear. I've tried to be better, I've rid myself of some stuff, but come on, I'm still me. I'm still mostly a mess.

"Dad?" I ask.

"Oh, Journey," he says, getting up. He looks so tired, like he fell asleep there with his head in his hands and just startled at my entrance. "Where the hell have you *been*? I've been calling your phone—"

"It's dead."

"I had no idea where you went—"

"On a walk. Dad, I've been gone less than an hour."

"I was imagining—I thought, I don't know," he says.

He shudders with a small sob.

"You didn't really think I was going to kill myself."

"I didn't *know*, Journey."

"Have I been acting suicidal?" I ask, offended that he would think this.

"I know it's your prom night, and I don't know—am I supposed to believe you would have told me?" he asks, raising his voice, which makes him near unrecognizable. My dad doesn't raise his voice. He gets quieter so you have to lean in. If my mother is fire, my father is water.

"Yes I would tell you!" I yell.

"Like you told me you went off medication?" he yells back. "Like that?"

I burn with this comment, then wither, like a paper ball turned to ash. Because I see in his crazy eyes and hear in his raised voice not meanness, but something shaken off its center. A bloodcurdling *fear*. A resentment and a sorrow miles deep and months old. My nose gets stuffy, my eyes wet, in one second.

I'm ready to scream "Get out of my fucking room!" when I instead hold my breath in for a moment and then let it out. I hate that he's right. Part right. I haven't been honest with him and Mom. And this new, painful paranoia of theirs—that's the price. Dad watches me, waiting, maybe, for an explosion. But I just breathe in and out again.

"Can I be alone, please?" I ask.

"Sure," he says, backing out with a bewildered look on his face.

He shuts the door, and I let loose.

I sink onto my bed and cry into my pillow.

After all the work I've done. Counting breaths. Taking walks. Dancing like an idiot in a pizza costume. Getting through a semester of big girl school.

Do they really think I'm the same as I was eight months ago?

Dear future self,

Please tell me it's over at some point. At some point, your mistake is erased. Your sin is forgiven. You don't have to feel guilty for what you did, or feel scared you'll do it again, and no one who knows you will associate you with that dumb thing that belongs to you and you only. You'll be able to pass Tylenol in a drugstore and not get a sick, bitter taste in your mouth. You'll be able to see the lake for what it is, a lake, and associate it only with the joy of childhood bike rides and your mom's wedding. Dear future self, I thought time was an eraser. It is, isn't it?

I told the other lovely humans I share a shift with that I have a deep affinity for poetry and it turns out I am not alone. Lydia was a creative writing major "way back in the Jurassic Period" and wrote her thesis on Anne Sexton. JD reads experimental stuff they find online by people I've never heard of. Beatriz has a deep love for prose poetry, poems that almost read more like stories to me, poems polka-dotted with Spanish. For the past few shifts, we each bring our favorites and when it's dead, when the lines are quiet, we read to each other and discuss.

Tonight, Beatriz brought some fat candles she made to add to the ambience. She makes candles, earrings, sews patchwork skirts together; she's crafty like that. The candles smell earthy when she lights them. She puts them on the long table she shares with JD and another on the table I share with Lydia. JD gets up and turns off the lights.

"I feel like I should put on some music," JD says, and scrolls through their phone. A moment later, some New Agey synth sounds emanate. They giggle. "Too much?"

"Nothing's ever too much for a poetry reading between suicidal compadres," Lydia says.

"Oh, come on," Beatriz says. "We're not suicidal, don't say that."

"I consider 'suicidal' to be like 'alcoholic,'" Lydia says. "You might not drink anymore but you've always got the disease."

"Well, that's dark as shit," JD says. "I don't agree with that. I tried, I survived, I'm here, I will always be here. This world is stuck with me." JD looks especially at me. "Don't listen to her."

"JD's right. I'm just a bitter old woman with major depression," Lydia says.

"I have depression, too, okay? But it's not, like, my identity," JD says. "Most of my life I take my Zoloft and then I don't even notice it's there."

"Lucky you," Lydia says.

"Have you ever tried acupuncture?" Beatriz asks them both.

"No," they answer together, in a pointed tone.

I don't say anything. Tongue officially bitten. I want to weigh in, but I'm not sure where I fit in here. I have meds prescribed in my name. I have a diagnosis. I'm not comfortable with any of it. But it makes me think twice to see these wise humans who I respect so much talking so openly about disorders, medication, things I've resisted so hard.

"There are so many paths to happiness," Beatriz says.

Beatriz always has to be the peacemaker. It's partly why she's so damn good at taking calls. She has this soft-spoken, focused way of talking anyone down.

"This one's a fun one," Lydia says, opening a battered paperback. It has coffee rings on the back of it and looks like something you'd find in a free box. "It's a poem called 'I Have Had to Learn to Live With My Face.'"

I inhale, lean back, taking in those words. Imagining a mirror, a long one, my dusty, imperfect face staring back at me. Lydia's voice is gravelly, deep, as she reads; I hear whiskey and tears. I hear age and fire. I lose myself in the rhythm and the words. Isn't poetry magic, the way it stops life in its tracks, the way it quiets the you in you? That's why I love it so.

I am barely breathing, I am so enthralled and aquiver in the listening. But then the sound of a phone interrupts. The long, loud, deep-throated ring of a rotary phone that vibrates the table underneath me. It's Lydia's. Beatriz flips the lights on, blows the candles out. Lydia puts down the book and groans as she moves her rolly chair back into the desk. She's clearly been in pain the past few weeks, her back a constant ache. "Goddamn bodies," she told me when I asked today. "Never make the dumb mistake of getting old, you hear?"

(Dear future self, you listening?)

"Crisis line, this is Lydia. Why, hello, Davis. No, you've never told me about your fascination with miniature trains. I'm setting my alarm right now for ten, just so you know . . ."

Maybe hang out this weekend? Etta texts, along with a video of adorable baby goats snuggling with puppies. I watch the video on my bus ride home, smiling. There's so much I want to say to her. And I do want to hang out this weekend. I start writing a whole paragraph about how distracted I've been lately, how I'm sorry I haven't been answering her texts in a timely way, and erase it and instead just give her a thumbs-up sign over the goat video.

I put my phone away and stare out the window at the dark town, the shuttered shops, the empty bus stops. How mournful and lonely the familiar world appears at night.

Once I get off the bus I'm walking past the garish glow of the supermarket at the end of my neighborhood, the quiet movie theater, the dark hardware store with its potted poppies out in rows, my sneakers pitter-pattering the pavement on this cricket-chirping night, everyone tucked neatly in their houses, cars quiet and shining under the streetlamps, front windows curtain-drawn and golden from hidden lamplight. And then I hear the squeak of a bicycle tire. A jolt of adrenaline freezes me to a stop. I don't know what I'm expecting. It's an empty street on an empty night and my first reaction is inexplicable terror. But instead I whip around and I see a sight that drops my innards down two stories.

There, five feet away, is Jonah Fucking Patterson.

I know every minute detail about him because he is not just a boy. He was a home. He was a country, he was a continent. Then I forced myself to forget him because to remember him was to love him and to love him was to lose my mind. But now here he is and even in the darkness, even with his

Thrasher hoodie pulled up around his head and tied tight, his eyes are bright enough to light the entire scene.

"Hey," he says.

"Hi?" I ask.

We don't say anything. I stand there in silence. I burn. Across the street, just a few hundred feet away, through the tall grasses and under the gnarled oak tree where we once first kissed, I tried to die. It all floods back to me, the pain, the pain so big it didn't just change me. It warped me. It made me question my identity, my sanity, how the two are interrelated. In one second, I look at him and I want him back so bad it has a taste in my mouth, sweet and overdone, burnt sugar.

"I was just thinking about you," he says.

"Well, you must have manifested this, then, right? Magical thinking?"

He and I had a passionate conversation about magical thinking once when we read the same book on it. When we thought we were important enough to conjure up realities.

"Must be," he says.

He has a maddeningly dry delivery, a suggestion of a smile but only a suggestion. I can never really tell how funny he finds me, or means to be. This is why, when we were friends and he first told me he loved me so bad it hurt him inside, I thought he was joking.

"Oh, Jonah," I say, looking away. "I hate you."

"Don't hate me," he says. "I don't hate you."

"What do you, then?" I ask. "You abandoned me. Never

called. Ended up with the girl I knew you'd been drooling over the whole last stretch of our relationship. What do you, then?"

"I'm an idiot, Journey," he says quietly, keeping his stupid gaze on me.

His statement shocks me so I run out of thoughts and words for a second.

"I knew if I reached out to you, well . . . I'd fall in love with you again," he says, voice cracking. "Because I can't resist you."

"Now I hate you even more," I murmur softly.

And I can tell, in the way his gaze hasn't wavered once, the hunger in it, the familiar hunger in it like the hunger that used to precede a long, deep kiss—I know, in a complete sucker punch to my soul, that he still loves me.

This I never, ever expected.

I moved on, see. I moved on not in some triumphant progressive march but in a wounded, half-dead zombie lurch. I moved on from him not because I wanted to, but because I realized that lingering and yearning for him would unravel me. I gave up on the idea there was a chance. I ripped the Band-Aid off and threw it in the garbage because, girl, that wound needed air to heal.

"What about Madison?" I ask.

"I'm not with her anymore," he says.

I'd be lying if I said I didn't fight the urge to grin from the sudden schadenfreude.

"Oh" is all I say.

"It was a rebound," he tells me. "She's so great, but . . . she's not you."

His mouth is a straight line the whole time. A straight line, revealing nothing. But his eyes. His goddamn eyes. Even this short, sudden run-in with him has me wanting so badly I swear I never wanted anyone like this and never will. Not even Etta and her red, perfect lips.

He reaches out and touches my arm. This used to be his favorite sweater of mine, the one with the roses, cashmere. "It's not too late, is it?"

"Why are you doing this?" I ask him, pulling my arm back. "Have you not hurt me enough already?"

My eyes prickle with tears, the words a lump in my throat.

"You were my best friend, you stupid asshole," I say, the words coming out hoarsely. "That was what hurt the most. Fine, don't be my boyfriend, but you didn't even care I tried to kill myself. You turned around and walked away from me."

"I was scared."

"Oh, well, boo-hoo."

"I was wrong. I'm sorry."

Those five words stop me short. I was ready to go on, berate him, tear him to pieces—but those five words were really all I ever wanted to hear.

For a moment, I can't even speak.

"You coming to graduation?" he asks.

"Yeah. My parents paid for the stupid outfit, I figure I owe it to them."

"You look like you're doing great," he says. "Marisol says you got a job, you're a semester deep into city college . . . that's amazing."

"Finals were last week," I say, unable to help myself from bragging just a little bit. "I can't believe I managed to get Bs."

"I can."

I roll my eyes.

"I'll be there, too, next semester. You'll have to show me around."

Now he smiles. And when he does, Lord help me. The word *charming* was invented for Jonah Patterson's wide, shining smile.

"How about you download a map and show yourself around next semester? I have a girlfriend." Yes, I exaggerate. *Girlfriend* is a term that might be a slight exaggeration, but how I enjoy the pinch of the news and the way he ever so slightly flinches at it as he keeps smiling.

"Good for you," he says. "She's one lucky girl."

The lump is still in my throat, no matter what words I say. Inhale. Exhale. The air feels colder somehow, stinging my eyeballs.

"I gotta go," I say.

His moon-blue eyes linger on me. They know me too well. They know every inch of my body, every ounce of my madness, every me I have been since I was a child. I feel naked. It's invasive. And yet, I am so myself with him. I don't have to explain anything. He knows, without any words. He just knows.

"Can we hang out again sometime?" he asks. "Like old times? Be buddies again?"

"My mom and Levi are getting married," I tell him. "You can come to that with me if you want. I mean, you were practically family, until you ditched me like a coward."

"I'm honored you're asking me," he says. "I'd love to come."

Why did I just do that? I was going to ask Etta. I really was. But, I don't know—even after everything, Jonah is a part of my past, my childhood, my family. It feels right to invite him instead, even if he's not my boyfriend anymore. He and I walk in silence, his bike wheels clicking as they rotate. When we get to my dad's house, he comments on the peonies in the yard, compliments my hair and how long it's gotten, my new necklace, because Jonah Patterson is the kind of boy who notices such things. He hugs me on the lawn and in one whiff of him—his stinging aftershave and his lemony soap—the smell that lingered in the sweatshirt so long—I get a wave of desire so big it threatens to eat every bit of progress I've earned since we parted ways last time.

I say goodbye. I head upstairs, get into my bed. But in the dark, here, under my covers, my heart is beating so wildly. I am thinking of Etta and our kisses and our laughter. I am thinking of Jonah and the mountain of emotions I hold for him. I am thinking of life and how wicked it is and how beautiful it is, the twisted strangeness of a lone walk home that turns into a reunion with a boy who broke my heart across from a lake where I tried to kill myself.

I wouldn't have wanted a yearbook—why commemorate the hardest year of my life, the school I left behind, the connections I no longer have? But my parents paid for one. I get to my dad's one night and open a brown box and find it there, shiny with our year screaming across the front in stencil lettering, the inner pages stinking of sweet glue and glossy paper. I look at my senior portrait, taken just weeks before I tried to end my own life. I feel so deeply for past me I shudder with a sob. And there's Jonah, that Jonah I loved, that Jonah I could maybe love again, and I recognize everything about him, from where his sideburns end to the collar of the shirt he's wearing. And Marisol, with her lop-sided smile and her old glasses. The nostalgia aches. We're already not them.

I flip pages, taking in the year I didn't have—the dances, the clubs, the student elections, the gags and inside jokes I don't understand. And then I get to the song team page and read down the list of girls' names. My breath stops short when I see the name *Nicola "Coco" Albierti*.

"No shit," I say aloud to no one, my finger tracing the outside of her flawless face, her careless hair.

*Aha.*

So that's you, Coco.

So that's been you all along.

My phone rings and I slip my headset on. I recite my greeting, the recording that lives in my throat. "Crisis line, this is Journey."

"My friend," Coco says. "There you are."

"Hey, Coco," I say.

It's strange saying it, this time, because I know who she is now. It's been weeks since she called. I picture her now in a way I never did before. I can see her, Nicola Albierti, there in her brown two-story house on Covington, lying on her bed, her hair a glossy spill on her pillow, her eyebrows shapely and striking, her eyes big and brown, her skin olive and flawless. I am not proud to admit how long I've stared at yearbook photos of her and social media pictures of her since I connected the dots and learned who she was.

"It's been weird," she says.

"What's been?"

"All of it." She's quiet. No background noise. Just the soft buzz of silence. "I'm drunk. I feel like I'm losing it," she says. "If there's an *it*. You can only think you're not alive for so long. I've been doing all I can to shock myself out of it, Journey. Drinking my mom's wine she buys in bulk for book club. Kissing boys like the world is ending. I crashed my car the other day and . . . you wanna know a secret? I did it on purpose."

"You crashed your car?!"

"Into a fence. At ten miles an hour. Don't flip. It's not like it was an actual suicide thing. I mean, I know where my dad keeps his gun. If I'd really wanted to off myself, I wouldn't be here talking to you."

I swallow.

"And guess what? It didn't do anything. It didn't even damage my fender, let alone shock me into life again." She exhales loudly. "I want it to stop."

I've never heard her this somber, this lifeless. She's almost someone else. And now that I can see her in my mind—see who she actually is, imagine her in her entirety—she's like a stranger all over again.

"That sounds so hard," I say.

"I've had this happen before, but never this long," she says softly. "Never for, like, months. I have gone so long now without feeling real that I forget what it's like. It's not even scary anymore. It's just . . . nothing. You know what it's like to feel nothing?"

I've felt too much, so much. I've wanted to die aplenty. I've had black holes open up in my path at moments when I least expected them. I've been so lonely I've been a raindrop. So upset I've been a roll of thunder. I've watched life happen outside me, spinning, moving, golden, and I could not touch it. But I have never really felt nothing.

"I can imagine," I say.

"You're so lucky," she says. "Because you're not me. I look at people all day long and think that now. I wish I were you, because you're not me." She sniffles. "And I'm walking soon. I'm supposed to give a speech about—of all things—hope."

"What are you going to say about hope?" I ask.

"A bunch of bullshit, of course." She laughs. "A bunch of memorized butt-kissing pseudo-Zen bullshit I stole from my mom's self-help library."

"Read me some of it."

"Journey," she says, sounding tired. "I didn't call you to practice my speech. I don't even know if I'm going to give it."

"Sometimes, we just have to plug on through, even when we're not feeling it. And later, you'll look back and be happy you did."

"Or not," she says. "Maybe I won't look back at all."

"What do you mean?"

I swallow. I look up at my fellow hotline volunteers, see they're all on the phone, having their own intimate, murmured conversations into their headsets, no eye contact. I swivel forward again and stare at the poster above my desk that is a crappy clip art printout of two hands holding a heart. I can't tell you how long I've stared at that picture, so long the shapes start becoming meaningless, more than hands, less than hands, more than a heart, less than a heart.

"I want to end this. I want to end myself at the height of me, stop this horrible nothing that is my existence."

She starts crying.

"I want everyone to remember me as being something. Not this nothing person I am inside. That should be how everyone remembers me. On a stage, in a cap and gown, young and beautiful forever."

My own eyes fill up with tears. "Nicola, if you're thinking about ending your life, you really need to get help."

She stops a sob and the line gets quiet.

"Wait—what did you call me?" she asks.

Oh no.

I didn't.

*Did* I?

"You said Nicola," she insists. "How do you . . . ?"

"I said Coco," I lie.

"I have to go," she says.

And the line clicks.

I guess it really was her, then. I was right about "Coco" being Nicola.

I stare at the tabletop in front of me, the useless binder, the stupid clip art on the wall. I take my headset off and listen to the quiet chatter of the other hotline volunteers.

"No offense, but your so-called friend sounds like a real piece of shit."

"In psychology, we call that 'projection.' You ever heard that term?"

"Have you tried acupuncture?"

*Suicidal ideation is different than suicidal intent,* Wolf always says. Maybe she was only saying the words out loud to frighten herself. Maybe she'll call back. She always does. And when she does, I'll say all the right things. I'll make sure she gets help.

Things could be a lot better for her, if she had a Wolf in her life.

I go to the bathroom, sit in a stall, wait for the mean self-destructive feelings to pass.

"Decompress?" Lydia asks me when I come back in. "You look . . . ruffled."

Her words make me angry, because she always looks ruffled. Her hair's a mess. Her eyes are bloodshot. She's knitting something that honestly looks like entrails.

"I'm fine," I say.

I am totally, totally fine.

For the next couple of days, I keep my eye on social media, checking Nicola Albierti's profile, noting that everything looks okay. And it does. Just smiling pics of friends and meals and gym trips and kitten memes. I channel Wolf and decide I've been overreacting. Nicola Albierti is not in the danger zone. She said she felt like she *wanted* to end it, not that she was *planning* to. Of all people, I should know there is a huge difference. Maybe she just needed to say the idea out loud to exorcise it.

But still I think how weird it'll be, being at graduation in just a week and listening to Nicola Albierti give her speech about hope, knowing she feels dead inside.

I am steeping like a human tea bag in a hot tub with Etta in the dark cricket-noisy night (yes, the same hot tub I skinny-dipped in the first night I almost died). During our quiet conversation about the semester ending soon, I confess I'm technically still a high school senior, expecting her to freak out a little bit. Instead, after assurances that I am indeed eighteen years old, she asks me if she can come watch me graduate. I don't immediately say yes.

I ran into Jonah the other night and asked him to my mom's wedding, and I've said nothing about it to Etta. Here she and I are, joking, flirting, touching, but she doesn't know a thing about me.

And across town there is Jonah, who knows everything about me, and totally wrecked me.

And I'm so conflicted, because part of me wants her—and another part wants to push her away.

It's like we're playing a game, she and I.

"What?" Etta asks, her hand on my thigh, squeezing. She has a damn hard squeeze, one that both tickles the crap out of me and hurts at the same time.

I yelp.

"You don't want me to come? You embarrassed by me?" she asks.

"Yeah right," I say. "I'm embarrassed by myself."

"Stop," she says, and leans over to kiss me, which makes every nerve in my body stand to attention. I get lost in her kiss for a minute, my fingers tangled in her hair. The Brazilians have a word for that, by the way: *cafuné,* to tenderly run your fingertips through your lover's locks. Those romantics.

I doubt so much with Etta, but never for a moment do I

doubt how completely magnetic she is and how completely attracted to her I am.

My problem is, I keep comparing. Even now, in the bliss of this kiss, I'm thinking of the ways she kisses differently than Jonah. How she has this grip to her kiss, and Jonah had this ease. How her tongue feels in my mouth, dominating, when Jonah's was passive, all softness. How I don't know what to do with my hands with Etta, if I'm allowed to, like, feel her up. With Jonah it was so clear how far he wanted me to go (far, as far as possible). But I don't know the rules here.

My problem is: thinking.

Etta pulls away, easy, and keeps her arms around my neck, looking into my eyes. The hot tub steams around us. She floats on top of me, straddling me, and kisses me again. I like this feeling, of being straddled. With Jonah, I did all the straddling.

See what I mean? Even when I'm thinking positive, I'm still comparing.

"But seriously," she says, holding me, her head on my shoulder. I breathe in the sweet coconut smell of her hair. "Can't I come?"

"It's dumb," I say. "Pomp and circumstance. Muumuu gowns. You did it last year. I don't want to put you through that."

"I want to be put through that," she insists.

She's pulling my bikini strings on my back, loosening

them, and now my top is floating in the water. She's kissing my neck.

I let her kiss me; I kiss her back; I taste chlorine; we laugh at the lipstick marks all over our faces. She has no idea. She has no idea about me. I can't let Etta anywhere near my shadows. It's like the hotline: I'm a different me here, one who has never screwed everything up.

I'm a me who gets to third base with a girl in the hot tub.

After we dry off and go in and shower together, I get dressed to go home. She sits there biting her nails as I wait for the Lyft to arrive.

"I really like you," she tells me, her eyes flickering. "Sometimes I get the feeling you're not all here. Am I making this up?"

"I'm here," I say, even though she's absolutely right. I'm here and elsewhere.

"If something was up, you'd tell me, right?" she asks.

She has a towel wrapped around her head, and for the first time maybe ever, she lacks her signature red lipstick.

"Of course!" I say.

It sounds so fake, so unlike me, so exclamation-pointy . . . I can tell she doesn't believe me.

We hug goodbye, a quick hug, and I hate myself for the relief I feel in the Lyft away from her. I don't understand myself. There should be a word for the simultaneous feeling of wanting Etta's nearness and wanting to run from her. I don't get how I can be so attracted to someone, so on-paper perfect for someone, and yet have a mind that keeps wandering back to an ex who shattered me.

I feel disgusting as I look at myself in the mirror tonight, getting ready for bed, a hint of lipstick still lingering around the edges of my lips. I feel like a bad person, a user, because even though I like Etta and I think she's the healthiest, most amazing person who's ever liked me, all I want is to run.

I put on a hideous gold muumuu, one a company had the gall to charge a hundred bucks for, and a silly matching cap with a tassel and a name as attractive as it looks, *mortarboard*, and merge with the sea of my fellow graduates on the football field, all in rows of plastic chairs under the terrible, terrible sunshine. A block away, calm as a storybook picture, orange orchards climb up the farm-striped hill. It's beautiful. It's wonderful. I'm going to be sick.

I'm supposed to be proud, or at least nostalgic. Although I know someday I will be looking back on this, I feel nothing right now but wanting this to be over with. This is no longer my scene, and I've never loved crowds and ceremony anyway. My fellow students have blown up beach balls and are painting their faces. The marching band plays cheeseball tunes.

"I didn't think you'd be here," Marisol says to me, sneaking up from behind.

I turn around, blindsided by her presence. Not that

I shouldn't have seen this coming—I've just been so preoccupied. We are standing in the aisle between seats before hundreds of butts sit in hundreds of foldable plastic chairs.

"I mean, deigning to come back and grace this horrible place with your presence," she says. "Are you going to ignore me in person, too? Or is that just something you do on your phone? Acting like you need 'space.' I mean, you couldn't even be original."

Marisol's manicured hands are shaking. She's not one to be mean. She probably rehearsed this speech this morning in front of her mirror. Again, I get a wave of déjà vu.

"I can't deal with the stress of fighting with you right now," I tell her.

"I never wanted to fight in the first place," she responds.

Her dad's entire family flew here from Puerto Rico for this. I spot them, a large family all in blue shirts with a sign that says "FELICITACIONES, MARISOL." Her parents wave madly at us. A man next to her dad with a long ponytail and aviators blows an air horn.

I take my seat, stepping on multiple toes and sticking my butt inadvertently into many faces as I find my place. Stuck, as with every yearbook, with the other Smiths, of which there are many. Isabelle Smith, who is eating a Costco-sized bag of Cheetos and has managed to get orange fingerprints all over her muumuu, somehow rendering the outfit less attractive, which I didn't realize was possible. Oliver Smith, who is wearing an umbrella hat unironically because he is whatever the next shade darker than albino is.

Jonah flashes me the peace sign and a maddeningly attractive half smile as he sits with the Ps.

I scan the audience, a sea of pinhead-sized people in the bleachers. Microbes, from here. Somewhere out there, Mom, Dad, Levi, Gary, Ruby, and Stevie all sit together like some new weird fusion of a family. I know Etta was hurt I didn't invite her. I wonder if she came anyway—but nah, she wouldn't.

It's bizarre being here, baking under the sun with my high school class. Like I stepped back in time. I thought I escaped these people, this place. These familiar strangers I aged with, some since pre-K. Now here we are, dressed alike, lined up in rows, ready to confront adulthood. Above my head, a cloud shaped like a hand waving, or maybe a bird. I get a strange sensation, warm invisible fingers on my neck, colors brightening. There should be a word for a moment you suspect you'll be looking back on later with nostalgia.

In the As, there up front in the left section (I'm in the right, near middle), first row, I see the shine of Nicola Albierti's long brunette hair and her movie star sunglasses as she laughs with fellow prep Laney Allston. Electricity surges through me. I open the program and see her name there, right after Principal Patrick, delivering a speech called "We've Been Given the World, Now How Can We Save It?" I watch Nicola do hair flip after hair flip. But then I see her lean down when she thinks no one is looking and reach under her chair, into her purse. She pulls something out—something flashing, a moment of silver—and she messes under her gown, tucking it away somewhere.

It happens so fast, no one saw it but me. But I almost pee myself. Because suddenly I'm remembering:

*Maybe I won't look back at all.*

*That should be how everyone remembers me. On a stage, in a cap and gown, young and beautiful forever.*

*I want to end myself at the height of me.*

*I know where my dad keeps his gun.*

*I didn't call you to practice my speech. I don't even know if I'm going to give it.*

I saw the flash. Something long and silver; something she's quietly adjusting in the neck of her gown, even now. This is a girl who has nothing to lose. Who wants to go out with a bang. This stupid moment on a stage in her cap and gown, that's the moment she's decided she doesn't want to live beyond.

Principal Patrick's speech booms in my ears, words with no meaning, and then everyone's applauding except me.

If I call the cops, they won't get here fast enough. Breathing's suddenly a task. She's really going to do it. And she's going to do it *here*. *Now*. In front of all these people.

Inhale, exhale. Inhale. Inhale. Inhale.

She called the hotline and told me what she told me because *why*?

Why tell someone you're going to kill yourself before

you kill yourself unless you want to be stopped? Remember, Journey, what that was like, standing in front of the medicine cabinet mirror, phone to your ear, telling Jonah you wanted to kill yourself. Did you tell him that because you wanted him to know, or because you wanted him to stop you?

The crowd is still applauding as Principal Patrick sits down in his foldable chair onstage and Nicola gets up from her seat to go up the stairs.

"Nicola," I yell into the applause.

Oh God, right now? I had no time to think this through. I stand up, program flapping away in the breeze, and make my way out of the row. My classmates I pass give me stink eyes, but they don't realize.

"Nicola!" I yell as the applause dies and Nicola takes her place behind the podium. "Nicola, wait!"

I run full speed toward the stage and I hear the hush—it's weird how you can hear a hush, same as a sound, a thing, not an absence, a heavy, heavy thing—as it ripples through the crowd. Nicola stands frozen in front of the mic. Principal Patrick and Mrs. Marston get up from their foldable chairs with pure confusion on their faces, arms out as if I'm a beast to be tamed.

"What is going on?" Nicola says into the mic, then backs up.

"Don't kill yourself!" In a second with no thinking, all body and no mind, I lunge at her so she can't reach into her dress.

In a moment that, like the car crash, feels like slow motion, she falls backward and I fall on top of her on the wood stage, which is hard, much harder than I would have imagined, had I taken the time to imagine.

She yells.

"It's Journey," I tell her loudly. "I—I had to stop you."

Her eyes, up close, are beautiful, deep set, so brown they're almost black, her mouth twitching. I can see her thick makeup. I can smell her—lavender—and feel the gun between us, a hard shape between our bodies. Holy shit, I can feel it, the gun, the touch of cold metal. Her expression stays frozen, but her eyes change. First they quiver with fear, then they flicker with confusion, then they glaze over with something close to rage.

"Get *off* me," she roars.

I feel hands on my shoulders, pulling me off. It's Principal Patrick.

"Ladies," he keeps saying. "Ladies."

The crowd starts buzzing with a mix of uncomfortable laughter, murmuring, and, somewhere, a distant air horn.

"I don't even know her," Nicola tells him, standing up and pointing an acrylic nail at my face. "She's fucking crazy."

"She's got a gun," I tell Principal Patrick as I scramble to my feet. "It's under her gown; I saw her put it there."

Principal Patrick, rubbing his enormous bald head with one hand, pulling his tie with the other, looks from her to me to her again.

"I felt it just now," I tell him. "She has one."

"Lift up your gown, Ms. Albierti," Mrs. Marston says.

"What?" Nicola shrieks.

"Lift up your graduation robe, Ms. Albierti, and show us you do not have a gun," Mrs. Marston says, voice raised.

The mic, though a couple feet away, is picking this up. Echoing in the speakers. Everyone in the crowd is, understandably, rapt. Facing us like we're players on a stage and it's the worst performance of all time.

Nicola gives me a look heavy with hatred and lifts her gown. There, tucked into the cleavage of her V-neck dress, is the shining silver thing. But it's not a gun.

It's a flask.

Mrs. Marston holds out her hand. Nicola gives her the flask. Mrs. Marston opens the flask and sniffs it, wincing from the vodka's stink that even I can smell from here. She puts the cap back on.

"Is this the 'gun'?" Mrs. Marston asks me.

"Maybe," I say. "I guess."

She wasn't going to kill herself; there was no emergency. My pulse does not get the message. Mrs. Marston turns to Principal Patrick and the two whisper.

Here we stand in front of hundreds of familiar strangers, me and this familiar stranger.

"I can't believe this," Nicola whispers to me, without looking me in the eye, keeping her gaze fixed on her four-inch heels.

"I was trying to save you."

"Take your seat," Mrs. Marston tells me sharply, and hands the flask to Principal Patrick. "You too," she tells Nicola.

We get off the stage in a state of shock, Nicola taking her seat and not looking back at me. Everyone's faces in the audience are frozen in the same state of lustful intrigue and Principal Patrick takes the stage and blathers on about technical difficulties. So many eyes watching me like I'm dynamite ready to blow. And you know what? They're right. They all see me, really see me, and it's terrible.

My parents are up there. And they see me.

Jonah is in the audience. And he sees me.

I couldn't even give them this moment.

I couldn't even let this be normal.

I don't take my seat. I don't care. I take my gown off and go running through the football field, away from the school and toward the parking lot, eyes full. And there, I sit between two cars and I bawl my eyes out. This, today, right here, is what the Germans call *verschlimmbessern*: to screw everything up when trying to make it better.

Dear future self,

If you even exist, I hope you have a terrible memory. I hope you completely wipe clean the worst day of your life when you ruined your graduation ceremony and everyone else's. I hope you forget not only those horrid details, but the details of the phone *call that came later that day from Davina, who told you that you violated hotline ethics rules by taking a call from a familiar person and then confronting said familiar person, and then let you go. Let you go? What am I saying. Fired you. Fired you from a volunteer position because, future self, that's how pathetic you once were, if you even are anymore.*

My phone is blowing up. My dad is knocking on my door. He comes in and tries to talk to me but I refuse, not moving, mannequin girl, trying to get to a place where, like Nicola, I do not exist.

"Dammit, Journey," he says, snapping his fingers in front of my face. "Do I need to call the doctor? I'll call the doctor."

"No," I mutter, angry that I have to break catatonia to answer. "Just leave me alone."

He breathes a sigh of relief and leaves the room.

On my phone, I see Etta's texted multiple times. Thank God she doesn't know, because I didn't invite her. Marisol called, too. So did Jonah. So did quite a few numbers with no names.

Within hours I was dismissed from the hotline. I'll never get to set foot in that Victorian house that was my Tuesday-night home again. And yet, with all these mistakes lined up in a row in front of me like pink pills, I still find myself just wishing I were dead, because it would be so simple.

I weep.

I read the texts from Etta. Dumb texts about musicals we should watch and how much she wants to kiss me. She doesn't even know me. She doesn't know what a black pit I am inside.

"Hey," I say, recording a voice message. "It's been fun, Etta, really, it has. But I can't keep it up." I stare at the phone, the seconds on the message adding up. "See, I'm a complete and utter mess. I've tried to keep it from you. You're so . . . amazing." My eyes fill with tears. "I am crazy. And I don't mean that in some manic pixie dream girl way. I'm not fun crazy. I'm just crazy. I do crazy shit, I say crazy things, I should be medicated but I can't bring myself to medicate myself because it's never worked and because most of the time I don't feel crazy." I wipe my nose, my eyes, holding the record button. "I did something dumb and big today, though, and I need space, okay? I need space. Maybe an infinite amount of space. I need you to get as far away from me as possible and not look back. Please don't try to contact me. I'm sorry." And *send*.

I delete her contact from my phone. Then I put my phone in the sink and run water over it, breaking it forever. It's that old feeling, remember? The *fuck it* feeling. The *burn it all down* feeling. I've lost it again, so much so that I lie in bed in my clothes all night, that I talk to myself, that I draw a spiral on my mirror in red lipstick.

It's like old times, this self, and in a weird way, it feels like home.

*Welcome back*, I say to no one in the mirror.

◆　◆　◆

I sleep for seventeen hours straight, like a sick person, which I am. I am a sick person.

I stay in my room all week at Dad's house, don't go to work or visit Mom's. I miss my appointments to see apartments. Instead, I lie in bed hugging Sprinkles and spacing out on Netflix and watching reruns. I go over and over all my mistakes in my mind. So many mistakes, so many wrong turns.

I relive the graduation afternoon a thousand times in my mind since it happened. There must be something wrong with me. Who would *do* that? What was I thinking? I ruined all my progress, all my work, in about three minutes' time. I see the whole scene from several perspectives, and in slow motion. I'll go an hour without thinking of the Incident and then I shudder, remembering with a wave of what can only be described as a nausea of the soul. I am nauseated with myself.

All my accomplishments this semester evaporate into the black hole along with every other speck of light. I don't let myself plunge to the depths I did last year, where I looked up suicide methods and crime scene photos, but I do catch myself lying in bed and just ogling that vein in my right wrist, purple, ticking there visibly below my skin.

My parents try an intervention-style meeting where they beg me to take meds again. I tell them I will think about it. I apologize for breaking my phone. I'm sorry I drew on the mirror with lipstick. I regretted it instantly, but then I had to live with it, like everything else I've done.

Mom's wedding is this coming weekend and I don't want her to be worrying about me. We can't get an appointment for weeks, because apparently Wolfman is in high demand these days.

"Will you live?" Mom asks me when she tells me my appointment date over the phone.

"I will live," I say, knowing she didn't mean it literally, but still somehow hearing it that way. I *will* live: it's true, and I'm almost disappointed.

Late, around ten, I hear a small knock at my door. I ignore it at first, but it persists.

"Fine, what?" I finally ask.

I expect Stevie, from the timid rapping, but am surprised to see Gary there. She has a cup of steaming tea.

"Can I sit with you?" she asks.

Reluctantly, I make space on the floor, plowing some books and sundresses aside with my slipper. We sit crisscross applesauce. She hands me the tea and I inhale the scent of peppermint. After a moment I take a sip. It burns my tongue. A welcome burn.

"It's been a challenging week," she says finally, which seems like the understatement of the century. "And I know this is no consolation . . . but I admire you."

I take another sip.

"You were just trying to help someone," she says. "You had a good reason to believe she was suicidal."

The tea sears my throat.

"I would rather be a person who goes too far trying to do good than a person who sits idly by while bad things happen." She gets up. "Enjoy your tea, and let me know if you need anything."

Her words linger after she leaves me alone again.

At my mom and Levi's wedding ceremony, the tables all have bouquets of peonies on them (Mom) in tiny glass boot vases (Levi) and the Elvis impersonator who officiates their wedding makes everyone laugh with his one-liners and random pelvis thrusts and constant interjections of *thankyouverymuch*. At first I kind of hate him but then I realize, standing in front of the crowd in my vomit-colored dress with a forced, frozen smile and my squeezed-back tears, that I'm only envious. Because he seems silly and carefree and everyone's looking at him and laughing and he's not a walking mess of a human like me.

Weirdly, I don't look like a mess. It was that way last year. I'd feel like a monster, imagining myself with feral-looking hair and crazy eyes. But when I go to the bathroom after the ceremony's over and everyone's hitting the catering line, I'm struck, in the mirror I encounter, by how grown-up I look, how pretty. I weep in the bathroom stall for a while, not sure why it feels like my heart is torn into little shreds. I beg myself silently to please get it together. I try to count my breaths but it doesn't work because counting breaths is idiocy. If I try to meditate, all I hear is an endless crap fountain of *I hate everything. I'm the worst. Why did I have to be born?* So I get up again, reapply my waterproof mascara, and go out to get my hot food.

I sit at the table with Jonah, Ruby, Stevie, and some ancient woman I don't recognize who I imagine is a professional wedding crasher. Ruby plays a video game on her phone under the table the whole time and is already changed back into her usual black tee and black jeans. The ancient woman is telling Stevie what it was like growing up without "cellular devices" and how exciting it used to be to "check the mailbox" when she was a child. I don't know why but it makes me think of Davis, and even the thought of Davis fills me with a dark, spiritual sadness of which there is no name. Maybe *toska*, an untranslatable Russian word for sadness, yearning, nostalgia. But sprinkled with a dash of shame. *Toska-plus*. I eat and don't talk much, though I'm aware of Jonah, Converse shoe next to my high heel, his leg jiggling, the feel of his gaze on my face. After the food's done, Ruby and Stevie leave the table to go find the other tweeners, the ancient woman falls asleep blissfully in the sun with her eyes closed, looking dead but hopefully not, and it's just me and Jonah and a bunch of paper plates mountained with chicken bones.

It's weird that if you walk down that pathway right there, the one through the eucalyptuses, and go on the main path around the turn, then you'd see the oak tree.

"You okay?" Jonah asks me. "You haven't been texting me back."

"I broke my phone. Haven't gotten around to fixing it yet."

"You want to talk about what happened at graduation?"

"I thought I was helping someone," I tell him. "Instead, it turned out I just ruined everything again."

"Don't be so dramatic. You do know she gave her speech right afterward and we all graduated and no one cared or remembered what you did, right?"

"I tackled a girl in front of hundreds of humans for no reason."

"You had a reason. You thought she was going to hurt herself. It makes logical sense."

"How . . . do you even know that?"

"Your dad."

"Why are you talking to my dad? I don't, like, talk to your mom."

"Your dad's cool, we email sometimes."

"My dad is *not* cool, and that's weird."

"Want to go for a walk?" Jonah asks me.

He reaches out and puts his hand on my wrist and then slides it up my forearm. I get a chill. A warm, sick kind of chill you get when someone you pine for touches you unexpectedly. I look him in the eyes and he's smiling that half smile. I must not be entirely dead inside, because I half smile myself.

We go for a walk in the sun-speckled shadows; in Japan, they have a word for that, *komorebi*, which is the light that comes through the trees. I tell Jonah this, and he looks up at the trees like he's seeing something new in them. He used to love all the untranslatable words I collected from other languages and carried around in my brain. He loved the poems I wrote, the little madnesses in them. His profile is exquisite. Someone should draw his portrait. I think of the night we lay on the trampoline and the world seemed full of magic, and for a brief adolescent moment, we seemed eternal.

He loved me, and let me count the ways: loved me first as a childhood acquaintance, next as a middle school friend, finally as a teenage lover. Even now, remembering his love makes me ache with a dry thirst that starts in my rib cage and echoes through my skin. I want him more than I want anything else in the world. We walk along a bridge together, my heels echoing on the wood, and stop there, leaning over the wooden railing, where reeds jut up from the murk for their taste of sunlight, and ducks quack between. Like no time has passed, we stand in silence—one that seems to say everything.

"I've missed you," Jonah tells me.

Our hands sit next to each other on the railing, his pinkie reaching out for mine and meeting it for an electric moment. My lips buzz because I can feel him looking at them.

"You broke up with me, remember?" I ask.

"What if I made a mistake?" he asks in a small voice.

Even though all I want is to put my lips to his and stick my tongue in his mouth, I look away, at the geese flying through the air. I ask myself why, if this is what I want—him—why does my heart still throb inside like some broken thing?

Maybe it's not my heart. Maybe I am the broken thing.

"I look at you now," he says. "And you're the girl I wanted before we were together. This . . . confident, mature you."

"Pffft" is all I say, thinking of the versions of me he didn't see just from today alone. The one who wept in the bathroom stall, the other who didn't want to get out of bed upon waking, the other who thought about killing herself and then thought about getting back on medication, back, forth, back, forth, like a game of shitbrain table tennis while getting dressed.

He puts his hand on mine. It just fits. Our temperatures match. It's hard to explain.

"It kills me knowing that you're better now and we're apart," he says. "That you're this . . . better version of you, Journey 2.0, and I don't get you."

I close my eyes and see nothing but gold, an imprint where the sun was shining from behind a cloud a moment before. The imprint stays on my vision like an ache. What Jonah just said bothers me so much my feet itch. I pull my hand away and open my eyes. He's still watching me with this smile like he thinks I'm so beautiful. Which maybe I am. But that's not all I am.

"Jonah," I say. "What if we'd just stayed together, and I had tried to off myself, and you'd been there for me?"

"I think we needed this to happen this way, right?" he asks.

I try not to get lost in his perfect imperfections: the mole on his left cheek, the scar on his chin from when he needed stitches in third grade, his hair that's always just a touch greasy. Even though I want to touch him, to hold him, I don't. Because I see him, but I don't think he truly sees me. I don't know that he ever will.

"No," I say. "I needed you."

"But now you're so independent," he says. "Stronger than ever."

"Jonah, this morning I woke up and honestly wondered if I will live long enough to get married someday and have my own wedding."

He rolls his eyes. "Come on. Of course you will."

"I wondered, will I ever be stable enough to be a mother?" I ask, my voice shaking. "Because right now I wouldn't even trust myself to pet sit, I'm that much of a selfish mess."

"You're eighteen," he says.

"He can count, too," I say quietly, but my heart's not in the sarcasm today, and it comes out sadder than I meant it to. I begin to cry.

"Journey, you're fine," he says.

"But I'm *not*," I tell him, wiping my eyes before the tears can wreak havoc on my made-up wedding face. "Don't you see that? Whatever I am, whatever you call me, I'm not fine."

"Oh, Journey," he says, opening his arms to wrap me up in them.

But I push him away.

"Journey," he says in that old tired tone I know so well. Once he gets into a place where he has no words, he just parrots my name. "Please."

"Please what?" I ask. "This is me. I still am *dramatic* or *crazy* or *bipolar* or *moody* or whatever the vocab of the day is. I'm still Journey. It's the one thing I know—I'm always going to be *this*."

He sighs and looks at the reeds. I can tell I've turned him off, the way I used to.

"You're disappointed, aren't you?" I ask him. "Here I am, same old me, and you'd hoped I was the 2.0 version."

"Don't be so dramatic," he says.

"Life is dramatic, you dumbass," I tell him. "Life is full of sadness and messed-up-ness. Everyone, even us, a couple of kids with as much privilege as is humanly allowed, living in a goddamn dreamtown with everything at our fingertips—even we suffer."

"I don't," he insists.

"You *don't*," I scoff, because what a dumb thing to say.

I stop and we stare at each other. The wind lifts my hair and gently sets it into place again. It's gotten long enough that it tickles my shoulders now. Jonah Patterson is so exquisite, so sad-looking sometimes when he's not stifling that charming smile. He looks like a boy who thinks deep things and feels deep things. But I realize right now, for the first time in my life, that he doesn't. He doesn't want to. He lives on the surface, which is where he's comfortable. When anything comes along and threatens that, it becomes too much, and he runs.

He abandoned me once. He will again. Look at the quiver in his blue eyes right now—he wishes he could abandon me at this exact moment.

That night on the trampoline? That magical night under the stars? Those were the only kinds of conditions where we could be truly happy. The tears let loose and he pats my back.

"Don't cry," he tells me.

Which . . . What an inane thing to say.

"It's okay," I say, wiping my eyes and sniffing back the emotion. "It's going to be okay."

It feels good, those words coming out of me. They would have felt better coming from him, but maybe it's better that they're mine. He watches me like I'm such a puzzle. He doesn't have that hungry look on his face anymore. And you know what? I don't give a shit.

We walk back and I go into the bathroom again, redoing my eyeliner in the mirror.

"Hi," I say, as if it's been a while since I saw me.

Strange, but it feels like it has.

*I don't miss him*
*Like fire misses its spark.*
*But he misses me,*
*Like an arrow misses a mark.*

◆　◆　◆

I get a new phone the next week and catch up on all the communication I missed being a depressed hermit. I'm surprised and disappointed that Etta obeyed my wish and never responded. I imagine her listening to that voice message, thinking, *This girl is off her rocker. Dodged a bullet with that one. Phew. Don't need another psycho ex-girlfriend, thanks.* Marisol texted me not once but twenty-three times. A third of the texts are about the graduation fiasco, a third are about how happy it makes her that we're on speaking terms again, the other third are about a *My Secret Obsession* episode concerning a man who comes home from work and dresses up as a dog and chews bones and lies on the floor and a pet sitter comes to take care of him.

I refuse to accept the fact my best friend is really actually leaving for Chicago in a month.

I delete all the texts Jonah sent before the wedding. Texts asking, in such a concerned tone and with such horrid grammar, how I'm "fairing." Funny how I get nothing after the wedding's over. I'd be insulted but you know what? I don't care anymore. The boy's basic. The apathy I feel for him, after months of sick-with-itself desire, is, quite frankly, bliss.

Tim-Tim sent me two messages.

Miss my fave dancin pizza slice!!!!!!!

All's well??????

Both feature random GIFs, one with an animated dancing pickle, another with a psychedelic cat changing colors.

I can come back Monday, I text back.

FUNDAY MONDAY!!!! he texts back, with a GIF of ever-flowing champagne.

I'm already exhausted by Tim-Tim's energy, but glad he values my pizza dancing so much and that I still have a job. Apparently I can relapse into crazytown and still resurface into the real world and be accepted with loving arms. That's something.

Hey, I text Marisol. I exist.

JoJo!!!! she texts back with so many hearts.

My eyes prick with tears reading that. Shallow boys come and go, almost girlfriends turn to dust, but Marisol, my soul mate, my bestie forever, will always be here for me.

We text back and forth for a while, first about graduation, which she thinks was entertaining and, once she learns the backstory behind my thinking, heroic. I tell her about Jonah and our frustrating yet enlightening conversation, which she is so relieved to hear.

Thank you! He is so vapid! Please never return to him again. What about Etta??

I also explain how I royally screwed that up forever.

Whyyyy, she responds, plus sad emoji sobbing face.

There are other bisexual fish in the bisexual sea, I tell her.

But she was so cute and so funny. Sadface and clown-face and sadface.

Yeah, I know, Marisol. I know.

I dull my thoughts with TV. There's a laugh-track-heavy show on about twentysomething people experiencing romantic mishaps in New York City. Ruby comes out in her penguin pj's, ostensibly for a glass of water, and sits on the couch with me in friendly silence as she gulps it down. I offer her half my blanket, and she silently accepts.

"I don't think you're going to try to kill yourself again," Ruby says. "Not now, anyway."

"Thank you?" I say.

The line between compliment and insult is so thin with Ruby Tuesday Smith.

On-screen, two of the characters kiss and the audience *woo-hoo*s. Ruby watches with a placid stare, takes her last sip of water. She puts her hand on my hand for a moment, her eyes ever so slightly magnified behind her glasses.

"You're not alone," she says. "You're never alone." She gets up. "No one is. Over ten thousand species of microbes occupy our bodies."

And with that, she heads to bed.

"But I'm the crazy one," I tell the muted TV.

I turn the sound back on. It's a commercial for the medication I was prescribed. The woman on the commercial goes from having unbrushed hair and not leaving her bed to happy, hanging laundry in the sunshine, in a matter of a minute. Meanwhile, a man rattles off an alarming list of side effects. It makes me mad that they sell it on people the same way they sell soda. It makes me mad people make money off sadness. It makes me mad that people have such sadness. It makes me sad it makes me mad.

Back at my mom's this weekend, my mom comes in and ruffles my hair and pulls tarot cards with me. I get the Star card—a woman crouched over a pond, one vase pouring water into the blue pond, another vase pouring water on the land. There are yellow stars around her. Mom puts on her reading glasses and reads from her phone. "The Star means you have gone and passed through a terrible life challenge. You have managed to go through this without losing your hope."

I begin to cry and she holds me tight. I close my eyes and go back to a place where I am small, where I can disappear into the comfort of my mother's arms. I think of the way she looked that night in the hospital after the pills, unrecognizable, frenzied. How different we both were then. How much I love her love, but even weightier—how much her trust means to me. How it helps me build faith in myself, to know that trust is there.

I might be too much. I'm always too much. But there is such a thing as unconditional love.

The next day, in what is possibly more shocking than me trying to end my life with pills or tackle a girl at graduation, Ruby is suspended from her gifted-and-talented summer school program.

"What?" I yell into my phone when Mom explains.

"I am speechless," Mom yells back. "I have no words. I have nothing to say."

I don't have time to explain irony to her, so I just repeat, "What?"

"My pepper spray from my purse?" Mom asks. "Ruby stole it. She brought it to school. Apparently some girls threatened to 'jump' her. She sprayed it in their direction and one of the girls got it in her eyes."

"What?" I say again.

"Are you broken?" Mom asks, annoyed.

"Basically."

"Well, we're on our way home. See you soon."

I'm eating cereal at the table looking at a catalog of hunting gear sent to Levi. I don't know why he has a hunting gear catalog. We don't hunt. We shop at Whole Foods. Anyway, I wait there with my empty bowl of cereal until I see Mom pull up in Levi's truck with Ruby staring out the window still as a bespectacled tween mannequin. They come inside in an icy silence that is clearly minutes deep and Ruby marches straight to her room.

"I don't know what the hell got into her!" Mom scream-whispers to me.

I pour more cereal. This conversation requires more cereal.

"She stole my pepper spray," Mom says to me, sitting at the table.

"You bought it for protection," I remind her.

"It's considered a *weapon*. One she technically discharged. She could get expelled."

"Why did she do it?"

Chewbacca comes in and slobbers all over Mom's lap. She pets his head absentmindedly, the stinky beast.

"Cindy's in a new group of mean girls," Mom says. "Apparently they've been picking on Ruby for months. I am in shock. I talked to someone in the district office and they said that while the vice president recommended expulsion, I could appeal, which I will. I have to go visit the district office with Ruby and she has to be willing to write a formal apology. Right now she refuses. Stubborn girl. I can't believe this. Ruby's a straight-A student!"

Guilt flutters in me. The text I saw . . . I should have said something.

"Mom," I say. "I saw a text on her phone awhile ago."

"Whose phone?"

"Ruby's."

"Go on."

"It was . . . a threat. Someone sent her a threat."

"And you didn't *tell* me?" she roars.

"Whoa, maybe because I figured you'd get like this."

"What the *fuck*, Journey?" Mom says.

"Geez, potty mouth," I say, pushing my dish away. "I was trying to help."

"By doing nothing?"

"Mom, she's thirteen. She has to figure her own social life out. How was I supposed to know she was going to steal your pepper spray? Maybe you shouldn't keep weapons in your purse—"

"It's for *protection*. It's not a weapon. You know how I feel about guns."

I push the hunting catalog toward her. She takes one look at it, gets up, and throws it in the recycling. More potty mouth ensues. Levi calls her phone, his special jingle that is a cow mooing. She reaches peak potty mouth. That's it, I'm retreating to my room.

"I want you to talk to her," Mom says, taking the phone from her ear.

"She hates me."

"She does not. You're her big sister."

"Yeah, exemplary screwup."

"Do you just say this crap for reaction, Journey? You're not a screwup. I didn't raise my girls to beat up on themselves. You're a warrior. Now go talk to your sister."

Warrior? I try not to let her comment affect my face, but I am savoring that word as I turn into the hallway. My mom doesn't shower compliments on people. Her expectations are high. Her opinions are typically low.

I knock on the "DANGER! HIGH VOLTAGE" sign on Ruby's door. She's playing the YesNoMaybe album. It's sweet. It softens me. I might be getting ready to leave home and she might be turning into a juvenile delinquent but some things remain the same.

"I am knocking," I yell, knocking louder.

The music gets turned down ever so slightly.

"I am not accepting company at the moment, Mother," she replies.

She calls Mom "Mother" when they're on the outs and talks in this affected, faux British accent.

"It's not Mother," I answer. "It is I, Journey, eldest sister of the house. I come in peace."

The door opens a sliver. Her eyes are bloodshot behind her glasses, although there are no traces of tears or emotion on her face. She lets me in. I take a seat on her bed, which is covered in clothes. They are all black. There's an open suitcase on the floor. It's a Hello Kitty suitcase, a relic from years ago, when she was a single-digit sweetie pie.

"I am running away," she tells me.

"Interesting," I say. "Where are you going to run to?"

"Iceland," she says.

"Because of the microbes?"

"No," she says, clearly offended. "Because of the Icelandic horses."

Random as this sounds, back when she was rocking Hello Kitty gear, she was also obsessed with horses. Horses were her microbes back then. She rode horses, she had horse pictures on her wall, she begged Mom to buy a horse. Then it passed. I haven't heard her talk about horses in years.

"How are you getting to Iceland?" I ask.

She holds up her passport. "I have savings, too."

"Ruby," I sigh.

I sit next to her.

"Did you really think pepper spray was going to fix everything?"

"I just wanted to wave it around and make Cindy pee her pants. I wasn't planning to *use* it. That thing went off without my meaning to, I swear."

"You realize what a mess you're in, right?"

"Whatever. You're in messes all the time. Who cares?"

I move on, not flinching. "I never got expelled."

"I never tried to kill myself. Do I get a cookie?"

Ouch. Seriously, I'm trying not to be hurt, but Ruby's got retorts like a scalpel.

"When did you become such a bitter little girl?" I ask.

"When I stopped *being* a little girl," she says.

Suddenly, in a complete break, she begins to cry. She removes her glasses and puts her face in her hands. I have not seen Ruby Tuesday Smith cry since . . . maybe since our parents announced they were splitting up. I put my arms around her and ache with her. I put my cheek on her greasy, bruise-colored hair.

"I just feel so much," she says.

I know what she means. I know how she hurts. I know, Ruby.

"Same," I say.

"Everything sucks," she says. "No one at school likes me. I am an actual pariah. Cindy is so *mean* to me—and I loved her like a sister. I don't understand."

I'm not going to say some dumb cliché like "this too shall pass" or "it gets better," even though those dumb clichés exist for a reason. Instead I hug her and let her be miserable.

"Ruby," I tell her. "I don't know much. I'm a mess. You know I am. But look—at least I'm still here. Intact. I haven't burned anything to the ground."

"Congratulations?" she says, wiping her eyes.

"No, I mean . . . I know what it's like to have cripplingly big feelings. To feel rejected from the people you expected to love you with lifelong fervor." My voice gets momentarily stuck in my throat as I see Jonah there in my mind, and he dissolves, engulfed by the ocean in me. "Those people who don't love you in your entirety—for the you you are today, for the whole-picture you—you don't need them. It hurts to know that. But you don't need Cindy. And even your screwups . . . they can turn out to be the most amazing gifts."

My eyes blur over and I have to pause a moment to will the tears away. It works. I swallow. Ruby leans her head on my shoulder.

"I went through hell," I tell her. "Now it's your turn."

"I'm sorry now," she says, sobbing once, then swallowing it back. "I was just so *mad*."

"We're going to appeal, we're going to get you back in school, don't worry." I take her glasses off, clean them with my shirt, put them back on her face. "You need to be willing to write an apology, and it'll all blow over. Okay?"

"Okay," she repeats.

We sit not speaking, YesNoMaybe whining over the speakers about a girl with red lips and mad hips. I think of Etta, although the thought of her seems too dignified for this poppy crap we're listening to. These lyrics, man. Once I thought they were Shakespeare. Past self, get some damn taste.

"If you could communicate one thing to your future self, what would it be?" I ask Ruby.

She thinks for a long time, chewing her hair, a habit I haven't seen since she was Stevie's age.

"I would ask, have scientists found a way to study microbial dark matter?" she asks.

This is not what I was looking for. But her face has lit up. That's all that matters, right? A little light escaping the darkness.

I take drivers' training and education and practice driving up and down the hill and on the freeway, breathing through near panic attacks, willfully forgetting the fiery crash. I, human pizza slice, dance with passion and am promised a twenty-five-cent raise and a promotion to busser. I pretend to be a grown-up and go view three apartments, nodding as the property managers show me the laundry rooms and the closets as if I know what I'm doing. I spend a lot of time alone reading poetry. Stacks of books from the library that smell like an intoxicating cocktail of ink, paper, and plastic. I write. I exercise. I go weeks without thinking of suicide, except to think, *Wow, look at me not thinking of suicide.* What a champ.

The hotline is done, and though I regret how it ended, I accept it now. It was what it was. Soon I'm going to start volunteering at a literacy program through city college instead, tutor ESL students. Training starts in August. So, I'm not done doing good.

JD and I still text sometimes. I never explained to them what happened, I made some excuse to save face about being too busy, but I'm flattered to know I'm apparently missed. A woman named Bethany who brings a footbath to shift and has a very loud voice has replaced me in our crew, and it sounds like she's not exactly beloved by all. JD and I keep talking about hanging out soon, maybe meeting up for tea with Beatriz and Lydia, but you know how it is with best-laid plans.

That's why, on August 1, a Sunday morning, a morning at Dad's when I am gleefully packing my room (I got an apartment! A complex around the corner from Etta's place, actually. But we won't think about that. No, that door has closed), I'm surprised to see JD's calling. We never talk on the phone, text only, and never on Sunday mornings. This is some kind of breach of our relationship's unspoken rules.

I answer the phone as I chuck the last of my ten thousand shoes into a box with a spirited, "Yelllllo?"

"Journey," JD says. "If you're not—well, sit your ass down."

"What's up?" I ask, correcting my tone.

"You sitting?"

"I'm sitting. Smelling salts in hand," I joke.

Because I'm nervous and you know how I get when I'm nervous.

"Lydia had a complete breakdown last week and was fired from the hotline," JD says.

"*Our* Lydia?"

"Yeah."

"What do you mean 'breakdown'?"

"She started screaming and cussing out Davis. Then she threw the phone and it broke the window. Beatriz and I didn't even know what to do. Lydia threatened to hurt herself. Then she checked herself into a psychiatric hospital that night after it all happened—that's what I heard."

I'm so stunned I have no response. Lydia, with her knitting and her acerbic wit and her good advice. Her heart-wrenching poems and her FaceTime calls with her dog and her weird green sludge teas. Her perfect, sarcastic kindness. The veteran, the mentor, the longest-lasting volunteer the hotline ever had. I can't picture her losing it like that.

"Lydia from the hotline?" I clarify.

"Yes."

I seem to have momentarily lost the ability to locate words.

"Maybe I shouldn't've called," JD goes on. "I just thought you'd wanna know. It was—so out of character for her. Scared the crap out of me."

My jaw has dropped, imagining this scene. Poor Lydia. Threatening to *hurt* herself? We were hotline volunteers! Lydia is a *grandmother*. She has gone through the darkness, emerged, and aged another generation. My heart cracks, like the delicate egg it is, thinking that someone as together as Lydia could have an episode like that out of nowhere and lose her hotline job and end up in a psych hospital. It makes no sense. I cannot compute.

"Have you talked to her since?" I ask.

"I checked in with her yesterday, yeah. She's back home now. She said she's been in a lot of pain lately, because of her back. And Camus died. I guess it all pushed her over the edge."

"Camus!" I say, my eyes watering. "Oh no. She loves that dog so much."

"Yeah, so . . . I don't know why I called . . . maybe give her a call or shoot her an email or something when you get the chance. She could use support right now."

"Thank you," I tell JD. "No—I appreciate it. I'll . . . I'll reach out."

I hang up. It's absolutely unbelievable that that woman, who I shared so many hours with, who counseled me and decompressed with me, who read poetry with me and gave me advice, who gave her own love and advice to strangers, for free, for absolutely nothing in return—could snap. I picture her screaming into the phone and breaking a window but it seems so ridiculous. Really? *Really*, Lydia?

I look in the mirror. If Lydia could break the fuck down at sixty-whatever years old . . . a grown-up . . . a mother, a grandmother . . . how in hell is there hope for me? And how selfish am I, to think of myself, to make this about me?

This is why my packing comes to a standstill and I lie on my bed in my piles of unpacked clothes.

This is why I crash, hard, back to earth with a sadness so big it should make a supersonic sound. But it doesn't. In fact, it sounds like nothing at all.

> Dear future self,
>     At some point, years past this, when you build up your death wish sobriety and walk to the furthest point away from your biggest mistake, is there a chance you would be willing to throw it all away again?
>     Dear future self, then what is all this for?

I've heard that suicide can be contagious, spreading through families and communities like viruses. There are copycat suicides and suicides inspired by irresponsible fiction. Even I was sucked into the fantasy of it when I tried, thinking it would be so exquisite, like an Ophelia painting, like a Sylvia Plath poem, *O romantic death.*

Even though I know now the ugly sick reality—the desperate, vomitous, embarrassing, regrettable reality—I find myself distracted by the thought of Lydia's breakdown after I learn the news. I reach out and send her an email asking if she needs anything and hear nothing back. I try to imagine the dark place she got sucked back into—was she in danger of trying to kill herself? Is that why she checked herself into the hospital? Is that what I'm going to be like if I make it to her age—still struggling with the same bullshit? I barely know Lydia, really, and it's dumb for me to be so preoccupied with her situation; I don't know the names of her children and grandchildren, or her age, her middle name, her address, or whether or not a potential suicide attempt was any part of her breakdown. But I am preoccupied. She haunts me during my driving lessons and my work days. She sits with me as I pick out cheap furniture at the thrift store with Marisol. I tell Marisol, lump in my throat, that I feel like Lydia's breakdown is seeing a depressing version of my future self.

"I can't believe a suicide hotline person spun out in a violent rage at one of your poor callers," Marisol says as we sit on used couches, trying them out.

"Well," I say. "First off, it's a crisis hotline, it's not just for suicide. Second of all, it's always the mentally unstable who are drawn to helping the mentally unstable."

"You think you're mentally unstable?"

"You think I'm mentally *stable*?"

"I don't know," she says, petting the rip in my jeans where my knee pokes through. "You're just Journey to me."

As usual, I don't know the answer to me, either. I'm too stable to be unstable; too unstable to be stable. I lose my mind and go into a catatonic state and draw lipstick spirals on my mirror and break my phone on purpose, and then, the next day, I'm sorry at my impulsivity. I snap out of it and apologize. I spray my mirror, shine it silver, and research how to fix my phone.

My problem is, I can't commit to either.

Lydia still doesn't respond to my email, and I notice an intense rage swelling up at her in the days after my call with JD. I know it isn't fair, but I'm disgusted with Lydia for being a mess. I'm repelled. I never want to be like her. In another way, I'm envious, like she's more authentically herself than I am myself for suffering a complete public breakdown and ending up hospitalized again. There are no words for this mixture of feelings, all opposite. Just a faint malaise. Just a bunch of pointless questions like is she sorry? What is her diagnosis? Did she regret it?

Did she wish she could undo it?

What was a nervous breakdown like for her?

Was it like it was for me?

I know what they mean about suicide being contagious because even after just the faintest whiff of it—someone else's hospitalization and breakdown—I catch myself thinking of suicide like this logical option again. I'm late to work and that old voice says, *Kill yourself.* I get a pang seeing Marisol's pics of her new roommate. *Kill yourself.* I stub my toe, I don't get into the class I want, I'm in a bad mood for no reason at all. *Kill yourself.* I don't mean it. The annoying voice buzzes around my ear like a fly I bat away. But occasionally, in dark moments, I catch myself thinking, if I were to do it, how? A gun and one bullet, a body of water with bricks tied to my feet, pills, razors, a bridge . . . I hate these thoughts, but they are familiar, and they park themselves in my brain and make a home as I perform life, buying furniture, autographing leases, signing up for classes. I should be so happy. Everyone keeps asking how I'm doing and I say fine.

Fine can also mean a very small particle, you know.

This summer is so lovely. I can smell the ocean from my new apartment and I'll be living there in less than two weeks. School starts again in four. I look up at the nonsensical clouds and the flame-blue sky and it's amazing how beyond them there is a universe scattered with so many stars they outnumber every grain of sand on every beach in this wide, unknowable planet.

I am a very small particle.

I force myself to keep going, a millimeter from madness. Blink open my eyes in the morning and enjoy a moment of quiet, pleasant blankness before the bad news comes in like brain rain: Marisol is moving away; I was kicked off a volunteer crisis line; I ruined my high school graduation; I will never fall in love; I am a joke no one is laughing at. Everything I ever thought I was, all those moments of joy, were fake and/or fleeting.

I hear myself. I hear how dramatic I'm being, and I know it's impossible it's all that stark and true. But the thoughts are so loud. They ring throughout breakfast, behind the chatter. Badger me while I go on my last driving lesson. I catch myself in the same patterns of thinking of death like a sweet vacation again, like I did back before I tried to off myself. How glad I am my driving teacher, a ponytailed surfer dude named Hal, cannot hear my thoughts.

"That driver's test's about to get *aced*," he tells me as he drops me off at my dad's.

"Thanks!" I say, smiling, waving, acting human.

I go upstairs and faceplant on my bed and hurt, from the inside out.

"No," I say. "No."

I thought I beat it. Lies. How I will ever escape the death-spiral thoughts without giving in to the death spiral is beyond me.

There is a razor in my shower and a ticking vein in my wrist. I keep returning to the thought of those two things, obsessively—razor. Wrist. Razor. Wrist. I can see how bloody the scene would be and it makes me sick and it also feeds something horrible in me, something embedded deep in me, but which cannot be removed.

This again.

I swear.

This monster in my head.

If I don't find a way to stop it, it's going to stop me.

I dial six out of seven numbers for the hotline and stare for a long time before entering the seventh and pressing the green button for go. This shouldn't be so hard. I was on the other end of the line. I don't judge people for calling. Or do I. Or maybe it's something like I don't think I'm crazy enough to ask for help.

Or is it that I don't think I'm deserving enough.

"Santa Barbara crisis hotline, this is Julie speaking," a woman says.

I don't know Julie. She wasn't part of my training group and she wasn't part of my shift. I breathe a sigh of relief and close my eyes, let them burn for a moment, before talking.

"Hi, Julie," I say. "Thanks for answering the phone today. Thanks for being here and all you do. I'm just going to verbally dump on you, and I apologize in advance. My whole life, I've had these big feelings. Since life. Since memory begins. If I felt, I felt big. Sometimes these big feelings make everything wonderful and Technicolor, and sometimes they make everything a parade of horrors. Sometimes I'm part lunatic and people threaten to call doctors and other times I'm passing classes and making people laugh. I've had lovely people fall in love with me. I've screwed that shit up real bad. Sometimes I'm behind the line, sometimes I'm on the line, sometimes I think I need help, and sometimes I think I'm the helper." I'm breathless. "What do I sound like to you? Like you're probably flipping through your binder right now. Honestly. What page are you flipping to? Be real. What do I sound like?"

Julie answers after a short static pop of silence between us. "You sound human."

I have not seen Wolf since the renovation, which took much longer than expected. The moment I step into his office, I think maybe I'm in the wrong place. This place is painted with an ocean mural, plants everywhere, fountain tinkling, a couch made of some kind of basket material, a couple hammocks. There are still books lining the walls, but otherwise, it's transformed. I take a tentative seat on the basket couch and Wolf sits in a basket chair across from me.

"This is different," I tell him.

"I'm sharing an office with another therapist now," he says. "She made some . . . choices."

"Are we supposed to be on the beach?" I ask, pointing to a potted palm, then the hammock. "Do you have a coconut phone somewhere?"

"I forgot how funny you are," he says, although he's not laughing. "How have you been?"

"I called a crisis hotline a few days ago."

I fill him in on Lydia's breakdown, on how it shook me, on my own morbid thoughts and how it's all so tangled I

315

can't pull it apart sometimes.

"Suicidal ideation is not the same as suicidal intent," he says to me.

The swell of relief I feel when he says that could move a mountain.

"You have been through trauma," Wolf says.

Ugh. *Trauma.*

"I hate that word," I say.

"Trauma?" Wolf asks, surprised. "Why?"

"I don't know," I say.

"Do you hate the word *grief*?" he asks.

"Also not my favorite."

"You are grieving," he says.

"Grieving what? Some woman I hardly know having a nervous breakdown?"

"You were in a very close, intense situation with her. But I'm not just referring to her—you were already grieving," Wolf reminds me. "There's been a lot of grief this past year for you; not just the suicide attempt, which I know you regretted. You mourned your parents, your family, your first love."

I break my "no crying in therapy" vow about three minutes in. I'm already on my second tissue.

"It's okay to grieve," he says. "It's okay to experience trauma. In fact, it's one thing we all share."

I close my eyes. The sound of the fountain is soothing, actually. For a moment I don't feel crazy at all. I feel sad, and older, and a sadness about being older, which there should be a word for. I think of my sister Ruby. I think of how beautiful my mom looked in her purple wedding dress and how I was so miserable that day I never even told her. I think of Nicola, and what a pretty package she is with such a canyon lurking in her soul. I think of Jonah when he first kissed me, the way I kept my eyes open the whole time because I wanted to see his eyes closed. I think of the car accident and the smell of burnt metal and gasoline, the way the glass shone crystal-like under the moon, the ambulance lights swirling. I think of Etta and her sweet voice singing in my phone. Life chokes me sometimes. Too much everything.

"Julie said I should maybe see a psychiatrist," I tell Wolf.

"Maybe you should," he says.

"But I thought I was grieving. I thought this was 'trauma.' Now, what, you think I'm mentally ill?"

Wolf doesn't answer.

"Am I?" I ask him. "Am I bipolar II? Or do I have a personality disorder or something?"

"Do you think you're mentally ill?" he asks.

"I'm mostly normal," I say.

"You do realize even mentally ill people are 'mostly normal,'" Wolf says, using air quotes. "Mentally ill people aren't 'ill' all the time. I invite you to question what you think of as normal and what you think of as mentally ill."

Hmm.

"We have this fixed idea in our culture of what mentally

ill means," he continues. "The reality is, most people who are mentally ill are functional people almost their whole lives who simply need treatment now and then."

"Medication," I say.

"Maybe," he says. "Some. Some people do with therapy. Some people try other methods."

"So you're saying I *am* bipolar," I say.

"*If* you are," he asks, "how does that change you? Or how *doesn't* it change you?"

I chew my lip. Now the tears have stopped, but my brain hurts.

"It's just so arbitrary, these designations," I tell him. "Like, we as human beings made up these categories: mentally ill; bipolar I, bipolar II—"

"We as human beings made up every word in every language," Wolf says. "Does that give some of them more meaning than others?"

I try to hold the tears back again, and fail again. Twice in one day, I have broken my no-crying rule. It's official: I am the worst.

"I don't know if I can do this," I tell Wolf. "I need help."

He nods, nudging the tissue box my way. "I really think it's time for you to set up an appointment with a psychiatrist, to at least *discuss* the option of a different medication."

I take a tissue, dab my eyes. He turns around and grabs a pad of paper, a pen, and writes a number down for me.

"No pressure," he says, handing me the slip of paper. "But

let's put one more tool in your toolbox. This is a colleague of mine. She works specifically with adolescents. I think you'll really like her."

I sniff, nod, and even though I want to resist this, I want to hand the paper back—I don't.

"Thanks," I say. "I'll give her a try."

Cleaning out my email in-box one day, Lydia's name appears and I let out a little yelp of joy at the sight of her response.

*Hiya J, thanks for reaching out. So I gather you heard all about my dramatic exit from the hotline. I'm sure I traumatized Davis and everyone else. What can I say, life is a real pile of shit sometimes. I've been having a rough go. Did you hear my dog died? And I threw my back out again? Honestly, sometimes I don't know why I keep going. But anyway here I am. You're all not rid of me yet. Maybe we can meet for coffee and I can fill you in soon.*

So Lydia, JD, Beatriz, and I meet up for coffee. It's at one of those too-hip places downtown, clean as a bank, all six-dollar pour-over coffees and baristas with a crap-ton of ennui. We sit together with our mini white paper cups. I've never been outside the hotline with them. Something about this, even though we're in public in a noisy open space, feels too intimate, like I've stepped into a stranger's house without invitation. I've never sat this close to them. I can see their pores.

Lydia shows up in a tie-dye dress over blue jeans, her hair

is pulled into a messy silver topknot. Though I wonder what is really going on behind her unblinking stare, she appears normal as ever, and tells us how refreshing it is to see our "sweet, uncrushed-by-the-weight-of-the-world faces."

"Lydia, the hotline's not the same without you there," Beatriz says, putting her coffee down as her bracelets jangle.

"And I'm not the same without the hotline," Lydia says. "I have all this *time* on my hands now. I'm considering taking up watercolor painting, that's how empty my schedule is. But you know what? I've noticed a surprising amount of *relief*. Relief it's over. I didn't realize how much giving all the time was sucking the life out of me."

Lydia worked more shifts a week than anyone else on the hotline. It was probably close to a full-time job when you added it all up.

"We miss you both," JD says, looking from me to Lydia. "I keep turning around to ask your advice and—and you're not there."

"Same," Beatriz says.

"It's strange," JD says. "In these last couple years, I spent more time with you all than I did with my own family."

"Right?" Beatriz says.

I'm overwhelmed suddenly by all this change—by the hotline being over, by my time with this group of people ending. I wipe my eyes.

"Honey." Beatriz pets my back. "Let it out."

I resent that I, of course, am the one who cannot hold it

together, who needs to be consoled by the hotline operators in diminutive terms like *honey* like I'm a human Chihuahua. I always knew I was on the wrong side of the crisis line. I should have been the one calling all along.

"It sucks that I won't be seeing you anymore," I tell them.

JD shakes their head. "Okay, come on, we're not dead."

"Not yet, anyway," Lydia says.

"Oh, Lydia," Beatriz says.

"Don't even joke about that," JD says. "You know we're here for you, right?"

"Yes, I know. It's what everyone keeps saying," Lydia says, smelling her coffee and putting it back down. "You're all *there* for me. And I know it's well meaning, but guess what, darlings? You can't fix what ails me."

"Being there has nothing to do with fixing, Lydia," JD says. "You of all people should know that."

JD has the most beautiful eyes. A deep brown, almost black, lit with a fire behind them that is infectious.

"You know who taught me that?" JD asks. "You. That night that guy shot himself on the phone with you it was this . . . complete crisis."

"Oh, God," Lydia says, shaking her head, clearly remembering.

"The ordeal took hours," JD goes on, turning to me. "The cops got involved. We had to call Davina in. She showed up in her bathrobe at ten p.m. It was the only time anyone calling the crisis center actually, like, *died* on the phone, then and there. All these people calling for suicide usually just want to be talked out of it, right? Well, this guy had made up his mind and he just didn't want to die alone."

"I haven't thought about that night in a long time," Lydia says.

"That night was something," Beatriz says, braiding her hair as she listens. "I'll never forget it."

"It was my third week on the hotline," JD goes on. "Third shift. Holy shit, right? My mouth was to. The. Friggin. Floor. Lydia swiveled around and told us everything, in detail, after it happened. In gory detail. Didn't flinch. When I asked how she was doing, you know what she said?"

"What did she say?" Beatriz asks, fascinated.

"Yes, what *did* I say?" Lydia asks.

"You were there," JD teases, hitting her arm.

"Well, I don't remember every nonsensical thing I say," Lydia says.

"You said, 'I'm honored to have accompanied him.' You said you felt like Charon," JD tells her. "The ferryman to the underworld in Greek myths. And then the bird."

Lydia hits the table for emphasis, shaking our coffees. "The bird!"

Beatriz rubs her arms. "Now I have goose bumps, remembering."

"A bird—mind you, it's after ten p.m. when this happened—a bird comes *hurling* itself into a window," JD goes on.

"Like it wanted in," Beatriz says, eyes wide as if she's remembering as she speaks.

"A crow," Lydia says. "*I'm* getting goose bumps now."

JD leans in. "Lydia, I just remember you looking up and saying, so casually, 'The bird knows.'"

"That was such a strange night," Beatriz says.

"One of the strangest nights in a long and very strange life," Lydia agrees.

"You said something that night that stuck with me. You said it was hard listening to a stranger die," JD says to Lydia. "But that . . . in the end . . . when it was quiet . . . you were just glad to have been there."

Lydia closes her eyes and breathes in and out audibly.

"So that's what I mean about being there, Lydia," JD says. "We're there for you. We don't want to fix you. We know you've had a rough time. But, here we are."

"Here we are," Lydia says.

I turn away for a moment, pretending to be interested in a bulletin board, to hide how emotional this is all making me. There's something deeply moving about knowing people see what a mess you are and keep loving you anyway.

Lydia, JD, Beatriz, and I finish our tiny coffees. Well, Lydia doesn't; she says this "six-dollar pour-over malarkey tastes like bile." As we start the goodbye process, putting on sweaters, checking our phones, Beatriz asks me a question.

"Not to pry," she says. "But what exactly happened to you? Why'd you leave the hotline so fast?"

"Yeah, Davina cited confidentiality when I asked, so I *know* this must be good," Lydia says.

"Oh . . . I broke a rule," I say, flooded with immediate embarrassment, wishing a hole would open up for me to jump into.

"What rule?" JD asks, with gossipy curiosity, leaning in on their elbows.

"I knew a girl who kept calling," I tell them. "Her name was Coco."

"I remember you talking about her," JD says. "Go on."

I tell them the whole story.

"You *tackled* her?" Lydia almost screams.

The three of them are covering their faces with their hands, Beatriz because she is wide-eyed and stunned, Lydia's got a double-facepalm going, and JD because they are laughing their ass off.

"I'm sorry . . . ," JD says.

Laughter, more than even suicide, is infectious. I see JD's shoulders heaving, their eyes tearing up in silent laughter, and I can't help it. I start laughing, too.

"Isn't that insane?" I ask, tears springing to my eyes as my shoulders rock back and forth. I can barely catch my breath. It's suddenly so funny, so incredibly funny, I can't stop.

"You didn't . . . ," Beatriz says, having caught the laughing bug, and now her eyes are rivering tears down her face.

"At least I didn't physically assault anyone when I got dishonorably discharged," Lydia jokes.

We clutch each other's arms in laughter so big there is no noise for a minute. JD stamps their boot on the ground and Beatriz puts her head on the table, her curls splayed everywhere. Lydia cackles like a witch. I wipe my tears away. It's weird how enough laughter can hit your heart in the same places as sadness, but backward. It's like putting a shattered heart together again.

"I'm sorry," JD finally gasps. "It's not funny."

"No," Beatriz agrees, putting her head up. Her face is red and she wipes her eye corners. "We shouldn't laugh."

"Too bad, because that was the funniest shit I've heard in a long time," Lydia says, reaching out to poke me in the shoulder.

I grin, wiping my eyes with a napkin, as my wild heart steadies itself back to its usual pace.

"You should," I say. "I deserve it."

"Coco, though," JD says, face slackening with such seriousness I expect them to follow up with some kind of joke on me. "Coco called once since you've been gone. Now with this context, maybe what she told me will make sense to you."

"What did she say?" I ask.

"Oh yeah, you told me about this!" Beatriz says, slapping JD's hand.

"Right?" JD asks. "So Coco called one night and asked for you, actually. 'Is Journey there?' I said you no longer volunteered there. Coco said, 'Oh. Well, I just wanted to tell her that I exist again.' I was like, 'Can you elaborate?' And then . . . *click*."

"She exists again," I say.

"She exists," JD says.

We get up and hug. We vow to start a text group, to have coffee more often. They're sorry I got kicked off the hotline, because they think I was a good volunteer. I appreciate their words, even if they're just the kind of words you say when you're inching toward goodbye. I take the bus home. It might be the last time, because I'm taking my driver's test in a few days, and Mom and Dad bought me a car for graduation, an ugly, horrid thing, yellow as mustard, old enough to be my guardian.

*She exists,* I think as I stare out the windows.

I see shadows, shaped like women's profiles, super-imposed against the dark parade of passing trees.

She exists.

While on the bus, staring out the window at the surf shops, the fancy churches, and the palm trees, I realize I still don't know which side of the crazy-person fence I land on. I remember that night Jonah and I ran around our childhood park and I caught up with him under the moon-light, my bisexual revelation giant inside me, quickening my pulse and filling me with a new electricity. It was the revelation of knowing I was both, or neither/nor. It was the revelation of knowing I didn't have to choose. That there was world enough for both inside me.

"You're just now realizing this?" I ask myself in the reflection of the window.

I look around. No one saw me say it. There's a woman with a paper bag on her lap, drooling and asleep, and three freshman-looking girls giggling over something on a phone. I laugh, too, even though I have no reason to.

I am standing in the sun, a giant pizza slice, and I am prancing. As mortifying as this is, it's somehow so much better than the ugly places I can sink to if you let my brain remain at rest. Since my Wolf appointment days ago, I've thought it over times infinity. I've set up an appointment with the psychiatrist he referred me to, a nice lady named Dr. Ng with tired eyes and shiny hair. I don't know if she'll prescribe me something, or what that something will be, but I'm open. I've gone on the forums my mom has squandered good years of her life in to read stories of people who are like and unlike me. And I don't know. I still carry around a brick for a heart some parts of the day. Other moments I feel it lift, get excited about the future like it's a promise. But not now. Now I prance.

Traffic light, *green-yellow-red*, you endless loop, you meditative escape.

"Werk it, pizza! WERK!"

"Oooh, I want a pizza that!"

"Hey, girl, need some sausage for that pizza?"

The moped in front of me at this stoplight looks familiar— bright blue, with rainbow streamers on the handles. Kind of looks like Etta's, actually, but the driver clearly has a huge head of platinum hair, so that can't be Etta. Notice, though, the arm of the driver, a white leather arm with dancing fringe. And the guitar strapped to her bike.

I get a sick flutter in my gut for her, something midway between desire and regret.

Like some kind of creepy wonderful mind reader, Etta turns and glances at me as she waits at the stoplight. She stares hard at my face. Then her eyes go wide behind her helmet. She points to me with excitement. The light goes green and she drives up on the sidewalk and gets off her moped. She pulls off her helmet, revealing the full absurdity of her messy-ass wig. Although I should be embarrassed, I can't help smiling so big when I see her. This sunshine pours over my insides. She walks up to me and stares for a minute, me in my pizza costume and Etta in her Dolly Parton outfit. Who moved first, I don't know, but in one hot second, we embrace.

"What *are* you?" I ask, pulling back.

"What are *you*?" she asks in disbelief.

"I'm a giant slice of pizza. I work at Crusty's."

"I'm Dolly Parton. On my way back from volunteering at the old folks' home."

"I can't believe this," I say.

"This is so crazy," she says, showing me her hand, which is shaking. "I was just thinking about you. And then you . . . appeared. I'm freaked."

"Really?"

"Yeah. I feel like I'm seeing a ghost. Maybe, because, I don't know . . . you ghosted me." She socks my arm playfully, and she's joking, but her eyes are not. "Oh yeah. Remember that?"

"I didn't mean to *ghost* you."

"Really?" She flashes me a mean smile. "Could have fooled me."

"I've got issues," I say. "I wish I didn't, but, I do."

"You think you're the only one with issues?" she asks.

She says it so friendly, smiling big, but her eyes are glossy with tears and her voice shakes a little. I crumble.

"I adore you," she goes on. "But I really don't understand you."

"You deserve better." I look at my sneakered feet, thinking, how do I begin to explain? How do I begin? "I tried to kill myself two months before we met. I am basically your psycho ex-girlfriend."

She sucks in air. "Oh, Journey . . ."

"And I don't know, I might be bipolar or some crap," I tell her. "And I might have to go on medication at some point."

Etta shakes her head. Her blond wig head. "And?"

"And . . . I don't want to put my shit on you," I say.

"That's *it*?" she asks, punching me in a pepperoni. Not hard. But not soft, either. "That's why you broke my stupid heart?"

"I didn't break your heart, did I?"

"You're so *oblivious*," Etta says, and her face crumples. I suck in air watching, not knowing how to comfort her.

"Sorry," I say. "I really like you, I didn't mean—"

"This is so dumb," she says, wiping the running eyeliner, struggling to keep her voice calm. "This is what I get for going after some girl in high school. Which I didn't know, by the way, for the longest time, BECAUSE YOU DON'T TELL ME ANYTHING!"

Here, standing on Fairview Avenue in front of Crusty's, is a flesh-and-blood human being I have hurt without realizing. I was so self-obsessed, I ruined something spectacular.

I feel like I trampled through a garden bed and only now just looked down at my feet to see the crushed flowers.

"Come on," Etta says. "We all have problems. Maybe if you'd let me get close to you, maybe if you were curious about what's inside me, you'd see that."

"I'm curious," I say.

"You have a stupid way of showing it," she says.

Her tears are dried, her eyeliner is still intact. She sniffs.

"I have crippling anxiety," she says. "I take meds almost every day to prevent panic attacks. Doesn't give me any excuse to ghost girls or push people away from me."

"Why didn't you tell me that?" I ask.

"I did say I have panic attacks. I said it a bunch of times."

"I thought you were joking," I say.

I really did. Every once in a while Etta would say, totally casually, something about a panic attack. Almost having one.

Or that time she had one. But she said it like she was kidding, in the same voice she said she was raised by wolves or joined a circus or was Jesus reincarnate.

"For once, I am serious," she says.

When she's serious, she's tired, and she's tired right now, in her Dolly Parton outfit and her wig.

"I didn't realize you *really* had panic attacks," I say.

"Oh, it's bad."

"I'm so sorry."

"It's okay," she says. "I manage it. Keep my pills close by and then I don't end up in the ER."

Medication, problem solved. So many people are like that. And it works, clearly. Maybe it would work for me.

"I'm a mess," I say.

I put my hands over my face because it's humiliating enough to be in a pizza outfit discussing my madness and my feelings on a busy street corner; I don't need to show everybody I'm crying now on top of it.

Etta steps closer to me and wipes under my eyes with her fingers. "You're not a mess," she says. "You're exactly what you need to be."

"I really like you," I say, welling up again. "I've been so smitten since I met you last year. But every time we started getting close—I kept pulling away. Then I got in this explosively shitty place. The bad place. I wanted everything to end. I sent you that message and screwed everything up."

"You haven't screwed anything up, though," she says, her eyes shiny. "I still exist."

Those three words seem to hold the world for a second. She and I, we are here. For now, for this brief little flash in the space-time pan, we are our own universe.

"Etta, you're too good," I say to her.

"I know I am. Guess what? I give people one chance to screw up. And this is your chance."

I breathe in, grateful.

"But that's it. Once chance. You screw me again . . ."

"I wasn't trying to screw you."

"That was the problem, really, but—" She laughs. I have missed her laugh.

There should be a word for when you only truly know that greatness of how much you've missed someone at that moment you see them again. The way it floods back, nervous. I've been pushing Etta from my mind, but I hurt exquisite when I see her.

"I'm not okay," I tell her. "I mean, sometimes I'm okay. Then I'm not again. I'm confused. They diagnosed me as bipolar and I tried medication but then got off it and I think I might go back to see a psychiatrist—"

Etta leans in and interrupts me with a soft, abrupt kiss, our lips one, her hand on the back of my neck and touching my pizza body, my hands in her wig. With my eyes closed, all I see is gold, sunshine filtered through my eyelids, and I think, for the first time in a long time, hell yes, life; I'm going to be okay.

Someone honks and we pull apart, laughing.

"Yeah, I'm sure this is a traffic stopper," I say. "Dolly Parton impersonator making out with a pizza slice on a street corner."

"Oh my God, Journey," Etta says, giggling into her hand.

"What?"

"Your face . . ."

I turn around and look into the moped's side mirror, where I see my lips are clownishly stained red.

"Goddamn your lipstick," I say.

She's laughing so hard she's silent for a moment. "I'm sorry."

"Okay, now we're even."

"Yeah right, you stupid heartbreaker," she says, wiping her eyes.

Who cares about the lipstick all over my face. The sun's starting its slow descent down. The sprinklers behind her sing.

I can't help it.

I kiss her again.


In a twist of irony, or more likely the limitations of health insurance options, Dr. Ng's office is in the same building as Dr. Shaw's. I sit in the waiting room with its enormous potted palm and outdated magazines fanned on coffee tables and get a flashback of the time nearly a year ago when I first came in here, desperate for clarity—an answer in the shape of a diagnosis. I left that appointment with a prescription and new word to describe myself, *bipolar*, lighter, inflated with hope, certain everything would get easier from there. Now here I am again, different year, different doctor, same clinic, same old mess.

When my name is called, I expect to walk into another dark room to another uninterested clinician with a clipboard and another multiple choice questionnaire. It surprises me that, on the contrary, Dr. Ng is warm and welcoming and her office is painted bright blue. She offers me a seat across from her on a plush chair and asks me to tell her about why I'm here. She doesn't give me paperwork, and she doesn't take notes. She sits intently with her hands folded and listens. I guess not all psychiatrists are the same.

How shall I construct the proper narrative of my downward spiral? Chronologically, beginning in childhood? Skip ahead to the traumatic events that led up to the nervous breakdown? The suicide attempt? A back-and-forth narrative sequence featuring my past and present selves? I don't know, but as soon as my mouth opens, I become a human gush of information, trying to squeeze in everything in a race against the clock—trying to construct a story of myself that most closely resembles the truth. When I get to the part about that first appointment with Dr. Shaw, how short our time together was, the lithium and how I went off, her eyebrows furrow.

"Did you get a second opinion of your diagnosis after that initial appointment?" she asks.

"No."

"Did you come back for follow up?"

"Not really. I saw other psychiatrists when I was hospitalized, though. And I have a therapist. That's kind of why I'm here—I was kind of hoping *you* would give me a second opinion."

"I'm a bit shocked you weren't followed up with and that you were diagnosed so quickly," Dr. Ng says. "That's not typical, at least not in my practice. We're frequently overbooked here, and that could be part of the issue—but a bipolar diagnosis and a lithium prescription require a lot of adjustment and I would expect multiple follow-up appointments."

My heart beats wildly at her admission. "Are you saying . . . I might not be bipolar?"

"Journey, we've been together a total of—" Dr. Ng checks her watch. "Twenty minutes? I wouldn't feel comfortable diagnosing you that quickly. I can say, based on what you've told me and reading your medical records, a bipolar diagnosis seems like it might fit. But I also see symptoms that could be major depressive disorder, a personality disorder, or even PTSD related to your accident. Or you could simply be a teenager going through a tough time. I can't say for sure if you have bipolar disorder or not in this first appointment. It's possible you were misdiagnosed. It's possible you weren't."

"Oh," I say.

"Mental health treatment is a journey, so to speak," she says, giving me an encouraging smile. "It takes time to get it right. It can evolve over years. Diagnoses are reassessed, medications are adjusted, the diagnostic manual is updated, treatment plans change. *People* change."

I let this information sink in, chewing the inside of my cheek. It's funny, isn't it, to be a poet, to be a writer of imaginary dictionaries, to be the person forever looking for words with no English equivalent to describe the indescribable—and yet to never feel like I find that proper word that fits me.

"How does what I've said today sit with you?" she asks.

"Well, on one hand, it sucks to think that maybe I'm not bipolar after everything, like I'm back at square one."

"I hear that. What about the other hand?"

"I do want to get it right," I say. "I want to know what I am, what to call myself, whether to call myself anything, what treatments there might be. I've doubted that I'm bipolar at times. Others I've felt like it fits. I hate the fact I have to label myself at all. But if I have to label myself, I want to get it *right*."

"We will, Journey," she says. "It just takes time."

"Well, you're in luck, because I have a *lot* of that," I say.

She laughs, pulling out her calendar to jot down our next appointment time. "I love a patient with a good sense of humor."

I think Dr. Ng and I are going to get along swimmingly.

I leave the clinic this time with no scrap of paper, no

word to Google, and more questions than answers. And you know what? I guess that's what progress looks like sometimes.

On the weather app, it says it's eighty-one degrees today in Chicago, which seems impossible, because it's eighty-one degrees here. Marisol and I go out to brunch. She's packed and is heading to the airport after we eat. This is it. From the diner, from our spot next to the window, we can see Crusty's two doors down, lights off, closed sign in the window. My world is too small. Even my new apartment is less two miles away. Not Marisol's world, though. Hers stretches into other time zones. I'm jealous, in a way, but I know she deserves this, she wanted this. And I've been too busy losing and not losing my mind to build anything resembling an adventurous life. But, dear future self, I'm sure you're out there exploring, and your world is impossibly large.

"What if I just brought you with me," she says, sipping her black coffee. "Stuff you in a suitcase and smuggle you into my dorm room."

"What if I kidnap you and lock you in my new apartment forever?"

"I'm going to miss my creepy best friend," she says.

"Same."

I put the ten thousandth tiny plastic container of cream into my coffee. There is a small mountain of empty containers next to my hand. Then I start on the sugar packets.

"Journey," she says, shaking her head. "You're going to give yourself a heart attack."

"I'm already giving myself a brain attack most days. Why not the heart, too?"

"I hope you're going to take care of yourself while I'm gone. Etta better be a good influence on you."

"Etta eats candy for breakfast and hates physical exertion possibly more than I do. She's wonderful."

Marisol lines her fork, knife, spoon up, straightens her napkin. "You're cute when you talk about her."

"We're just friends who make out." I take a sip of my coffee, the sweet screaming taste. "No big."

"Anyone but Jonah."

"I can't believe I ever loved that empty vessel."

"We all date mistakes. Remember Lloyd?"

Lloyd, Marisol's boyfriend last summer, was the whiniest wisp of a manboy who I basically ignored, hoping he would go away, and he eventually did, and now Marisol makes herself gag whenever she thinks of him and his—I quote her, here—"eel-like tongue and sweaty fingers."

"I'm about to *eat*," Marisol says.

Alejandro, our old favorite waiter, brings us our usual. Marisol cuts our chicken-fried steak with a lovingness that can only be described as maternal.

"We're always going to be best friends, though," Marisol says, putting my plate in front of me, as if she's continuing some conversation. "And we can FaceTime anytime, day or night, and I can text you dozens of times while watching some show on TV."

"Sure," I say.

She stares at her plate for a moment, her exactly half a meal that looks so scrawny on its own. She looks up at me. "Journey, we've got to talk about what happened between us."

I don't say anything.

"What happened between us?" she goes on.

"Does this matter now?"

"Yes, of course it matters. It's been bothering me for months. This has gone on for *months*. And then you just want to move on and not talk about it—how can we do that? We used to talk about everything."

"I'm tired of looking backward," I say.

"Yeah, I got that. And I'm glad your life is going well for you and you're moving out and all that. But you know what? Ever since you attempted suicide, it's like you survived by not being able to look behind you. And maybe that served you well. I'm sure it did. But it cut people like me out of your life."

"I didn't mean for it to be like that."

"It was almost like the whole essay thing was just an excuse," she says, her voice shaking. "An excuse to cut me out."

I roll my eyes.

"No, really. I've thought about this a lot."

"Why would I want to cut you out?" I ask.

"Because you're so afraid of being abandoned like Jonah abandoned you, and you know I'm leaving. Because you didn't want to fall back into old patterns and I'm part of those old patterns. You've been building a future for yourself— which is amazing! Which is great! But in doing so, JoJo, you've completely forgotten your past."

A fist closes over my heart. "My past is a bunch of pain, Marisol, maybe that's why."

"Not all of it," she says. "I'm part of your past, too."

"It's not like that."

"Stop it," she says, raising her voice. "It *is* like that. I've watched you sabotage relationships because of this stupid fear of yours. You've got to give that up."

"What *relationships*?"

"Etta, for one," she says.

Neither of us have touched our food. We sit, motionless, her eyes on me, my eyes on my food.

"I know you too well to let you burn this down," Marisol says. "I swear if I wasn't relentless, you'd have just let me go. And that hurts me so bad, JoJo."

"I wouldn't have let you go."

"But you *did*."

"Temporarily."

"Are you even sorry?" she asks, tears in her eyes. "Did you even miss me?"

"Yes," I say, looking her in the eyes, blinking tears away.

"But I had to just—just focus on other stuff. To survive."

"I'm glad you survived, obviously, but don't let survival be an excuse to push people away," she says. "Because that's not truly living."

Dumb stupid uninvited tears prick my eyeballs. And they are contagious. So now Marisol's sniffing hers back, too, dabbing behind her glasses with a napkin.

"I'm really sorry, Marisol," I say.

"It's okay. And I'm sorry, too. I just wish we hadn't spent our last year together this way."

I put my head on the table and sob. She pats my hair. When I'm done with my mortifying display of emotion in a public place, she hands me a napkin.

"It's like no matter what I do, when I look back, all I feel is regret," I say.

"Stop being so hard on yourself. Have some compassion. Those regrets are just getting in the way."

I blow my nose on a napkin. "I hate that we're spending our last moments together mopping up the mess I am instead of being excited about the future."

"Are you excited about the future?"

"Weirdly, yes."

"What are you going to do?"

"Keep living," I say. "Go to school. Maybe study psychology, English. Save my money, I don't know, travel somewhere—"

"Chicago," she interrupts.

"Have my own apartment. Write some more poems. Maybe not screw it up with Etta."

"And what if you get depressed?"

"I will get depressed," I say. "If there's one thing I know, it's that I'm not getting off this roller coaster entirely." I grab a triangle of jammy toast and chew it. "Right now, though, I really am okay."

Marisol nods. I can tell my words didn't really assuage her worries. But it's not like she can argue with me.

"Keep writing poems," she says. "Keep going to school. Send me pictures of how you decorate your apartment. Don't forget about me. Come visit me in Chicago."

"I will."

"But no, I *mean* it. Come out for Halloween. We'll go to a dumb party."

"I would love that."

She comes and sits next to me and shows me pictures of the campus on her phone, and I, in trade, show her some pictures from the listing of my apartment. It's nothing fancy. Dim-lit photos with blah-colored carpet and blah-colored walls. It's a studio, and you can practically reach both the toilet and the stove from the only place my bed will fit. But I paid the deposit. I signed the lease. It's mine.

She leans her head on my shoulder. I lean over and breathe her in for a moment. Her smell comes with an entire history—like I'm breathing in not only us, but another time and place, another self I once was. The freshman girl with long hair and blue eyeliner, who scribbled in composition books all day long, who hadn't yet fallen in love or been broken. Whose big feelings shone in her eyes and were kept quiet in her heart and hadn't yet spilled over. It's weird how different yet the same you can be. It should be a contradiction, shouldn't it? But it isn't. It's life.

"I love you, Journey," she says, hugging me. "Love you so much. The world is such a better place with you in it. I hope you know that."

"I do," I say.

And I'm not lying; even when the black hole tempts me, I know my absence would only bring more pain, more emptiness, to a world desperately in need of more joy, more sunshine, more pretty things.

"Good luck. I want to hear all about your adventure," I say.

Each word hurts. I miss her already, and she's standing right in front of me. Please leave some space in my dictionary for that definition.

"Journey, I loved you then, I love you now, and I'll love you forever, okay? I love every Journey. Every one."

"You too," I say.

We say goodbye. I want to say more, but she has to get going, and so do I. Some poor girl was just hired at Crusty's and I'm about to train her in the art of pizza dancing. As I watch Marisol drive off, a pit manifests in my stomach, a sour cramp, regret physicalized. Then I breathe in and out, count-ing. I let the feeling stay there. I feel unfulfilled, unresolved. But that's okay.

Because real life?

It has no resolution.

Dear future self,

I see you there, stumbling, mucking things up, not knowing which direction to choose. Making wrong turns and then doubling back to find your way again. Reaching your hands into the darkness, feeling for the light switch, falling down. I know you're going to fall. It hurts to know this.

But you know what else I see? I see you reaching for hands to help you up, laughing at yourself, dusting yourself off. Admitting when you're wrong. Learning. Growing. Writing. Verbing all the nouns.

Most importantly, dear future self, I see you. Not your shape; not your details. I just sense your shadow. I see you're there. And guess what? I like you.

And I think I want to keep you.

Dear future self, my composition book says. Dear future self.

And I realize something.

I'm here.

# ACKNOWLEDGMENTS

Thank you first to Claire Anderson-Wheeler, who always goes above and beyond as an agent—not only guiding me through the business side of book writing, but helping shape my messy first draft ideas into something so much stronger in the end. I'm ever grateful for your patience and support every step of the way.

Thank you to Kristen Pettit; I'm still pinching myself that you're my editor. It's truly been a dream to work with someone so brilliant who has such an appreciation for the complexities of this story and Journey's voice.

Thank you to Dr. Jessi Gold for your invaluable input as a mental health professional.

Thanks to everyone on the HarperTeen team for their work on this book, and to Darren Booth for the gorgeous, thoughtful cover design.

Thank you to Gordon Hess, one of the kindest, most generous people I have been lucky enough to cross paths with, who met me during the hardest period of my life and saw me as a whole person, who taught me to learn to love my "big engine" despite how difficult it can be.

Thank you to all my friends who supported and loved me during the times echoed in this book: Paul Isham, Isaiah Klein, Ida Ruff, Jared Blankenship, Christine Lewis Giffen, Jonathan Pugh, Tawnie Cameron, Dan Weiss, Erin Cantelo, Steve Gross, Heather Stevenson, Wyatt Lavasseur, Alyson Gove, and so many others I'm sure I'm forgetting.

Thank you to the Santa Barbara Rape Crisis Center for making me a hotline volunteer and a better feminist.

Thank you to my best friend in the wide world, Ramona Itule-Patigian, for not only your sisterhood, but for your support for my ideas, my writing, and my mental health.

Thank you to my lovely friend Eliza Smith, for some important conversations early on in the writing process as I thought through the complexities of mental illness and identity.

Thank you to my friends at the Ralston retreat, where I first started this story; a special thank you to Jane Martin-Gilmore for being the heart of that retreat and a champion of young writers and readers.

Thank you to my tribe who has seen me through the best and blurst of times: Mom, Dad, Matt, Jackson, Micaela. Thank you too to all my extended family for the constant support: Katie Gardner, the Sanitates and Ellen Martin, the Richardsons, the Woods, and all the Gardners in North Carolina.

Thank you to my daughters, Roxanna Tulip and Zora Fire-lily, who bring a special sunshine to my life I never knew existed.

Thank you lastly, but most of all, to Jamie—my partner, my best friend, and someone whose understanding and love reaches impossibly far back in time. I still remember sitting shotgun with you as a teenager while we drove around our little paradise and exchanging stories about our struggles. I felt so wholly known, respected, and adored, despite all my mistakes. Decades later, I still feel the same. I'm so grateful to still be riding shotgun with you everywhere we go on this wild journey.

# RESOURCES

If you or a loved one are struggling, there are many resources to support you through crisis. Here are just a few:

- **National Suicide Prevention Hotline (https://suicidepreventionlifeline.org):** "The Lifeline provides 24/7, free and confidential support for people in distress, prevention and crisis resources for you or your loved ones, and best practices for professionals."
    - o **Call 1-800-273-8255 or chat online at https://suicidepreventionlifeline.org/chat/.**
    - o **https://youmatter.suicidepreventionlifeline.org** is "a safe space for youth to discuss and share stories about mental health and wellness."
- **The Trevor Project (www.thetrevorproject.org):** "The Trevor Project is the leading national organization providing crisis intervention and suicide prevention services to LGBTQ+ young people under twenty-five."
    - o **Trevor Lifeline (1-866-488-7386)** is "the only national 24/7 crisis intervention and suicide prevention lifeline for LGBTQ+ young people under twenty-five."
    - o **TrevorChat (www.thetrevorproject.org/get-help -now/#trevorChat:** is a "free, confidential, secure instant messaging service for LGBTQ+ youth."
    - o **TrevorText (text START to 678-678)** is a "free, confidential, secure service in which LGBTQ+ young people can text a trained Trevor counselor for support."

- **Crisis Text Line:** "Text HOME to 741741 from anywhere in the United States, anytime. Crisis Text Line is here for any crisis. A live, trained Crisis Counselor receives the text and responds, all from our secure online platform."
- **NAMI (National Alliance on Mental Illness) (www.nami.org):** "The nation's largest grassroots mental health organization dedicated to building better lives for the millions of Americans affected by mental illness." Their website includes tons of resources including connections with local chapters, statistics, educational information, and more for people with mental illness or friends and family who want to support them.
  - o  NAMI also has a HelpLine open Monday through Friday, 10 a.m. to 6 p.m. ET, reachable at 1-800-950-NAMI (6264) or by email at info@nami.org.